The October That Changed Everything

Connie Lacy

Wild Falls Publishing
~ ~ ~
Atlanta, GA

Copyright © 2024 by Connie Lacy
Cover design by James at GoOnWrite.com
All rights reserved. No part of this publication may be reproduced, distributed or transmitted in any form or by any means, including photocopying, recording, or other electronic or mechanical methods, without prior written permission of the author, except for brief quotations in book reviews.

This is a work of fiction. All names, characters, businesses, organizations, places and incidents are either fictitious or are used fictitiously. Any resemblance to real people, living or dead, is coincidental.

ISBN-13: 978-1-7374552-6-4

Published by Wild Falls Publishing
Atlanta, GA

WildFallsPublishing@outlook.com

For Doug

~~~

Also by Connie Lacy

Livvy and the Enchanted Woodland
A Suffragette in Time
The Time Capsule
The Going Back Portal
The Time Telephone
VisionSight: a Novel
A Daffodil for Angie
The Shade Ring, Book 1 of The Shade Ring Trilogy
Albedo Effect, Book 2 of The Shade Ring Trilogy
Aerosol Sky, Book 3 of The Shade Ring Trilogy

1

October 15, 1962

Outmaneuvering the boss's roving eye and wandering hands was an essential job skill at Carlisle Realty. Cheryl Donovan learned that lesson the hard way. On this Monday morning in mid-October she was battle ready when his voice exploded through the intercom summoning her to take dictation. She reached for an important weapon in her arsenal – brown cat-eye glasses. She put them on and wiped the lipstick from her mouth with a tissue.

Only then did she press the "talk" button.

"I'll be there in the blink of an eye." Releasing the button, she whispered to herself, "Or two blinks. Maybe three."

To complete her camouflage, she removed her jacket and hung it on the back of her chair, then partially untucked her white blouse from the waistband of her skirt. Good. She'd ruined the classy look of her royal blue suit, achieving a lumpy, frumpy effect. She left her auburn hair loose on her shoulders.

Cheryl was expected to wear fashionable clothes in primary colors to coordinate with the Danish modern furniture in the lobby. Naturally, there was no clothing allowance to pay for her wardrobe. Sometimes it seemed as though she was little more than a decorative lamp.

Disapproval painted Mr. Carlisle's jowly face when she entered his office with her steno pad and pencil. Taking a seat in one of two chairs facing the desk, she angled her legs to the side to thwart his prying eyes. She was on her guard. It had been several days since he tried anything.

"About time, Miss Donovan!" He sounded like a drill sergeant browbeating recruits.

It was hard to believe Mr. C. had once been a good-looking guy. But proof hung on the wall behind him in a framed eight by ten. Wearing his football uniform, a muscled young Harry Carlisle gloated as if he'd been given the key to the head cheerleader's dorm room. But his fondness for steak, cigarettes and top-shelf whiskey had transformed him into a paunchy, greying, red-nosed man who looked a decade older than his fifty-three years.

He paced around the office, fiddling with his tie as he dictated a letter to Perry Odom, president of a competing real estate firm.

"Dear Perry, thank you for speaking with me last week about the possible merger of our two companies."

A skilled stenographer, Cheryl's pencil flew over the paper, her shorthand materializing like an elaborate secret code.

"As we discussed," he went on, "growth at Fort Bragg means more military families are looking for homes in the Fayetteville area. I believe combining our inventories will create a company that can compete with the largest realty firms in the state. As for a name, I think Odom and Carlisle

Realty has a nice ring to it. I look forward to our next business lunch at the country club. Etcetera, etcetera."

He paused behind her, leaning close. "Don't worry, Cheryl. Your job is safe."

When his lips brushed her neck, she leapt from the chair and bolted for the door.

"I'll type this up right away," she said, reaching for the doorknob.

"I'm not finished!" The threatening tone was new. "Not only do I pay you for your secretarial skills, I also pay you to present an attractive face to the public. And to *me*! One of the reasons I hired you is that you're easy on the eyes. " He tugged on his earlobe. "So you might want to spruce up a bit. You've been letting yourself go lately."

Her high heels ticked like a time bomb on the parquet floor as she scurried to her desk. Grabbing her pocketbook and jacket, she made for the ladies room to freshen up. And to calm down. She was sick of her boss's skirt-chasing ways. Now he had the nerve to send her a not-so-subtle message that if she didn't measure up in the beauty department, he might let her go. She growled under breath. Unfortunately, flouncing out in a huff was not an option. There were only seven more months of night classes before she got her accounting degree. She couldn't risk a detour at this late date. All she had to do was play it cool and keep that lecher at arm's length.

After removing the glasses, tucking in her blouse, slipping her jacket on and applying a fresh coat of lipstick, she took stock in the mirror. While she spent more on the suit than she could afford – the blue tweed was perfect for the lobby color scheme – she admired the smart styling of the pencil skirt and fitted jacket. Besides, a polished wardrobe was a step in the right direction. When she left secretarial work behind to become an accountant, she would look the part. If there was one thing she wanted, it was a professional job where she wouldn't always have to be on the alert for an ambush.

Walking across the lobby to her desk, she glanced out the wall of windows along the front of the building, spotting two men in Army dress greens headed to the entrance. She made it to her chair in time to stow her purse and load paper in her typewriter. Watching them out of the corner of her eye, she saw them remove their garrison caps as they stepped through the double glass doors. They were both tall and lanky with lieutenant bars on their shoulders and spit-shined jump boots on their feet.

"I guess it's true – nothing could be finer than to be in Carolina on a Monday morning," said the dark-haired one, giving her a lop-sided grin that was, no doubt, intended to make a woman's stomach turn cartwheels. "Top of the morning to you, Miss Donovan! We're looking for a house to rent."

Hm. The nameplate on her desk might need to go.

Fayetteville being an army town, she'd had her share of wolf whistles and shouts of "hey baby!" She usually let it roll off her back. But after the boss's conduct this morning she was in no mood to have a GI flirt with her, even if he was an officer instead of a private. No doubt, he'd ask for her number and insist that having a drink with him would be the highlight of her life. That guy needed a slice of humble pie.

Wishing she hadn't already spruced up, as Mr. Carlisle put it, she took advantage of another secret weapon to repel unwanted advances. She smothered them with southern graciousness. But instead of speaking in her smooth feminine voice, she used the grating nasal tone she perfected when she was thirteen trying to drive her older brother crazy.

"I wish I could help but we don't have any rentals. Plenty of homes for sale though."

Equal measures of surprise and discomfort washed over the lieutenants' faces as they tried to reconcile what their eyes were seeing with what their ears were hearing.

"I can round up a salesman for you," she said, gesturing in the direction of the sales offices.

She sounded so obnoxious, even her own ears rebelled. It was all she could do to keep a straight face as she watched them squirm.

The one who greeted her a little too warmly a moment before couldn't make his mouth work now, leaving his sandy-haired friend to do the talking.

"Would you happen to know of any rental houses?"

"I've seen a couple *For Rent* signs on my way to work," she replied, keeping up the charade. "But I don't know anything about them. You can check with Odom Realty over on Yadkin Road. They handle rentals."

"Thank you. We'll do that."

They double-timed it through the front door, bugging out as fast as they could in a flashy blue 1959 Corvette Stingray.

She couldn't help gloating in triumph as she turned her attention to typing the boss's letter.

*

She knew why the telephone was quiet that afternoon. She also knew why one of their top salesmen was leaving early. Jerry Inman stopped by her desk a few minutes after two.

"Roger is number one on the floor," he said. "He'll take any calls that come in. I'm meeting a sergeant and his wife to show them a couple of listings in Forest Hills."

She raised a skeptical eyebrow.

"He wants to keep his commute to Fort Bragg to a minimum," he explained. "And Forest Hills is close."

"It's also where you live, isn't it?"

"Which is why I can personally recommend it."

She retrieved a pocket-sized transistor radio from a drawer and placed it on her desk. "First pitch is at three, right?"

He was caught and knew it. It was common knowledge that today was game six of the World Series. People also knew that every working man who could get away with it was taking the afternoon off to watch the game on TV, either at a bar or at home.

"Don't tell the boss," he said.

"I'm pretty sure he knows all about it."

She gave him a little wave as he went on his way.

That's when she noticed the flirtatious dark-haired lieutenant who stopped by with his friend that morning. Standing in the middle of the lobby, the cocky expression on his face made it clear he'd overheard the banter between her and the salesman.

"I've been feeling sorry for you all day," he said, mischief in his eyes as he approached. "Worried about how that voice must've ruined your life."

Like the salesman, she'd been caught in a deception.

"You deserve a prize for most original brush-off." He was having too much fun at her expense. "As much as I dreaded hearing your not-so-golden tones again, I came back to ask about the *For Rent* signs you mentioned. We're having a tough time finding a house. By the way, I'm Paul McIntyre."

Maybe she overreacted on their first meeting, allowing frustration with the boss to cloud her judgment. She tore a page from her steno tablet and wrote two street names on it. "These are streets where I've seen rental signs," she said, using her natural voice. Retrieving a city map, she handed it to him along with the slip of paper.

Her phone rang then, for which she was grateful.

"Good luck, Lieutenant."

She nodded at him as she lifted the receiver, surreptitiously watching him drive away in his Corvette.

Later, she was filing paperwork while listening to play-by-play of the World Series game when the boss's wife called. She was not her usual composed self.

"I'm sorry, Mrs. Carlisle, he's on another line. I'll have him return..."

"Interrupt him! This is urgent!" She sounded truly alarmed.

"Of course."

She put Mrs. Carlisle on hold and pushed the button on the intercom.

"Excuse me, Mr. Carlisle. Your wife is on line two. She says it's urgent."

"I'll get back to her. I'm on an important call."

Her finger hovered over the button. Mrs. Carlisle didn't often ring the office. And when she did, she was never high-handed. She pushed the intercom button again.

"I think there might be an emergency."

"Take a message!"

She braced herself as she picked up line two.

"Mrs. Carlisle, he says he'll ring you back in…"

"You tell Harry if he doesn't pick up this instant, the next call I make will be to the divorce lawyer who won a big fat settlement for my sister!"

"Yes ma'am."

This time she hurried to the boss's door, tapped softly, then opened it.

He glared at her, holding his hand over the mouthpiece.

"She says pick up now or she's calling a divorce lawyer."

A large vein bulged on his forehead.

By the time she sat down again, she could see by the lighted buttons on her phone that he had hung up on line three and picked up line two.

Thirty seconds later he raced past her desk, yanking his suit coat on as he went.

"Going to the hospital! My son was injured at football practice. If I'm not back in time, lock up!"

He didn't return.

At six o'clock, after the salesmen cleared out, Cheryl gathered her things. But through the plate glass windows, she saw a blood red Cadillac pull into the parking lot, its taillights resembling fire shooting out the back of twin chrome rockets mounted on soaring tail fins.

Two men emerged. One was a brawny guy with the hard-edged look of a nightclub bouncer. The other wore expensive slacks and a sport coat but no tie. He marched toward the building at a rapid pace, leaving the tough guy smoking a cigarette by the Caddy.

"Dang it," she grumbled.

The last thing she needed was the boss's brother delaying her departure.

Eddie Carlisle owned several high-priced restaurants, including Carlisle's on the River, which served steak and lobster. He had the swagger of a four-star general accustomed to being saluted. She'd seen him come and go from time to time but hadn't interacted with him. Lately, though, he'd been stopping by every week. He had dark hair, as yet untouched by grey, and he was younger, taller and thinner than Harry Carlisle. In fact, he might be considered middle-age handsome. Until you looked into his eyes, that is.

"Where the hell is Harry?" he demanded, storming into the lobby.

He could've been a heavy on a TV show with a gun concealed under his jacket.

"Something important came up. He had to leave. I was about to lock up."

"Something important? Well, I've got something *important* right here and the bastard knew I was coming!"

He withdrew a white business envelope from inside his coat, slapping it angrily on his other palm. He did it with such force, the unsealed flap opened, spilling the contents on the floor. Stooping to pick up a pile of loose bills, he stuffed them back in the envelope and got to his feet. There was a one thousand dollar bill on top.

He looked at her then, seeming to choose his words more carefully.

"It's for the closing tomorrow on a house I'm buying. Harry knew I was bringing it over. He shoulda let me know he wouldn't be here, the asshole. Now he's put me in a bind. I've gotta be somewhere in twenty minutes and I can't have all this dough on me. You got the combination to the safe?"

"Well..."

"You better have it."

If she'd felt uneasy before, she was fast developing a case of jitters.

"I haven't got all day!" he bellowed.

"I need to type a receipt so there's a record of how much…"

"Ten grand."

"Oh, great," she mumbled, more agitated by the minute.

"Did you say something?"

"I have to count it."

"Christ!"

"I'm a fast counter."

He slammed the envelope on her desk. "You got sixty seconds."

She sat down and thumbed through the bills at high speed. The envelope contained fifty well-worn hundred dollar bills and five one-thousand dollar bills.

"Ten thousand dollars," she announced.

"You don't say."

There was a sneer on his face the size of a howitzer.

She loaded two sheets of paper in the typewriter with carbon paper in between. While she typed the receipt, he slid the cash back in the envelope.

After they both signed it, she gave him the original and took the copy to Mr. Carlisle's office. Reluctantly, she pulled a framed landscape painting away from the wall like a small cabinet door, revealing a wall safe. Using her body to block Eddie's view, she turned the dial back and forth and back again, unlocking the safe. Once she opened the thick door, she took the envelope from his outstretched hand and placed it inside along with the receipt. When the safe was secured, she took a deep breath, realizing she'd been bracing herself for a whack on the head.

Eddie marched out without a word just as his brother drove into the lot in his white Lincoln Continental. From her desk she watched the two exchange angry words, hands slashing the air between them. The argument was over as quickly as it began. With Eddie at the wheel, his bodyguard beside him, the Caddy burned rubber as it fishtailed onto Raeford Road.

Mr. Carlisle rumbled through the door like a battle tank.

"My brother was supposed to drop off some paperwork today and bring the money to the closing *tomorrow*. Of course, he did the opposite. He said you typed up a receipt."

"In the safe with the money."

"Good, good."

She turned to leave, anxious to go home, but he stopped her.

"I assume you know the meaning of confidential, Miss Donovan."

She nodded.

"Swear you won't tell anyone." His words were softly spoken but it didn't make them any less threatening. That he felt compelled to say them at all suggested something shady was going on.

"I swear."

"Not a word to the sales team. No chatting with your roommate. No letter to your family. Not a single soul."

An implied "or else" hung in the air.

2

God, she wished she'd never seen that wad of bills. On the drive home from work Cheryl couldn't stop thinking about it. Ten thousand dollars was enough to buy a modest house, one Eddie would never live in. Somehow he didn't seem the type to rent such homes as investment properties. And what was that yelling match all about in the parking lot? Afterward Mr. Carlisle made what could only be described as a veiled threat, warning her that his brother's purchase was strictly confidential.

She was relieved when she turned into Pinetree Heights. The residences on Loblolly Lane were small ranch style homes. Hers was red brick with a picture window and a porch big enough for a porch swing and a rocking chair.

Walking through the front door, a whiff of garlicky tomato sauce drew her to the kitchen. Her mother called the kitchen cheerful, and no one could argue that. It had a yellow stove, yellow refrigerator and yellow Formica table with vinyl chairs to match.

Cheryl's roommate moved back and forth fixing spaghetti and setting the table, a floral apron tied over dark slacks and a turtleneck. Tina Rossi was a divorcee, which sounded modern. But her office wardrobe consisted of skirts that fell below the knee and buttoned-up cardigan sweaters, straight from the 1950s. Tall, with a direct gaze and short dark hair, she'd been Cheryl's best friend since ninth grade and roommate since her divorce.

"Can you go out back and keep Ricky company?" Tina said, dumping noodles into a pot of boiling water. "He had a cruddy day."

"Mine wasn't exactly a bed of petunias," Cheryl said.

"That makes three of us."

"When it rains, it poo-poos." Cheryl chuckled, snitching an olive from a bowl on the table.

"Don't let Ricky hear you say that." Tina gave a little snort in spite of herself.

"What happened at school?"

"Red Rover is what happened. Bullies turn into demons on the playground. Me and Miss Dunn are gonna have a little set-to. I don't know why she lets the kids play those rough games."

"Be careful. She's twice your size."

"She's also twice my age."

"Ricky's dad could go with you."

"Wyatt, the Paleolithic father?" Tina slammed a lid on the pot. "He thinks this kind of stuff makes his son a man."

Cheryl hung her pocketbook on the doorknob and stepped onto the back stoop. Pinky greeted her as if she was Queen for a Day. Pinky was the imperious calico cat who thought she owned the place. Her coat was a crazy quilt of orange and black on a silky white background. She also had a pink nose. Thus, the name. Cheryl stroked her soft fur, receiving a quiet purr in appreciation.

She sat down on the top step, watching as Ricky picked up a ragged baseball.

The little boy was a blond dynamo with a buzz cut almost as short as an army recruit's shaved head. There was an ever-present glint in his big brown eyes. His dungarees and striped tee shirt made it clear that playing outside meant rolling on the ground. It appeared he'd forgotten his bad day at school – at least for now – as he rollicked with his beloved doggy.

The long-haired mutt with the reddish-brown coat and a white patch on his chest was named Max. His tail resembled a fan when it wagged. And it wagged a lot.

"Watch this, Cheryl!" Ricky threw the ball beyond the clothesline, barely missing a row of towels drying on the line. "Fetch, boy!"

Max raced across the sparse grass and retrieved the ball as Ricky clapped his hands. The dog dropped down on a bare sandy spot and gnawed the ball.

"Come on, boy! Bring the ball!"

Max chewed happily, ignoring his young master. When the silly dog loped toward him, he left the ball on the ground in the distance.

"Aw, Max!"

"Try giving him a treat when he brings the ball," Cheryl suggested. "Keep some treats in your pocket."

Before serving dinner, Tina spooned cat food into a bowl by the back door for Pinky while Ricky fed Max on the porch. When they sat down at the table Ricky was his usual bubbly self.

"Guess what, Cheryl," he said between mouthfuls.

"What?"

"My peepee smelled like soup today."

"Ricky!" Tina cried.

"What kind of soup?" Cheryl said once she recovered from nearly choking on her iced tea.

"Chicken noodle. We had chicken noodle soup in the lunchroom."

"Both of you!" Tina tried her best to contain her mirth. "Not at the table!"

"You think your peepee will smell like spaghetti tonight?" Cheryl asked.

A big laugh escaped Ricky's mouth, along with some noodles and spaghetti sauce that spattered his jeans and the table.

Tina grabbed a wet dishcloth to clean up the mess while changing the subject.

"My boss started the week with a bang," she said, scraping spaghetti from Ricky's pants. "Would you believe she chewed me out for not wearing nylons? She said wearing flats doesn't mean I can go without hose."

"How would she know?" Cheryl asked.

"She rushed up to me at lunchtime, leaned over and ran her finger down my leg."

"The nerve!"

"She said if she caught me without stockings again, a formal reprimand will be placed in my file. Two violations and I get the boot. It's a cockamamie rule for keypunch operators like me who don't interact with the public."

"You don't have any stockings, Mommy?" Ricky said, a troubled look clouding his face.

"Don't worry." She patted his arm. "I've got two pairs. But it gripes me that women have to wear them. It also gripes me that Mrs. Sheahan has been giving me grief since my first week on the job. Of course I'm not the only one who had a bad day. You had a tough time too, didn't you, sweetie?"

"I hate Red Rover!"

"Why's that?" Cheryl asked.

"Miss Dunn always lets Butch or Junior be captain. They're mean. And they pick mean boys for their team. When they yell, 'Red Rover, Red Rover, send Ricky right over,' I don't wanna go. They hold their arms real tight and make a fist so I can't bust through. It makes my tummy hurt."

Deciding to lighten things up, Cheryl was ready with her own story.

"This was definitely a rusty-nail-in-the-foot kind of day," she said. "I had something happen too."

She didn't share anything about Mr. Carlisle's behavior or his brother's envelope of cash. Instead, she entertained them with how she discouraged the lieutenants from flirting with her by using her nasal voice. When she demonstrated, Ricky giggled as if someone had tickled his armpits.

"You sound like a oinking pig!" he spluttered.

He asked her to do it again and again. Which she was only too happy to do if it picked up his spirits.

*

Mr. Carlisle usually started the day bombarding Cheryl with orders and questions: When would the new Xerox machine be delivered? Did she order the new brochures? Bring him the paperwork on the Montclair home that sold two weeks ago. Not Tuesday morning though. Instead, he stayed in his office with the door closed. When she delivered his morning coffee, she took her steno pad, ready to take notes.

"How's your son doing?" she said, placing the mug on his desk.

"Got his bell rung during practice, that's all. Concussions don't kill anybody. They sent him home after watching him for a while."

"Glad to hear it. Do I need to gather documents for the closing?"

"Closing?"

"The one your brother…"

"Everything's taken care of. I'll be driving over there in a few minutes."

He gave her an approving once over, his eyes taking in the blue floral sun dress she'd worn with a white summer sweater draped over her shoulders. Perfect attire with temperatures getting into the eighties again this afternoon despite being October.

He left midmorning. She assumed after his brother's hush-hush closing he would celebrate by having his usual porterhouse steak and several Manhattans at the country club. Then he'd watch game seven of the World Series with friends, accompanied by too many glasses of whiskey on the rocks to keep track of. Which meant tomorrow morning he would be cranky.

In any event, it was another quiet afternoon at the office. Jerry Inman, who decamped yesterday so he could watch game six, was stuck holding down the fort today as number one on the floor. He had a transistor radio on his desk too.

It was still scoreless in the fourth inning when Lieutenant McIntyre walked through the door carrying a bouquet of deep pink chrysanthemums in a cut glass vase. No uniform today. He was dressed in grey slacks, a blue sport coat and loafers.

She was surprised when she felt heat blooming in her cheeks.

"I had to stop by and thank you." He set the flowers on her desk. "We rented one of the houses you told us about. Do you live in that neighborhood?"

"Not far from there," she said, not entirely certain she wanted him to know where she lived.

"Do you know of a nice place to eat close by?"

"By 'nice,' do you mean classy or yummy?"

"Yummy."

Her face was very warm now. "There's a Japanese restaurant down the road from here with good sukiyaki."

"That would be a new experience for me. I don't suppose you could be my guide. How about tonight?"

She had the perfect excuse. Suddenly she wished she didn't.

"I have accounting class after work on Tuesdays and Thursdays."

His left eyebrow rose, suggesting he might be impressed.

"Tomorrow night then," he said.

"No offense, but I don't even know you."

"Yeah, it makes me a nervous too. I mean, yesterday you could've passed for an axe murderer in a horror movie."

Her cheeks were blazing.

"But I'm willing to take the risk if you are," he said. "As long as we meet at a crowded restaurant where we're surrounded by lots of people so I feel safe."

She couldn't help laughing.

Cheering erupted from her little radio. They listened as the announcer narrated the action on the field. Yankee shortstop Tony Kubek hit a grounder into a double play, knocking in the runner on third, giving the Yankees the first run of the game.

"I can't believe you're listening to the World Series," he said.

"Why not?"

"Well, you know. You're a woman."

"Lots of women enjoy baseball."

"Enough to listen at work?"

She shot him a challenging look. After which, they agreed to meet at the Sakura Restaurant the following evening.

*

She was a few minutes late leaving work after the ninth inning turned into a nail-biter. When all was said and done, the Yankees held on to win the game and the series. She tucked the radio in her bottom drawer and rushed out the door for class, eating a sandwich as she drove.

She tried to ignore all the pawn shops, used car lots and mobile home sales lots along Bragg Boulevard. There were also several massage parlors. That was one of the downsides of living in an army town overrun with young soldiers.

Leaving the highway behind, she parked in front of the Business Department classroom building which was ugly enough to pass for a barracks at Fort Bragg. When she reached for the canvas bag containing her textbook and notebook, she found the passenger seat empty. It was still in her desk.

For an instant, she considered muddling through. But this had turned out to be a tough semester and she needed her book and notes if she was going to do well. She cranked the engine and raced back to the office, regretting rushing out of there with baseball on the brain.

Two cars were parked out front when she pulled off the highway – Mr. Carlisle's Lincoln and his brother's flamboyant 1959 Cadillac with the biggest tailfins on the road. Maybe she should do without her book and notes. No, she was here. She knew exactly where she left her bag – in the bottom drawer with the transistor radio. She would zip in and out in less than a minute. No one would be the wiser.

She eased the front door open, then gently closed it. The men were in the midst of a heated discussion in the boss's office. As fate would have it, the door was open and she could hear every word.

"I'm selling it next month, as soon as I get the deed."

"We agreed you'd wait a year, Eddie," said Mr. Carlisle.

"You *told* me to wait a year. I never agreed."

"The whole idea was to wait so you wouldn't cause uncomfortable questions."

Cheryl tip-toed across the lobby to avoid the click-clack of her high heels. She slowly pulled the bottom drawer open and retrieved her carryall bag.

"It's *my* money, Harry! And now it's *my* house. The last thing I want is to be a landlord to a sergeant and his family, collecting goddam rent!"

She left the drawer open and noiselessly retraced her steps to the front door.

"It's not just *your* skin in the game, Eddie! If you don't play by the rules we agreed on, you can count me out!"

"I don't have time for this bullshit."

Cheryl had the door halfway open when angry footsteps echoed behind her.

"Well, what do we have here?" Eddie's voice made her hands shake.

She turned around, concentrating on not looking guilty.

Suspicion radiated from his body. "Harry!" he called out.

Mr. Carlisle rushed from his office. Standing side by side, the two brothers were like soldiers on the battlefield who discovered the enemy had breached their defensive perimeter.

"Sorry for the interruption. I had to come back for the transistor radio I borrowed to listen to game six," she lied, trying to sound calm. "It belongs to my roommate. She'll be upset if I don't return it tonight."

The men exchanged a glance.

She recrossed the lobby to her desk, pretending she was arriving rather than departing. Her high heels click-clacked conspicuously. She hoped to convince them they would've heard her if she'd snuck in earlier. Slipping behind her desk, she reached into the open drawer to get the radio.

"I'm late for my accounting class."

She opened her bag, dropped the radio inside, then hurried toward the entryway, her heels clicking loudly once again.

Eddie gave his brother an ominous glare.

"Women don't listen to the world series," Mr. Carlisle said.

"A friend said the same thing to me this afternoon. But I assure you, this one does." She attempted a smile, unsure whether she succeeded.

"Why?"

"I'm partial to baseball. I used to watch with my dad when I was growing up. My brother plays first base on a Navy team. And believe it or not, I was pretty good at softball in high school."

"Who won the Series?" her boss asked.

"The Yankees."

"Who won game seven?"

"Yankees."

"Who knocked in the winning run?"

"The winning run – the only run actually – was in the fifth inning. Tony Kubek grounded into a double play, knocking in the runner on third."

"Who was the runner?"

"Bill Skowrun."

He gestured with his chin for her to go.

"Harry!" There was a warning tone to Eddie's voice.

Mr. Carlisle held up his hand to silence his brother.

3

Cheryl could hardly keep her eyes on the road for checking the rearview mirror. She was terrified of being followed or run off the highway. Mr. Carlisle was a middle-aged Casanova whose libido was out of control, but she didn't believe he would hurt her. His brother, on the other hand, had an aura of menace about him.

If only she'd left the office before Eddie showed up yesterday. If only she hadn't laid eyes on all those bills. And going back to the office tonight was a blunder of epic proportions. She should not have pulled in when she saw their cars in the lot. Eddie wasn't fooled by her attempt at subterfuge. He was convinced she overheard them. She checked the rearview again, eyes peeled for a red Cadillac the size of an armored personnel carrier.

Still, it was possible she was blowing things out of proportion. Quite possibly her imagination was getting out of control. She needed to calm down.

Mr. Klein hardly gave her a glance when she stole into class. As usual, he was manipulating a length of string as he played Cat's Cradle, his feet resting on the teacher's desk at the front of the classroom.

Taking a seat in the back, she opened her notebook and clicked her pen. Ironic that tonight he was lecturing on conducting audits to uncover fraud. Were the Carlisles engaged in fraud? The last thing she needed was to be dragged into any dirty dealings. Being employed by a company with a dicey reputation could tarnish her record. She needed to find another job, even if it meant a smaller paycheck.

She shook her head to dislodge that train of thought so she could concentrate.

When class was over Allan stopped by her desk, ready for their calculus study session. Tall and trim with thick brown hair, he had the physical grace of a quarterback. But his interests ran more toward world affairs.

"Let's adjourn to Johnny's so you can pay me for my services with a couple of beers," he said.

She met Allan in high school. In fact, he'd been her date to senior prom. But they became friends, not sweethearts. Now he was a high school math teacher who was also working toward an accounting degree. Thankfully, he agreed to help her with the calculus requirement.

She drove her old Volkswagen and he drove his pickup. Parking side by side, they walked in together and chose a small table in the front corner. After ordering beers, she told him about the ten thousand dollars and what she overheard, making it clear not to spread the story around.

"I'd say it's a money laundering operation," he said.

"Drug money?"

"That would be my guess."

"Ugh. That means I need to get out of there."

"The secretary at my school has given notice, in case you're interested."

She sipped her beer. Then she opened her notebook and scooted her chair over so they could get to work.

*

By the time she got home, Ricky was asleep. Seated on the couch, Tina stretched her arms above her head as *The Untouchables* theme music played. The aroma of popcorn lingered in the air.

"Long day?" Tina asked, crossing the room to turn off the television.

"I'll be glad when I finish my classes. Accounting two nights a week and calculus on Saturday morning is a bit much. On top of that, now I've got to search for a new job."

"I thought you had the boss under control."

"A new problem cropped up. I think he may be involved in something illegal. And I definitely don't want to be considered guilty by association."

"Illegal?"

"He warned me to keep my mouth shut. So you can't pass anything along to Peggy or anyone else."

Tina crossed her heart.

Cheryl explained about the cash and what she'd overheard. "Allan thinks it's money laundering, probably drug money."

"I don't like the sound of that."

"Me neither. The secretary at his school is leaving so I'm going to apply."

Tina gave her a thoughtful nod.

"Speaking of Allan," Cheryl continued, "he's currently not dating anyone. I was thinking I could set you two up for a…"

Tina's hands flew to her hips in exasperation.

"He's a good catch," Cheryl argued.

"If he's a good catch, why don't you catch him?"

"We're just friends. But he's good looking, he's funny, he's..."

"He was my classmate too. I know his good qualities. I don't need a matchmaker, thank you very much!"

"When was the last time you had a date?"

"When was the last time *you* had a date?"

"I have a date Friday night!"

"Don't tell me – one of the horny lieutenants."

Cheryl replied with a mischievous shrug.

"The blond or the dark-haired one?"

"Dark hair."

"Tall, dark and handsome." Tina pursed her lips as she handed Cheryl a letter lying on the lamp table. "From your mom." Then she carried her glass and empty bowl to the kitchen.

Cheryl sat in her dad's Early American wing chair. Upholstered in a hideous brown print fabric, it was as comfortable as it was ugly. Before her family left for Okinawa, her dad said he expected her to take good care of it for the three years they were gone. She was lucky her folks agreed to rent her their home for seventy-five bucks a month while they were overseas. Splitting the rent with Tina meant they both had a safe, affordable place to live with three bedrooms and a fenced back yard for Ricky, Max and Pinky.

As she ripped the envelope open, Pinky jumped into her lap, turning around twice before lying down. Cheryl stroked her fur as she started into her mother's chatty letter. Tina plopped down on the sofa.

"Mom says she joined a bowling league. The team name is – get this – the Naha Devil Dames."

"Devil Dames?" Tina looked genuinely shocked.

"Their team shirt has horns on it."

Tina's mouth fell open.

Cheryl licked her pointer finger and swiped the air, giving herself a point. "You're as gullible as you were in high school! Their name is the Naha Angels."

Tina grabbed a throw pillow and lobbed it at Cheryl's head, but missed. "Such a comedienne! But you'll never be Phyllis Diller!"

They stuck their tongues out at each other, something they'd done a zillion times, prompting Pinky to leap from Cheryl's lap onto the sofa where she curled up next to Tina.

Cheryl continued. "Wayne is playing jayvee football."

"He loves the rough and tumble."

"Get this! Vicky's dating a private named Brad from California. Mom says he's nineteen years old, only two years older than Vicky. My parents must be going soft in the head letting her date that guy. I'm definitely writing my little sister a letter."

"What if it's true love?"

"Says the woman who knows firsthand what happens when you marry too young."

"I wasn't sure what I wanted back then."

"I rest my case."

"Once the class know-it-all, always the class know-it-all."

"Listen to this! Mom says she ran into Audrey Quinn at the PX!"

"What's Audrey doing in Okinawa?"

"Teaching fifth graders at one of the schools for Army kids. Now she's heading home to Fayetteville. Mom gave her our number."

"Wow."

"Audrey was so quiet and studious in high school, she's the last one I would've predicted to become the adventurer while you and I got stuck here in Boringville, North Carolina. First, she went to college, then she taught school in Germany and traveled around Europe. She taught kids in Panama and traveled to Aztec and Mayan ruins. Now the Far East!"

"I'd love to hear about her experiences," Tina said.

"Not me. It would make me feel even more boring."

"You have a point."

Cheryl read the next paragraph aloud.

"Your father has been sent to supervise training of troops in the Vietnamese army. He'll be gone for six months! Please don't tell anyone besides Tina. It's supposed to be on the QT. Some words of warning for you, my dear. You need to be madly in love with your man to live the army life. It's all about training for war, going to war, burying those who die in war, trying to heal those wounded in war and cleaning up after a war. So here I am, nearly eight thousand miles from home while my husband is stationed in another country I know nothing about. It's hard to sleep at night, the room is so quiet without the comfort of Arthur's snoring."

Tina smiled. "Your mom's a good writer. It's a shame she didn't follow her dream."

"Once she fell in love with Dad, her priorities got rearranged several times – first, with baby number one, then baby number two, then baby number three and baby number four."

"Now your dad's in Vietnam. He better retire before we get dragged further into that war."

Cheryl shook her head. What a scary thought.

A short time later, the phone rang as she was rolling her hair, getting ready for bed. Dashing to the kitchen, she answered it before the ringing woke Ricky. When she said hello, there was silence on the other end. She said hello again. Although she could hear someone breathing, there was no response, so she hung up. Wrong numbers were common. Usually the caller apologized. "Sorry, wrong number." Although sometimes they didn't. Could this have something to do with Eddie Carlisle and drugs? No. Even if Allan was correct that Mr. Carlisle and his brother were involved in money laundering, there would be no reason for anyone to dial her at home, then breathe in her ear. Yet, standing barefoot in the kitchen in her pajamas, she couldn't help wondering. Hopefully, it wasn't paranoia kicking in.

*

If she'd been playing by the rules, she would've worn her red suit on Wednesday to complement the precious lobby décor. But Cheryl wore her brown corduroy skirt and a cream blouse and sweater, even though it was once again supposed to be a warm day. She planned to drop off her resume at Sandhills High School on her lunch break. That's where Allan taught math and where the secretary's job was up for grabs. While she wanted to look nice, she didn't want to come across as a show off. So the red suit would stay in the closet.

She sniffed as she entered the lobby that morning. As usual, it reeked of cigarette smoke. She waved a can of air freshener around, then checked her inbox. There were two letters to type – one for Mr. Carlisle and one for a salesman following up with a prospective seller. She was trying to decipher Mr. Carlisle's scrawl when the intercom roared to life.

"Cheryl, get in here."

She cringed as she grabbed her steno pad and pencil and hustled to his office.

He ordered her to close the door, waving her toward a chair. She pursed her lips and waited.

He picked up some documents, tapped them several times on the desk to make the edges line up, then set them down again.

"How long have you worked for me, Cheryl?"

"Almost two years."

"As I recall, you'll be getting your degree in accounting next spring."

She nodded.

"Then you'll be looking for another job so you can make more money. That's the objective, right?

Great. He was going to threaten her with bad references. A low blow considering how diligent she was.

"There are other ways to make more money, you know," he continued. "Selling real estate, for instance."

"Pardon?"

"It occurred to me last night that you might make a good sales person. We could get some excellent publicity if Carlisle Realty announced its first woman real estate agent. I'll pay for you to take a real estate class. Then I can pay for you take the state exam. While you're learning the ropes I can continue to pay your secretarial salary. If you have a talent for it, there's good money to be made selling homes in a boomtown like Fayetteville."

He leaned back in his chair.

"Well?" he said.

"Me, a real estate agent?"

"It's the chance of a lifetime! There's a lot more to be made in real estate than there is being a glorified bookkeeper."

Why would he offer her this *chance of a lifetime?* He hadn't mentioned anything about wanting a woman sales agent. And she hadn't expressed an interest in selling. Driving strangers around in her tiny VW was laughable. Encouraging them to buy a home they couldn't afford would be wrong. In addition, there was no way she would feel safe holding an open house alone.

Then the events of the previous afternoon came rushing back. Was he offering her a sales position to keep her from going to the police about what she overheard?

"Of course, if I invest in your career development," he continued, "I would expect loyalty. I couldn't have you jumping ship to another company after I train you."

She would never accept the offer but it was probably to her advantage for him not to know that. If he and his brother thought she was interested, she'd be better off.

"Thanks, Mr. Carlisle. I'll give it some thought."

"You do that."

When noon arrived, she was out the door, driving directly to Sandhills High. It was a tan brick building shaded by an abundance of tall pines. Sand and pine straw carpeted the ground.

She reported to the front office, introducing herself to the woman whose job she hoped to fill. Mrs. Welch was all politeness, clarifying that the principal would hire the new secretary but it was still necessary to fill out an application at the superintendent's office. Cheryl had hoped to at least say hello to the man who would hopefully be her next boss, but she merely left her resume and thanked Mrs. Welch, glad she'd worn a skirt and sweater so she would fit in.

*

The clock read five till seven when she pulled into the parking lot at the Sakura Restaurant. It was located along a stretch of Raeford Road where homes used to line the street. Those homes had been rezoned commercial as traffic increased. The restaurant was inside one of them, which was now painted pale green with red accents.

She was alarmed when she spotted Paul in slacks and a tweed sport coat. His back was against the door beneath the entrance overhang that resembled a red Shinto Shrine. He jerked his head this way and that, scanning the surroundings. But what was he looking for? Bad guys? Instead of parking her Beetle, she came to a halt in front of the door and rolled down her window.

As she was about to open her mouth, it hit her. He was pulling her leg. "Hop in!" she cried. "We'll make a break for it!"

He ran around the rear of the car and jumped in beside her. "They're armed and dangerous!" he said. "But you can strike terror in their hearts with your secret weapon."

Without missing a beat, she shifted into her nasal voice, squawking through the open window. "Drop your weapons, you stinking skunks!"

He was convulsed with laughter, which gave her a giggling fit. They reined in the silliness as she parked the car and they made their way to the restaurant door.

"Stinking skunks?" he said. "Is that the best you could do?"

Still in high spirits, they were escorted to their table by a hostess in a traditional kimono with white tabis and wooden getas on her feet. Following her through a maze of Japanese folding screens to their own dining area, they settled onto tatami mats across from each other at a low black lacquer table.

"You can't be too careful," he said. "Who knows what you're getting into at a restaurant you haven't been to before? Especially on a first date with a diabolical woman!"

"Diabolical woman?"

Warmth enveloped her. And it wasn't the burgundy corduroy pants and jacket she'd changed into before leaving the office. Funny that she'd done her best to give him the brush-off and now she was falling for him. This, despite knowing almost nothing about him except he had a sense of humor and was a good looking man.

He had a masculine jawline, a straight nose and expressive dark eyebrows. His features were softened by his inviting hazel eyes with longer eyelashes than a man deserved, and lips that whispered, 'kiss me anytime you want.'

"All I know about *you* is that you're a first lieutenant with a kooky sense of humor."

"This from the woman who uses an invisible clothespin on her nose to drive men away!"

She rolled her eyes.

A pretty waitress in a pale blue kimono stepped around a decorative folding screen that enclosed one side of their enclosure. Charming screens surrounded them, with other tables and diners seated beyond them. She set a tray with a teapot and tiny teacups on the table. Her black hair was arranged in an artistic Japanese style. She handed them menus before serving tea with quiet grace. Bowing in the traditional Japanese manner, she left them to make their selections.

Paul gestured after her with his head. "If the food is half as good as our waitress..." He didn't feel the need to continue.

"So, Lieutenant McIntyre, what exactly do you do for Uncle Sam to justify the bars on your uniform?"

"I'm a pilot with the Eighty-second Aviation Battalion, part of the Eighty-second Airborne Division. I fly Hueys mainly."

"Wow."

"Yeah, I'm a lucky guy. I've got a fun job. As long as we're not at war, that is."

"Your roommate, is he a pilot too?"

"Affirmative."

"Affirmative?"

"Top secret military jargon."

"Military mumbo jumbo, you mean."

Cheryl couldn't believe how free and easy conversation was. She'd only met the guy a couple of days ago. After placing their order – sukiyaki for her, teriyaki salmon for him – questions and answers flowed from one side of the table to the other in an unhurried fashion, peppered with sparring and teasing.

They were both Army brats. He had a brother and sister and had moved around growing up. His parents now lived in Washington DC. His dad was a major general stationed at the Pentagon. Having gone through college as an ROTC student, he was kicking around the idea of following in his father's footsteps. Cheryl thought he would see her in a different light once she told him her dad was a master sergeant. But he was unfazed by the chasm between his father being a high-ranking officer while hers was an enlisted man. She told him her family was in Okinawa and her brother Mike was a sailor aboard a ship based in Norfolk.

As dinner progressed, so did they, never lacking for things to chat about. She didn't want the evening to end and was positive he didn't either. After paying the check and leaving a generous tip, he professed as much on the way to her car.

"You may think I'm a little over eager, but I'd like to take you out to dinner again Friday night. I can pick you up at your house as a gentleman should now that I know you're not Lizzie Borden's cousin."

She hadn't felt so drawn to a man. She imagined asking him to follow her home, fantasizing about his lips on hers. But this was their first date. She hardly knew him.

Still, maybe she could invite him over. She pictured sitting on the couch, having a glass of wine and talking into the wee hours. Could she trust him? More importantly, could she trust herself?

Her heart felt all fluttery. Realization dawned that she'd been *in like* several times, but she'd never truly been in love. Was this love? One thing was certain: she had never experienced the dizzying sensations that made her want to slip her hands beneath his shirt and caress his chest.

"How about coming over to my house?" she blurted.

His eyes widened in surprise.

"For a family dinner," she added, flapping her hand nervously.

He gave a big, slow nod.

"All I know how to make is old-fashioned southern food," she said. "I'm thinking fried chicken, mashed potatoes, biscuits and gravy?"

"It'll be torture but I'll force myself. You *are* a diabolical woman."

In the parking lot afterwards, he waited until her engine was running before crossing to his Corvette.

She backed out of her spot, then shifted into first gear, driving slowly toward the exit. When she turned the wheel to the left, her low beams swept across a bright red car. It was a fifty-nine Cadillac with white sidewalls and tailfins that she would recognize anywhere.

4

Cheryl sprayed Pledge on the coffee table, still dressed in the burgundy pants outfit she'd worn to the restaurant.

Tina emerged in her PJs and robe. "You do know it's almost eleven o'clock," she said, massaging lotion onto her hands.

"I invited Paul for dinner Friday night."

"And that means you have to…"

"Tidy up, yes. I can't do it all tomorrow night. I have class." She gestured at the mess, including Ricky's Tinker Toys dumped willy-nilly in the center of the room, several toy cars lined up on the lamp table, a cowboy gun and holster draped over the back of the couch, a Davy Crockett coonskin cap on the floor and the magazine rack by her dad's chair overflowing with magazines and newspapers. "God, what was I thinking? I need to clean the bathroom and mop the kitchen too."

"Cancel! Tell him your roommate is a slob and refuses to clean up her mess on two days' notice."

"I don't have his number."

"Why not?"

"I didn't want to seem forward."

"Of course. Better to seem backward."

Cheryl gave her a smirk.

"So inviting him over for dinner is not being forward," Tina said, returning Cheryl's smirk and raising her one. "That must've been one helluva first date!"

Cheryl suddenly saw herself as Tina did – all worked up about making a good impression on a guy she didn't know existed until two days ago.

"Cut class tomorrow night and do your cleaning then." Tina leaned down to pick up the coonskin cap before strolling into the kitchen for her nightly glass of milk. On the way, she covered her mouth in a futile attempt at suppressing an enormous yawn.

Cheryl had been on the verge of telling her about seeing the red Caddy at the restaurant but the yawn stopped her. Tina needed her sleep.

*

She had removed the dust cover from her typewriter Thursday morning when Mrs. Carlisle swept into the lobby showing off the spoils of a shopping trip to her favorite Raleigh boutique. She wore an ivory wool suit and matching pillbox hat atop her teased hair, which was dyed a dark brunette at an exclusive beauty parlor to cover the grey.

"It's yellow dress day!" she said, pointing at Cheryl's outfit as she hurried through the lobby. The secretary dress code was Mrs. Carlisle's idea to increase sales. "Excellent choice, dear!"

Cheryl assumed Mrs. C. was one of those cheerleaders her husband drooled over when he was young. Although there were some lines on her face, she was a good-looking woman with a 'rah! rah! sis-boom-bah!' personality.

Cheryl jumped up, hoping to delay her.

"I only need a couple of minutes," Mrs. Carlisle said, waving Cheryl off. "I'm on my way to a Junior League meeting."

Without slowing her pace, she continued to her husband's office. With a quick tap on the door, she ducked inside, not waiting for an invitation.

The boss didn't approve of people showing up unannounced. Even his wife. Cheryl could probably count on being dressed down for letting this happen. But what was she supposed to do?

As she loaded paper into the typewriter, an angry interchange was underway in the boss's office. The words were muffled but it was plain that Mrs. Carlisle was letting her husband have it about something.

"Well, if it isn't the company's first *saleslady*."

It was Roger Buckley, the agent who won last year's award as Carlisle Realty's million dollar salesman.

"Sleeping with the boss, huh?" he went on.

"I can't believe you just said that! At no time and under no circumstances would I ever stoop so low."

He replied as though he hadn't heard her. "Remember, real estate is a man's world."

Spoken like a strutting rooster pushing the hen around to preserve his place at the top of the pecking order.

In one fell swoop, Roger was her enemy. They'd been on friendly terms for two years. He'd flirted with her a few times early on, but once she made it clear she wasn't interested, and Mr. Carlisle let it be known that he *was*, Roger backed off.

Which begged the question: why did Mr. Carlisle tell Roger? Did he think Roger would mentor the first woman agent at the company? That he would encourage her, give her advice, make her feel welcome? If so, he seriously misjudged his top seller.

She stewed over the encounter, eventually deciding to give Mr. C. the benefit of the doubt even though she'd already dismissed his proposal out of hand. Why would she want to work for a company that laundered drug money?

Leaning down to fetch her purse from the bottom drawer, she overheard a couple of salesmen heading out for lunch. Because she was hidden from view, they thought she was already gone.

"She must really deliver the goods behind closed doors."

"Mark my words. Nobody's going to take him seriously when this gets out."

It was Walter Sutherland and Dan O'Keefe who shared an office and a passion for golf.

"Yeah, it's one thing to have a pretty young thing as your secretary. Quite another to let her do a man's job. Like I said, she must be damn good between the sheets."

She sat up once they were out the door in time for Mrs. Carlisle to stop by on her way out, her chipper tone long gone.

"Did you work late on Tuesday?"

Which struck Cheryl as a question in search of trouble. She answered truthfully, but kept it vague.

"I had accounting class Tuesday night. I went directly from work."

"Hmph!"

With that, Mrs. C. did her usual hoity-toity strut through the front door and across the parking lot to her pink Grand Prix.

Cheryl stopped by Jerry Inman's office as she was leaving on her lunch break. He was on the schedule to cover the phones while she was gone.

"I'm leaving now." She turned to go but he stopped her.

"How'd you convince Harry to let you do sales? We don't take beginners. We let them get their feet wet elsewhere."

Unlike Roger, Jerry was a loyal husband. Also unlike Roger, the expression on Jerry's face wasn't sarcasm mixed with condescension. In fact, his objection was that she was inexperienced, not that she was a woman.

"It was his idea, not mine. An idea that doesn't have much appeal at the moment."

"Glad to hear it. You'll be getting married before long. Then family will be your top priority, as it should be."

He wasn't being nasty like Roger and the other guys, but his reaction annoyed her just the same. She wouldn't be surprised if he had the same feelings about her plan to become a CPA. She didn't have time to argue. That job application needed filling out.

Her trip to school district headquarters went off without a hitch. On her way back, she stopped at a payphone to dial Sandhills High School to arrange an interview. The secretary said Mr. Swaney could meet with her next Wednesday at ten.

*

It was pushing four when the boss returned from a long lunch with Mr. Odom to discuss details of the proposed merger. Cheryl waited half an hour before knocking on his door.

"I'm busy!" he barked.

Determined to have her say, she barged in anyway. He was hunched over his desk, studying a document. His suit jacket was draped over the back of his chair, his sleeves rolled up and his tie loosened. She closed the door, crossing the room to stand before him.

"Why did you tell half the staff about offering me a sales job?"

"I said I'm busy." His eyes remained focused on the paper in front of him.

"Or did you tell the *entire* staff?"

"Are you deaf?"

"They're accusing me of sleeping with you in exchange for special treatment."

He ignored her.

"Tell them it was your idea, not mine," she said.

He looked up, glaring at her. "Not now, Cheryl. I've got more important things to deal with!"

From a distance the document on his desk could've been a contract.

She stood her ground, jaw tightened, a torrent of words locked and loaded. But once that angry outburst began, she knew there would be no applying the brakes. So she took a deep breath and forced the bile back down her throat. She needed this stupid job a while longer. She couldn't afford to walk out. She had to have another job locked in first. Now that she had that interview scheduled for next week, she hoped it wouldn't be long before she could give her notice and flounce out of here however she pleased.

After stopping by A&P to get ingredients for tomorrow night's dinner, she arrived home to find Tina and Ricky at the kitchen table. Ricky's face lit up as she bustled through the door.

"Mommy made tuna roll-ups, Cheryl! With graybee."

"Oh boy! Tuna roll-ups with gravy!"

"And French fries with ketchup! And baked beans too!"

"I've gotten so good at gourmet cooking," Tina said, straight-faced, "I may apply for a chef's job at that new French restaurant, Le Bistro des Dumdums."

Cheryl tittered as she put her few groceries away, then took her seat across from her favorite first grader. "Well, good golly, Miss Molly," she said, lifting two roll-ups onto her plate and spooning cream of mushroom soup – the gravy – over them.

"Good golly, Mister Jolly!" Ricky shot back with glee.

Once supper was over, Cheryl changed into cleaning clothes and got to work. By eight-thirty, she'd scoured the bathroom, mopped and waxed the kitchen floor, cleaned the refrigerator, vacuumed the house and tidied up. Tina and Ricky stashed his toys and games in his bedroom, which was a major undertaking that would be completely undone within a day and a half. Tina thought Cheryl overdid it, arguing that they kept a clean, if somewhat messy house. But being her mother's daughter, Cheryl couldn't help herself when it came to preparing for company, especially when the guest for tomorrow night's family supper was the guy she was falling in love with.

She was setting out crackers and cheese on the kitchen table when she heard Allan's pickup. Tina and Ricky got the door while she dashed to her room to change out of her pedal pushers and old top into jeans and a decent shirt.

When she joined them in the living room, Ricky was showing Allan his Halloween costume. It was a homemade soldier uniform – dark olive drab pants, matching jacket and a toy army helmet.

While Tina tucked him in bed Cheryl led Allan to the kitchen where her textbook was waiting. Setting two cans of Schlitz on the table, she took the seat to his left so they could share the crackers and cheese.

"I'll be so glad when the blasted calculus test is done," Cheryl said. "Tell me why we need to learn calculus to be accountants?"

"Universities are always looking for ways to make money. If they require students in the accounting program to take calculus, then that's one more class we have to pay for."

"Cynical."

"Can't help it."

"You think I can pass the exam next week?"

"You'll do fine. All you have to do is keep studying. Once the test is over, you won't ever have to use that stuff again."

"Hallelujah!"

"I've been thinking that when we get our degrees, we could throw in together to set up an accounting business. Partners, you know?"

Cheryl always imagined hiring on at a company that could pay her well and provide good benefits.

"I don't know."

"We could start out small, then hire a couple of others. We could incorporate as Donovan and Blake, Certified Public Accountants."

He was serious.

She opened her book, eager to get through all the material she needed help with. His idea would have to simmer a while.

It was almost ten o'clock when Tina moseyed in.

"Join us," Cheryl said, jumping up to get a can of mixed nuts from the cabinet. "We're done." She dumped nuts in three small bowls and set them on the table as Tina poured herself a beer.

"I was telling Cheryl that Ricky is one heck of a great kid," Allan said.

"He's a bundle of energy, that's a fact. The best part of my life."

"Which is why I don't mind babysitting," Cheryl said. "Most people don't want to look after their roommate's kid, but Ricky's a blast to be with. I always tell Tina she can go out for the evening anytime she wants to."

Tina gave her a wary look.

"By the way," Cheryl said, "did you see the story in the paper about The Carolina Trio performing next weekend at Methodist College?" She was all innocence. "I hear they have a Kingston Trio sound."

Tina shot her a warning look.

Allan changed the subject.

"Either of you been contacted about our ten-year class reunion?"

"It has *not* been ten years," Cheryl said.

"It's been eight years. Which means it's time to get the ball rolling. I got a call from Nelson Bartlett. You remember Nelson. He was president of our senior class."

"How could we forget?" Tina said with a hint of sarcasm.

"They need someone here in Fayetteville to head the reunion committee," Allan said. "He asked if I would do it."

"You said no, of course," said Cheryl.

"I told him I'd do it. But I need a co-chair." He gave Cheryl a hopeful look.

"Don't look at me."

"Aw, come on. We'll be finished with accounting next spring."

She crossed her arms and shook her head.

"You're a good organizer," he said. "And the committee will have eight members. Plenty to share the load."

Cheryl looked at Tina for her take but Tina made herself busy wiping a wet spot on the table with a napkin.

"I'll think about it," Cheryl said, figuring that would give her time to come up with a good excuse.

Once he was gone, she sat down in the living room, organizing her notes. Tina wandered in, picked up a book she'd been reading from the lamp table and sat down on the leather hassock at Cheryl's feet.

"You're an idiot," Tina said.

"I'm..."

"An idiot."

Cheryl's response was a look of indignant innocence.

"Unbelievable that you tried to set me up with Allan after I asked you to cease and desist," Tina continued. "Besides, it's as plain as that dense expression on your conniving face that it's *you* he has eyes for."

"He does not!"

"He didn't ask *me* to work with him on the reunion committee."

"We're old friends, that's all."

"Uh-huh. Regardless, I want to make something perfectly clear. He's not my type. How many times do I have to tell you?"

"Who *is* your type?"

Tina gave her the evil eye, then tucked the book under her arm and disappeared into her bedroom.

*

Friday morning it seemed to have been ages since she'd seen Paul even though it was only night before last. She was on pins and needles worrying about dinner, afraid her cooking wouldn't measure up. More importantly, she hoped the growing affection between them was real.

A note from the boss put her in a bad mood right away. He was out of the office all day, which meant there was no chance he'd tell the salesmen she wasn't sleeping her way to the top.

She was cussing under her breath when she turned her attention to a shopping bag on her typewriter with her name on it. She pulled out something wrapped in tissue paper. When she unwrapped the mystery gift, heat flooded her cheeks.

In her hands was a sheer red nighty the likes of which she'd never seen. It had cheap lace around the edges and was barely long enough to reach the tops of her thighs. So thin, it would leave nothing to the imagination. The finishing touch was a pair of crotchless panties.

That's when men's giggles floated into the lobby. She resisted the urge to toss the tacky lingerie in the trash can. Instead, she dropped it back into the bag and wrote a note. It read, "Mr. Carlisle, this was left on my desk by some of your well-mannered sales agents who think you're offering me a sales job because I sleep with you. Do you want that reputation? Are you going to allow this to continue?"

Taping it to the outside of the bag, she took it to the boss's office, using her key to let herself in. She left the bag on his chair so he couldn't help but see it when he returned.

Back at her desk, it occurred to her that if a potential employer asked for references, any of the Carlisle Realty sales agents could spread the salacious rumor. She was outraged that one of those numbskulls could ruin her career with a single nasty comment.

She remained at her desk all morning and afternoon, answering the phone, typing letters, purchase offers and other documents and filing paperwork. Instead of delivering them as she normally did, she arranged them on top of her file cabinet, silently pointing them out to salesmen when they came searching.

When Eddie Carlisle showed up around three-thirty, she turned away, hoping to somehow avoid being on his radar by making herself invisible. It didn't work. He came straight for her, demanding to know where his "half-wit brother" was. He was indignant when she said Mr. C. was gone for the day. He found his way to Roger's office. After the two of them chewed the fat for half an hour, Eddie sauntered back through the lobby. He stopped to give her a lingering once-over, sizing her up with fresh eyes. Very fresh eyes.

"You had everyone fooled, Miss Donovan. The guys thought you were a bona fide goody-two shoes. Now we know that's a bucket of horseshit."

"Your brother offered me a sales job. I didn't request it and I didn't sleep with him. Roger is so full of it, he could manufacture a cow patty big enough to pave Hay Street!"

His smug grin made her want to slap his face. He walked out before she was tempted to satisfy the urge.

She was livid. Intensely livid. At the razor's edge of violently livid. Was this how Ricky felt when bullies at school picked on him? She was being bullied too. First, by Mr.

Carlisle with the constant threat of being touched or kissed. Then there was Eddie who literally made her fear for her life. And the mean-spirited, sexist salesmen who thought of women as a lower species. She wondered if being hounded by a pack of rabid Rottweilers could be any worse.

Covering the Smith Corona, she announced in a booming voice that she was going home. The boss had approved her request to leave at five today. Bearing in mind that she was already on the verge of punching anyone in the face who said another asinine word to her, she concluded that making her exit at four was the prudent thing to do.

5

As luck would have it, the house was empty when Cheryl got home. That meant there were no judgmental eyes to watch her select a juice glass with oranges painted on it and fill it with Chardonnay. She took a sip on her way to the bedroom.

She made the mistake of looking around her room as she set her glass on the chest of drawers. Above her bed hung a charcoal portrait of her parents she did in high school. There was an abstract collage made of buttons, jewelry, scraps of cloth and other odds and ends. When she completed it in ninth grade, it spoke to her of happiness and hope. Now it pulsated with regret. Her youthful drawings, pastels, paintings and collages covered the walls, all of them created before she graduated high school, back when her imagination was brimming with ideas. That her bedroom looked this way eight years later was depressing. It was as if she'd died and her mother insisted on keeping as it was.

The realization only served to make her even more out of sorts. Which was bad timing with Paul coming over for a homecooked meal tonight.

Hanging her work clothes in the closet, she donned an old shirt and pants. Returning to the kitchen, she poured more wine into her now empty glass, then wrapped an apron around her waist. She put her Peter, Paul and Mary album on the stereo and sang along with "500 Miles" while peeling potatoes. Dinner would be at seven. She needed to calm the fury in her chest. She couldn't afford to waste any more energy seething about being bullied by morons.

By the time she sang along with the last song on the album, her glass of wine was empty again and she was feeling less like a prickly cactus.

Thankfully, Tina and Ricky had smiles on their faces when they arrived.

At twenty till seven, the biscuits were arranged on a baking sheet waiting to be popped in the oven while the rest of the food simmered. Cheryl set the oven to pre-heat, then freshened up before changing into the outfit she'd chosen for the evening. She paused in front of the full-length mirror, eyeing her tapered black pants, black and white houndstooth vest over a white shirt with black flats. Her hair hung loose on her shoulders. She'd worn pants to the restaurant Wednesday night, and she was wearing them again tonight. It was an easy way to let Paul know she didn't aspire to hobnob with the conventional ladies of the Junior League who wouldn't approve of pants for an evening date.

Ricky acted starstruck when she arrived in the kitchen.

"You look like you're on the *Dobie Gillis* show!"

"Yeah, you could pass for a beatnik," Tina said, gathering plates, silverware and napkins.

"Cool, daddio," Cheryl said, snapping her fingers as she crossed the kitchen to retrieve her apron. "I don't want to come off as a square. Dig it?" She tied the apron on before sliding the biscuits in the oven. Then she gave the chicken gravy an energetic stir.

"All you need is a beret and a cigarette and you could be Maynard G. Kreb's girlfriend," Tina said.

"Yeah!" Ricky cried.

"I'm not sure Maynard has a girlfriend," Cheryl said.

A knock at the door sent Ricky tearing through the living room as Cheryl mashed the potatoes. Tina hurried after him to greet Paul, who presented her with a pot of orange mums.

"Ah, the man of the house," Paul said, reaching out to shake Ricky's hand.

Ricky's response was little-boy awkward.

"The flowers are for the ladies," Paul said, giving the little boy's small hand a quick shake. "And this is for you."

He gave him a blue Matchbox pickup truck. Ricky looked at his mom, beaming.

She mouthed 'thank you,' and Ricky thanked their guest.

"Man, it smells good in here!" Paul said, stepping into the living room.

Cheryl materialized in the wide archway to the dining room. "Thank goodness even bad food can make your mouth water while it's on the stove."

"Oh no," Tina said, "not again!"

"Well," Cheryl said, wiping her hands on her apron, "if at first you don't succeed, fry, fry again!" She whirled around and returned to the kitchen.

A concerned expression crept over Paul's face.

"Don't worry," Tina said, "if the second try is as bad as the first, there's a Kentucky Fried Chicken ten minutes from here."

"But Cheryl," Ricky said, following her into the kitchen, "you make the bestest fried chicken in the world!"

"You two are good," Paul said, catching onto their shenanigans at his expense. "Right up there with Martin and Lewis!"

After the introductions, there was a flurry of activity as the food was served and they took their seats around the dining room table spread with a pale blue tablecloth. The pretty mums sat on the sideboard adding a splash of color.

Paul watched Cheryl as she removed her apron. His eyes took in her beatnik outfit. Anyone paying attention could see he was besotted. It was an old-fashioned word but the only one that truly fit the expression on his face. It appeared he was struggling to come up with a compliment.

"I guess you like pants," he said, his tone uncertain.

"Looks like you do too."

Tina laughed. Paul laughed too.

"Look what your boyfriend brought me, Cheryl!" Ricky showed her the little metal truck, bringing an end to Paul's awkward moment.

Now it was Cheryl's turn to feel uncomfortable. She tried not to blush at his use of the word 'boyfriend,' but failed.

"How about you store it in your pocket while we eat?" Tina said.

Sitting on a seven-inch thick dictionary in one of the upholstered chairs, Ricky crammed the toy in his pocket, then rushed through his "God is great" blessing so they could get down to business.

"I want a drumstick, Mommy!"

"Hold your horses, Little Joe."

"Don't forget a biscuit and graybee."

She loaded his plate. Then the adults passed the bowls, Paul oohing and aahing over each dish.

"Finger lickin' good!" he exclaimed, holding a breast with both hands. "It may be the only kind of food you know how to cook, but like Ricky said, this is the best fried chicken I've ever tasted!"

"Yup," said Ricky, his mouth full.

"A woman who can whip up such a fine supper is going to make *someone* a good wife!" Paul closed his eyes in ecstasy.

Tina snuck an amused glance at Cheryl, then wiped a dollop of mashed potatoes from the front of Ricky's shirt.

"Do you cook, Paul?" Cheryl asked.

"I make a mean tuna salad sandwich."

The women cracked up.

"What?" he said.

"I don't think that qualifies as cooking," Cheryl said.

"It's the masculine form of cooking."

"You mean, without fire?" Tina asked.

"The feminine form of cooking is *real* cooking. That's a woman's domain." He took another bite of chicken.

"Tell that to all the French chefs who answer to monsieur!" Cheryl said.

He didn't argue.

"I'll bet Ricky would enjoy hearing what you do," Cheryl suggested, deciding to change the subject.

"So would I," Tina said.

Paul obliged, explaining that he was a pilot who flew helicopters and planes. He described how a helicopter lifted straight up into the air and how it could hover in one place. His descriptions came alive with pantomimes of a helicopter's movements and sound effects of rotors spinning at high speed.

If Ricky had been a dog, his tail would've been wagging.

"Can you take me for a ride?" he asked.

His mom told him it wouldn't be possible with a military helicopter.

The banana pudding was a big hit for dessert. Afterwards Paul and Ricky played with his cars and trucks in his room while the women did dishes.

Once Ricky said his good-nights and Tina escorted him to the bathtub, Paul declared that it was a perfect evening for a drive.

Parked along the street, his Corvette resembled a teal gemstone, gleaming in the light from a streetlamp above. She'd seen him drive it with the top down but the weather had turned cooler, so the hardtop was in place.

He cranked the engine, revved it a couple of times, put it in gear, then took it slow and easy through the neighborhood before picking up speed once they were on the main road. When they reached Highway 301, he headed south, winding it out on the divided highway. He was doing seventy, but when Cheryl noticed the speedometer went all the way to a hundred and sixty, she grabbed the armrest.

"Don't worry, I never exceed a hundred miles an hour." He chuckled as he slowed to turn off the highway.

In moments, they pulled into a dirt parking lot beside Hope Mills Lake. Zipping up their jackets, they strolled along the shore, their eyes drawn to the three quarter moon reflected off the surface of the water.

If only he would take her hand.

No sooner had the thought flitted through her mind than his warm hand enveloped hers. What gave her away?

"A perfect night," he said. "Well, almost perfect."

Moving slowly, giving her time to demur, he took her in his arms and leaned close until they were nose to nose. "This will make it perfect."

As his mouth gently settled on hers, his lips tingled with invitation. It was a take-no-prisoners kiss, his hands softly mapping the terrain of her back. When he paused, his eyes searched hers.

"Any chance you love me as much as I love you?"

A 'yes' was on the tip of her tongue, but she hesitated. There was a hunger in her belly that had nothing to do with food. It could also have nothing to do with love. But she'd learned that lust could be a booby trap. Things were moving too fast.

"I felt it in your kiss," he said. "Even by the moonlight I can see love in your eyes." He entwined his fingers with hers, holding their clasped hands on his chest.

She amazed herself by kissing him, which fanned the flames.

"Actions do speak louder than words," he said softly.

She eased out of his embrace and slid her arm through his, pulling him forward to resume their stroll. They were navigating new territory a mere four days after they met.

The way his eyes drank her in, the way his body molded to hers and the way his lips tasted, made her want to ignore the little voice in her brain nagging her to slow down while her heart pounded. She felt as though she was being tossed about by gale-force winds.

She was reminded of her mother telling the story of how she and Dad had a whirlwind romance. She always said it with a loving glance at her father. When Cheryl was a little girl, she imagined younger versions of Mommy and Daddy being blown off their feet by a storm as they kissed. Now she knew what her mom was talking about.

It was no wonder she suffered emotional vertigo. It was unnerving how fast she'd fallen for Paul. She'd always imagined that falling in love would be gradual. First, she would feel some attraction. Slowly, she'd get to know him. Then she'd feel a growing attachment, deep affection and desire, until she knew in her heart that she was in love. But with Paul, she felt as though she'd been injected with a love potion that sent her tumbling head over heels.

"This is the kind of night that comes along once in a lifetime," he said, looking down at her by his side.

"The moon on the water is lovely." There was a dreamy quality to her voice.

"It's you. You and the moon and the pretty lake created this enchanting night."

He had stopped walking, turning to face her. He pulled her into another sweet embrace and kissed her again.

"Mm-mm, your kisses are sweeter than wine," he whispered.

It was *his* kisses that were sweeter than wine. She craved more.

"You're shivering," he said. "We better go."

As they walked back to the Vette, she didn't explain that the shivering had nothing to do with the cold.

On the drive home, he told her that while the Corvette was a blast to drive, there was one drawback – the bucket seats.

"If I still had my fifty-seven Bel Air with that nice bench seat, you could slide over next to me and I'd wrap my arm around your shoulders and kiss you at every red light." He reached for her hand, glancing her way in the dark. "We could sit hip to hip, thigh to thigh."

She kept her eyes on the road.

"I could trade this beauty in for a bigger car."

"I'm partial to the Corvette."

"Yeah, but it may not be long before I need a family car."

In the dark, he couldn't see the infinitesimal shake of her head.

As they turned into her neighborhood he reached for her hand again. "What say we take in a movie tomorrow night? *Cape Fear* just started playing at the drive-in."

"I think I'm babysitting for Tina." It was a lie but she thought she could convince Tina to ask a friend out.

The last thing she needed was an evening at the drive-in where couples missed the feature entirely, otherwise engaged in the back seat.

"If you're babysitting, I'll come over and help," Paul said. "I can play with Ricky while you cook and wash dishes."

"How about *I* play with Ricky while *you* cook and wash dishes."

He laughed, missing her sarcasm completely.

When he walked her to the front porch, they paused at the door.

"You know," he said, "the first time I saw you – before you opened your mouth, that is – I thought to myself, that's the woman I want to be the mother of my children. Then you spoke." He chortled at the memory. "But when I came back that afternoon and heard your real voice, I was in fourteenth heaven. That's two seventh heavens rolled into one. Besides striking me as a perfect mother, you had two things I prize: a wacky sense of humor and great feminine beauty."

He meant it as a high compliment but, for some reason, it reminded her of June Cleaver, the mom in "Leave it to Beaver." And who wanted to be June Cleaver?

She had intended to invite him in. Was it a good idea? Before she could make up her mind, Tina opened the door.

"Good timing! I'm making hot cocoa!"

And so it was that the low-key, family dinner date Cheryl had been waiting for with bated breath stretched out for another hour just when she was having doubts.

"Cheryl tells me she's babysitting Ricky tomorrow night." Paul's eyes were on Tina.

"Well, I..." Tina gave Cheryl a look that was part question and part accusation.

Cheryl broke in. "I think you said you're going out with Peggy?" She nodded her head, hoping Tina could read between the lines.

"It's kind of up in the air."

"I volunteered to help out," Paul said. "I understand why Cheryl enjoys babysitting for you. It's fun hanging out with Ricky. It's also good training for when Cheryl has children of her own." He turned to Cheryl then. "I'll bet you already know how to change diapers, feed a baby, rock him to sleep, and do all kinds of things a mother needs to know."

"Gosh," Tina said, "maybe I should live here rent-free since you're making use of my little boy to prepare for motherhood?"

Cheryl responded with a tight-lipped smile.

Paul seemed to pick up on the tension, choosing that moment to shower them with praise for the food and the company. He said goodnight to Tina and followed Cheryl onto the front porch.

"Thanks for the drive," she said. "Riding in your Corvette was fun. And the lake was lovely in the moonlight."

"It was the loveliest moonlit night I've experienced in my life." He took her hand in his, tugging her closer. "Of course, it had a lot to do with the beautiful woman I was with."

He wrapped his arms around her and kissed her tenderly.

"I'm so glad fate sent me to your office on Monday," he said.

She didn't respond, afraid she'd say the wrong thing.

He stepped back, digging in his pocket for a tiny notebook and pen. He wrote something on a page, tore it out and handed it to her.

"That's my number. Let me know if you end up babysitting. If not, we can go to the drive-in after all."

She studied the paper to avoid meeting his eyes. Folding her arms across her chest, she watched him drive away. When she turned to go inside, something caught her eye down the street. Parked along the curb in the dark was a big red car. It was too dark to make out any details.

She hurried inside where Tina was cleaning up.

"There's a red car parked a few houses down. I have to find out if it's Eddie Carlisle's Cadillac."

"How do you propose to do that?"

"I'll drive my car down there and turn my lights on. I need you to stand on the porch and watch. If he rams me, call the police. Oh, and an ambulance."

"Great."

"I'll get my keys. You turn the front porch light off, then stand in the shadows and keep your eyes peeled."

"This is not good. You know that don't you?"

Cheryl tiptoed to her bedroom, grabbed her keys and soundlessly made her way out the back door and around to the driveway. She took a deep breath to steady her nerves, then cranked the engine of her VW, put it in reverse and without turning her lights on, slowly backed out of the driveway. Shifting into first gear, she hugged the left curb as she crawled down the street in the dark.

Passing the next door neighbor's driveway she turned the headlights on and hit the brights. As her high beams lit up the other car, his brights suddenly came on too, blinding her. Was he coming at her? Was he about to ram her head on? She slammed the brakes and braced for impact. In that instant, she realized the other car was getting smaller, not larger. He was backing away. Fast.

"Oh no you don't!" She moved her foot from the brake to the accelerator and gave chase.

Now that his high beams weren't so close, she could see that it was, in fact, a large red car with fins. But they were different from the fins on a Cadillac. They were more subdued. And this car had a front grille that reminded her of monstrous teeth ready to devour its prey. The grille was battered, making it look like a couple of teeth were missing. If it wasn't Eddie, it had to be one of Eddie's flunkeys. The guy wouldn't have reacted as he did if he wasn't spying on her.

He raced down the street in reverse. Then, with her gaining on him, he performed a one-eighty and streaked away.

It was gut instinct that caused her foot to step on the gas, sending her little Volkswagen on a reckless game of chase. Her brain knew there was no chance in hell she could catch that big red bomber. Her brain also knew there was a real risk of killing someone in the process, perhaps herself. When she reached the intersection, there was no sign of the mystery car.

On the one hand, she was frustrated. On the other, she was relieved. Although she'd raced after him, she had no idea what she would've done if she'd caught up with the guy. She would probably have become road kill, joining the carcasses of raccoons and possums along the shoulder.

Returning to the house, she found Tina standing in the street.

"God," Tina said, "I thought you'd been…"

"I wasn't."

Cheryl parked in the driveway. She was a little shaky and didn't protest when Tina gave her a hug.

They waited to talk about it until they were ensconced on either end of the couch, knees up, sipping on a juice glass of wine.

"If it wasn't Mr. C.'s bad-to-the-bone brother, who was it?" Tina asked.

"When I got close enough to see him I was blinded by the headlights. But now that I think about it, there was a second or two after I turned on my brights before he did the same. That's when I got a glimpse of him. He was wearing a hat, you know the kind gangsters wear on TV. And he had sunglasses on." She cocked her head. "Who wears sunglasses at night?"

"Elvis?"

"I think I would recognize Elvis. Even in the dark."

Which Tina found entertaining.

Cheryl was lost in thought for a moment.

"You know what else I saw? Big, fuzzy dice hanging from the rearview mirror."

"So you're being tailed by a tacky gangster wearing sunglasses."

Cheryl chuckled although in reality, she wasn't the least bit amused.

6

Ricky was lying on the living room floor eating a bowl of Cheerios while watching *The Bugs Bunny Show* when Cheryl got up Saturday morning. Hearing her footsteps, he whirled around.

"I'm the Cheerios Kid! Big-G, little-o, Go-power!" He flexed his right arm, squeezing his bicep to prove that eating Cheerios was making him as big and strong as the Cheerios Kid. Turning back toward the TV, he tipped his bowl over and spilled cereal and milk on the rug.

"Uh-oh," he said.

"I'll clean it up." Tina hurried in from the kitchen with a wet rag.

"I only took two bites, Mommy. I'm hungry."

"You're in luck," Cheryl said. "I'm making a big breakfast this morning – bacon, eggs, and grits with cheese."

She headed to the kitchen. Tina followed, leaving Ricky to enjoy his Saturday morning cartoons.

"Did you and your boyfriend have a good time last night?" Tina pulled a bag of grits from the cabinet.

Cheryl wrinkled her nose. "I wouldn't say he's my boyfriend."

"I could've sworn you were madly in love. I mean, you couldn't wait for last night to get here!" Tina eyed her friend as she set a pot on the stove. "Oh, I get it. It's something to do with cooking being *a woman's domain*. And that comment about using Ricky for mommy training."

"I couldn't believe my ears!" Cheryl made quick work of cracking six eggs. "It gripes me that he thinks cooking has to be a woman's job. Even though it usually is. And all that baloney about training to be a mother, sheesh!"

"The guys I know would say the same thing."

"That gripes me too!"

"You're turning into a radical."

Cheryl dropped the eggshells in the garbage, bumping the trash can with her foot. The can tipped over, spilling coffee grounds and egg shells on the floor. She threw her hands into the air in frustration, then cleaned up the mess, resuming her rant without missing a beat.

"When we got home from the lake he said the first time he saw me, he knew I was the woman he wanted to be the mother of his children. Who thinks like that?" She shook her head. "And what kind of woman wants to hear a man say that?"

"A woman whose priority in life is to have the babies of a handsome fast talker."

"A handsome fast talker." Cheryl snorted.

"Let's see – and who was it who fixed him a homecooked meal, coming across as the Julia Child of the south?"

Cheryl grunted in frustration, placing six strips of bacon in the pan. "You know what else he said? He said I have two other things he admires – a sense of humor and great feminine beauty. Ugh! I do *not* have great feminine beauty."

"Sure you do."

"I do not!"

"Do too!"

Cheryl gave her friend a dismissive flap of the hand.

"Okay, you're ugly," Tina said, "but men love your hair."

Cheryl tossed a stray piece of eggshell at her smart-aleck friend.

Tina was unfazed. "It's shoulder length and wavy and the auburn reflects the sunlight. It's the kind of hair men dream of running their fingers through."

"That's ridiculous! Listen to yourself!"

"I don't understand why you're so angry. If he's not your cup of cocoa, give him the heave-ho. Simple as that!"

"*I* like him," Ricky said from the doorway, the cat in his arms. "And Pinky and Max like him too."

Cheryl was embarrassed that she'd let Ricky hear her gossiping about Paul. Bad form.

"He's a good guy," she said.

"He knows the names of all my Matchbox cars. And he makes good engine noises!"

"Desirable qualities in a man," Tina said.

"Maybe he could be *your* boyfriend, Mommy."

Tina hooted with laughter. Cheryl chuckled, but still wished she'd kept her big mouth shut.

When the phone rang, Tina picked up. "That's awfully nice of you." A pause. "Will do." Then she hung up.

Cheryl looked at her expectantly.

"Believe it or not, that was Paul," she said, measuring water into the pot. "He asked us to take Ricky to the empty lot at the rear of the subdivision at three o'clock. He's bringing something to show him. He wants you there too."

"Does he now? Sounds rather mysterious."

"Oh boy!" said Ricky as Pinky jumped down and hurried to the back door, meowing.

"We better get breakfast on the table," said Cheryl. "I've got calculus class this morning. Double ugh!"

*

That afternoon, Tina parked her Fairlane along the road at the rear of the subdivision a few minutes ahead of time. It was scheduled to be paved in the near future as new homes were built. For now, though, it was a dirt road that cut through a big sandy patch of land with weeds and spindly pines around the edges.

Ricky grabbed the bucket and shovel his mom brought for him to play with and settled down to dig. Cheryl and Tina strolled in a circle, smoke from backyard leaf fires drifting by. They kept their eyes peeled for Paul's Corvette, curious what he had up his sleeve.

They looked up when they heard a rumble above them. Living not far from Fort Bragg and Pope Air Force Base, they were used to the sound of military aircraft. But this was closer.

"Look, Mommy!" Ricky pointed to a helicopter approaching from the north.

It was olive drab with an elongated profile flying lower than usual. As they watched, it veered toward them, the thunder of rotors growing louder.

"It's Paul!" Ricky cried.

Cheryl was about to gently explain that there was no way it could be Paul, but that's when the copter dipped even lower. Amazingly, it was coming right for them. Ricky jumped up and down in excitement as his mother ran to him and lifted him into her arms.

"It *is* Paul! It *is* Paul!" he cried.

It appeared the chopper was going to land right there on the empty lot. As the blades rotated, there was a whoop, whoop sound. It slowed its forward motion, descending gradually, finally hovering about fifteen feet in the air. The rotating blades stirred up a sudden sandstorm which caused Tina to turn away, shielding Ricky's face. Intent on watching, Cheryl held her hands in front of her eyes, peeking between her fingers as her hair thrashed around her head.

Ricky was right. It had to be Paul. Nobody else would land an Army helicopter here in Pinetree Heights. Had he lost his mind?

The aircraft descended bit by bit for the final few feet until its skids lightly touched down on the sandy ground. The sandstorm intensified, forcing her to turn away. When she heard the rate of rotation begin to slow and the engine shut down, she turned around, spotting Paul in the pilot's seat.

Despite Tina's best efforts, Ricky broke free and ran toward the chopper, Tina close behind him. The door on the pilot side opened and Paul waved. He and the man beside him wore fatigues and helmets.

In spite of her muddled feelings, Cheryl was captivated. He seemed larger than life, like an actor in a war movie. Her eyes lingered on his uniformed silhouette.

Ricky reached the aircraft as Paul jumped down. He lifted the little boy up, yelling in his ear to be heard over the noise.

"Can I sit in the driver seat?" Ricky shouted.

"I can't go that far," Paul replied. "Want to see what's inside the back of the helicopter?"

Ricky performed a cartoon nod of the head.

Paul carried him to the rear door, pulled it open and set him inside the cabin, climbing up after him.

Cheryl knew Ricky would remember this experience for the rest of his life. In spite of being a thoughtful gesture, she couldn't fathom why Paul would jeopardize his career.

She watched him from a distance as he gave Ricky an animated first person tour, wishing she'd brought her camera. If only she'd known what he had in mind! After a couple of minutes, he handed Ricky down to his mother and jumped to the ground.

"I have to get back to work."

He turned to Cheryl then.

"Won't you get in trouble?" she said.

"Not if they don't find out."

"What if your co-pilot tells?"

"That's my roommate, Chuck. I trust him."

"But..."

"I only need a minute."

"A minute for what?"

He took her arm, leading her far enough away from the others so they wouldn't be heard. When they stopped, he gave her a searching look.

"I sensed a change in your feelings as the evening wore on last night. I think I said something wrong. I don't know what, but I'll have to find out when I get back."

"Get back from where?"

"Leaving for maneuvers this afternoon. I don't know how long I'll be gone. A few days. A few weeks. Hell, it might be a few months."

"And you only found out today?"

"I did. They won't tell us where we're going until we get there."

"So you flew your helicopter here to tell me goodbye?"

"That, and to ask you to forgive me. When I come back, you can spell out exactly what I said."

"But..."

He didn't let her finish. Instead, he pulled her into an unexpected embrace, transporting her back to Hope Mills Lake under a silvery moon. "I love you, Cheryl. It's not a passing fancy either. It's a fierce love that makes me tremble. Remember the song, *Fever*? That's what you do – you give me fever." He kissed her then, pressing his body against hers. When he stepped back, he gazed into her eyes with an earnest look that said, 'wait for me.'

Then he turned and jogged back to the chopper, climbing into the cockpit where his co-pilot waited. When the doors closed and their helmets were in place, the engine sprang to life and the rotors began to spin.

Cheryl, Tina and Ricky moved a safe distance away. They watched as the blades spun faster and faster, once again blasting sand in all directions. The roar overwhelmed their ears, the wind whipping their hair. When the chopper lifted off, it rose into the air with that whoop, whoop sound and flew off to the north like a hawk sweeping across the sky in search of prey.

He could've been a hero riding valiantly into battle. Which made her feel guilty about her negative reactions the night before.

Ricky chattered non-stop on the short drive home about Paul flying the helicopter. About Paul letting him get in the cabin where wounded soldiers were flown to hospitals. About how loud it was, and about sand getting in his nose and ears.

At home again, he ran outside to play with Max, leaving the house quiet in his wake. Too quiet. Cheryl had to get out of there. She changed into a nice Saturday dress and some comfortable flats.

Stopping by the kitchen before she left, she found Tina browning a roast and onions.

"Paul must be crazy in love with you to land in our neighborhood, then kiss you while we watched!"

"I hope he's not court-martialed."

"Why would he risk everything doing that?"

"He says they're going on maneuvers. The top brass isn't even telling them where they're going."

"He flew here so he could kiss you goodbye?"

"Apparently."

"Ricky thinks it was all for him."

"Don't tell him otherwise."

That's when Ricky barged into the kitchen from the yard, the screen door slamming behind him.

"I'm hungry, Mommy! Can I have a cookie?"

"You can have one Oreo, a glass of milk and some apple slices."

Tina turned away to fix his snack as Cheryl headed for the front door. She ran her hand over Ricky's soft buzz on her way out the door.

Several neighbors on their street were raking leaves. She needed to get busy too before the yard was knee deep. She admired the watercolor vista with a sprinkling of red, orange and gold in the treetops, experiencing a peaceful moment that was all too fleeting. It vanished when her thoughts turned to Paul again.

He was begging for her forgiveness without knowing what he'd done. How many men would do that? He had sensed the cooling of her affection. Although she was justified in her feelings about his backward expectations, she still felt bad for causing him distress. Unlike some of her friends, her dream had never been to become a housewife. She didn't want to be judged by her cooking skills. With luck, she could make him understand. He was a man who stirred her.

She pulled into the recently opened Tallywood Shopping Center. All the stores were new, including the Winn-Dixie, a steak house, a fabric store and the Belk-Hensdale department store. Which was her destination.

It sounded odd to say she needed to do her Christmas shopping on October twentieth. But anyone who had to mail gifts overseas knew packages could take weeks to be delivered. She would scout around for presents for Mom and Dad, as well as her sister and little brother.

With Muzak playing softly in the background, she walked to Men's Casual Wear, buying a summer shirt for her dad and a polo shirt for her brother. Then she browsed around the ladies department in search of gifts for Mom and Vicky. She was working her way through a rack of blouses when a woman spoke behind her.

"Well, if it isn't my husband's pretty secretary."

She turned to find Mrs. Carlisle eyeing her, an expensive green dress draped over her arm. Her tone was sharp and the look in her eyes was withering.

"Mrs. Carlisle, good to see you."

"Did you know I've been asking Harry for five years to let me be a sales agent? Five years!"

"Mrs. Carlisle..."

"Then, after telling me repeatedly that women aren't suited for real estate sales, he goes and offers you – his young *secretary* – a sales job! No doubt, you *paid* him with services rendered!"

Everyone in the Ladies Department could hear.

"Mrs. Carlisle..."

"The office trollop! I didn't realize that's what you are until now."

Cheryl was stunned. And angry. She resisted the urge to match Mrs. Carlisle's volume, but she gave as good as she got.

"What an ugly thing to say. I'm guessing you're getting your information from pea-brained salesmen who can't imagine a woman is smart enough to do sales. That a woman is smart enough to do much of anything for that matter. I don't know why he offered me the position. I don't want it. It's all yours! I would never do anything unethical to get a job, including granting favors. Talk about trashy!"

"Uh-huh!"

It was galling that everybody who heard the revolting rumor believed it! For some reason, it bothered her more that the boss's wife fell for it than the men who thought of women as having one asset only – their bodies. But arguing with Mrs. Carlisle in front of a growing audience at Belk's would accomplish nothing. She turned on her heel and left.

Christmas shopping was forgotten as she drove home, blood simmering. She was still fuming when she turned onto Loblolly Lane, barely avoiding a car making a left without so much as pausing at the stop sign. It was an oversized red car!

She twisted her neck trying to see more but it vanished around a curve in the road. She thought she saw dice hanging from the rearview mirror.

She wheeled around and did what the driver of the other car did: ignored the stop sign and barreled down the road. A glance at the speedometer told her she was going way too fast. She lifted her foot off the accelerator. The other car was long gone.

*

Falling asleep that night didn't come easy. So many things ricocheted around inside her head – red cars, money laundering, the confrontation with Mrs. Carlisle, her feelings for Paul – all of it.

As difficult as it was drifting off, it was worse when she was awakened by a noise. Sitting bolt upright, she tried to get her bearings. There it was again. A whining noise?

She wrapped her robe around her, put on her slippers and opened her door. Someone was inside the house. In the kitchen? The back door creaked. She reached for the heavy vase atop her chest of drawers. It would make a good weapon.

Tiptoeing from her room, she made her way to the darkened kitchen, straining to hear. A scuffing noise near the back door drew her eyes. She relaxed when she saw Tina peering out through the door.

"I heard it too," Tina said, flashlight in hand.

She set the vase on the counter and followed Tina onto the small porch, both of them shivering in their robes in the brisk night air. Tina swept the yard with the beam of light, coming to rest on Max as he stumbled drunkenly in a circle. Aiming the light at his doghouse, they could see an unfamiliar bowl on the ground beside it. Tina jumped down to examine it.

"Someone fed him meatballs!" she said. "I think he's been poisoned. Stay here with the flashlight. I have to get something."

She handed it to Cheryl and dashed inside, returning with a brown bottle in one hand, a soup spoon in the other.

"Come on," she said, leading the way to where Max stood weaving and drooling in the middle of the yard. "Hold him."

Cheryl set the flashlight on the ground, then wrapped her arms around poor Max while Tina poured the liquid into the spoon. Tina raised his head with one hand while she slid the spoon into his mouth. He tried to pull away but was too weak with Cheryl's arms clamped firmly around him. Then Tina gave him another spoonful.

"Now it's wait and see," she said, releasing Max's head.

"What are we waiting for?" Cheryl asked.

"For him to upchuck those meatballs."

"What did you give him?"

"Hydrogen peroxide. When I took him to the vet last year, Dr. Hahn had recently had a poisoning case. The collie died. Dr. Hahn said if they'd known to give him a little hydrogen peroxide, they might've saved him. Sometimes it works, making the dog throw up, getting rid of the poisoned food. He said if you can't take a dog to the vet, try hydrogen peroxide. It doesn't always work, but doing nothing definitely doesn't work."

After retrieving a couple of blankets, they sat side by side on the porch steps wrapped up to stay warm while keeping Max company. He alternated between whimpering, lying listlessly on the ground and meandering aimlessly around the yard, stretching his neck this way and that. Fifteen minutes later he vomited.

"Thank God," Tina said, a hitch in her voice.

"I second that."

It would've been unbearable having to tell Ricky that his doggy had died. Cheryl put her arm around Tina.

As they watched, he vomited again. They kept watch for more than an hour until Max stopped leaving little piles of vomit all over the yard. Cheryl wrapped the bowl and the uneaten meatballs in Saran wrap and placed the whole thing in a grocery sack.

They knew the worst was over when he drank from his water bowl.

"Good boy," Tina cooed, then turned to Cheryl. "Who would do such a thing? That's what I want to know."

"Someone who wants to send a message."

"But who would want to send me a message?"

"Not you, Tina. Someone is sending *me* a message."

She felt beleaguered. She'd been hammered by one thing after another, at work and at home: Ricky was bullied at school; Tina was harassed at work by her boss; she, herself, was intimidated by Mr. Carlisle, then his down and dirty brother and those yapping chihuahua salesmen. Now the boss's wife had accused her – in public – of having sex with her pot-bellied, grey-haired husband whose nose hairs were as bushy as his eyebrows! If that wasn't enough, the intimidation had now escalated with this despicable attempt to poison Ricky's dog!

Cheryl was frightened more than she let on. Not only was *she* in danger. Tina and Ricky were too.

7

Tina was on cleanup patrol in the back yard when Cheryl got up Sunday morning. Max seemed a little less bouncy than usual but Tina's quick thinking the night before saved his life. The two friends agreed not to mention any of it to Ricky.

"If the poisoning has something to do with the crap going on at Sleazy Realty and Money Laundering Incorporated, you have to go to the police," Tina said, shoveling a pile of dog puke into a garbage can.

"But I need ammunition before I go making accusations," Cheryl said. "You know, proof!"

Tina huffed, continuing the nasty cleanup.

Max wagged his tail at Cheryl. She sat down on the first step and clapped her hands to beckon him. He wiggled with pleasure when she scratched behind his ears.

"You'll need to wash your hands," Tina said. "He rolled in his vomit. When it warms up this afternoon, he's getting a bath."

Cheryl headed inside to wash up, then dialed police headquarters. Because Max was fine this morning, she was asked to stop by the station and fill out a report. It was obviously a low priority.

After breakfast Ricky was ready in no time for a big Sunday with his dad.

"Daddy says it's gonna be an afternoon of adventure!" he said for the umpteenth time since jumping out of bed.

Pickup was supposed to be ten-thirty. But ten-thirty came and went. Ricky was still playing with his toy truck while keeping watch through the window when his tardy father pulled into the driveway at eleven forty-five.

"You should pee before you go," Tina said, shooing him toward the bathroom.

"I don't need to, Mommy."

"Yes you do. Now go!"

As he charged into the hallway there was a knock. Tina opened the door, stifling her irritation.

Cheryl watched from the couch where she'd been reading the paper and keeping Ricky from becoming fretful. Wyatt was always late. For all Tina's comments about Allan not being her type, it was hard to believe that Wyatt Armstrong would ever in a million years have been anything close to her kind of man. There was something about him that screamed "I don't care about anyone but me." Or as he put it, "I don't give a green goddam about your stinking opinion!" It was the look in his hooded eyes, the nonchalance of his full lips and the way he sauntered, rather than walk like a regular guy.

"Had to pick up my girlfriend," he said, giving Tina a devil-may-care shrug.

"He needs to be home by six for supper."

"You're a regular killjoy, you know that? And a goddam square."

"Please watch your language around him."

Ricky tore through the living room, squeezing past his mother and sidestepping his father on the way to his afternoon of adventure.

Without another word, Wyatt followed his son to the driveway. They climbed into his Chrysler New Yorker, which was light blue with fins nearly as big as Eddie's Cadillac. How he afforded it working a job at the gas station was anybody's guess.

Tina glanced at the wall clock, then at Cheryl. "I'll be leaving in fifteen minutes." She headed to her bedroom.

Cheryl folded the newspaper and placed it in the magazine rack. That's when she heard car doors out front. Had Wyatt forgotten something? She looked through the picture window. It wasn't Wyatt. It was Tina's parents. They'd come straight from church. Mrs. Rossi's greying hair was teased and sprayed so that even hurricane-force winds would be no match.

"Mrs. Rossi, Mr. Rossi, come in," Cheryl said.

They called to mind a pair of matching salt and pepper shakers, Mr. Rossi in a grey wool suit that probably fit him twenty years ago, his wife in a grey tweed suit that accentuated her large bosom. Both of them wore World War II vintage hats.

"Did y'all attend services this morning?" Mrs. Rossi inquired.

Plainly, she was fishing for an opening so she could launch into one of her never-ending lectures.

Cheryl sidestepped her question. "Ricky is spending the afternoon with his dad."

"Today isn't Wyatt's visitation day."

An explanation about why the date was switched was more trouble than it was worth so Cheryl didn't bother. Instead, she arranged her features into a reasonably pleasant expression and gestured toward the sofa.

"I'll tell Tina you're here."

She withdrew to the back of the house, relieved she'd been able to keep a promise to herself to ignore any feeling of obligation to make uncomfortable small talk with people whose real goal was to get under her skin. She was also relieved for the millionth time that they were not her parents. It was no wonder Tina's older brother left town when he was still in high school.

She tapped on Tina's door, then opened it a few inches.

"Your folks are here. I'm sorry."

Tina responded with a wry smile.

Cheryl ducked into her own room. She had to finish ironing her clothes for the coming week. She left the door open so she wouldn't overheat. She was pressing a blouse when Tina walked into the living room.

"Why isn't Ricky here?" Mrs. Rossi asked, not bothering with hello.

"We changed to a different schedule."

"You didn't tell me."

"I hate to rush you but I'm meeting a friend for lunch and I need to go."

"You can't offer your parents a glass of iced tea? Having lunch with a friend is more important? And what friend are you meeting? Do I know him?"

"I can walk you out to your car as I leave," Tina said, refusing to take the bait.

"Why didn't you take Ricky to Sunday school this morning?"

Tina turned up at Cheryl's door, exasperated.

"I'm leaving," she said. "I'll be home by four-thirty."

Her mother continued her incessant badgering when Tina returned to the living room.

"Who is this *friend* you're having lunch with?"

"I'm meeting Peggy St. John. My old high school friend."

"Cheryl!" Mrs. Rossi shrieked.

Cheryl almost burned her finger on the iron.

"Cheryl, come in here please!"

"Oh brother," Cheryl muttered, carefully setting the iron on the metal stand. She braced herself as she peeked into the living room from the hallway, which was as far as she was willing to go.

"I want to know why you haven't set Tina up with a man. I thought you were going to give your best friend a helping hand. You're falling down on the job!"

"Rosemary!" Mr. Rossi cried.

"Don't Rosemary me! You ask me the same question at least once a week!"

He stared at his shoes. Which made Cheryl wonder if his wife had cowed him for the twenty years he was in the Army and the dozen years he was a Fayetteville Police officer.

"Ricky needs a father!" Mrs. Rossi brayed. "He also needs a little brother or little sister!"

"Mom, I have to go." Tina tucked her handbag under her arm, pulled her keys from her pocket and headed for the door. "You can see yourselves out." Said without so much as a glance over her shoulder.

Before Mrs. Rossi said another word, Cheryl followed Tina's lead, making herself scarce. A moment later, in her bedroom, she heard the front door close and breathed a sigh of relief.

She ironed a dress with a full skirt that took a while, then an apron. She paused to turn the fan on, then spread another blouse on the ironing board. She lifted the iron, but a sudden racket from outside stopped her.

A few quick steps and she was peering through the picture window. Wyatt's big blue New Yorker had returned. As he lifted Ricky from the back seat Tina dashed toward them from her car, which was now parked on the street. From the back yard, Max barked his head off.

Cheryl opened the front door as Wyatt bounded up the porch steps, Ricky in his arms. Tina was behind him, her face twisted into a knot of worry.

"What were you thinking, Wyatt?" she shouted, not even pausing as she ran through the living room and dining room to the kitchen.

"I thought he had more sense than to put his hand between them," Wyatt said.

"Between what?" Mrs. Rossi said as she and Mr. Rossi rushed in through the front door. "We saw you both on the highway headed this way."

From the kitchen came a loud cracking noise followed by the sound of a tray of ice cubes being dumped.

"Is that how you take care of your son?" Tina bellowed from the kitchen.

"He's not gonna die!" Wyatt fired back.

"What did he put his hand between?" Mrs. Rossi said.

"Bowling balls." Ricky's words came out a bit shaky. He cradled his left hand in his right hand, ignoring his runny nose. Cheryl plucked a couple of tissues from the box and sat down next to him on the couch.

"Blow," she said.

She held a tissue over his nose as the sound of hammering and splintering of ice jarred their ears.

Ricky blew his nose, looking defeated.

Tina rushed back into the room placing a rolled dish towel containing crushed ice on his left hand.

"That's too cold, Mommy."

"Why did you put your hand between bowling balls?" Mrs. Rossi said.

"You should've driven him to the emergency room," Tina said.

"His fingers aren't broken. I checked," Wyatt said.

"You wouldn't know what to check for!" Tina snapped.

Cheryl leaned close to Ricky. "Can you feel your fingers?"

"It's too cold," he whined.

"Let's take it off for a minute." She lifted the towel from his hand. "Can you move your fingers?"

He wiggled them gently.

"Does it hurt when you move them?"

"A little."

"He's too young to go bowling," Mrs. Rossi said.

"All he needs is someone to teach him properly," said Mr. Rossi.

"That's why we were there!" Wyatt roared. "I told him to go find a ball."

"By himself?" Tina said.

Wyatt raised his eyes to the ceiling, aggravated.

"Wyatt! Can we leave now?" a honeyed voice said.

They all turned to stare at the blonde who had quietly slipped in the front door.

"We've gotta go, darlin'," she said, waving her hand impatiently.

"I'm taking him to the emergency room," Tina said. "I want a doctor to examine his hand."

"I'm thirsty," Ricky said.

"Wyatt!" The blonde stretched his name into three syllables.

"Hey, little pardner," Wyatt said to his son, "next time we'll definitely have that afternoon of adventure. I can take you to the State Fair!"

With that, he got to his feet, squeezed between his former in-laws, took his blonde girlfriend by the hand and left.

"Let's go, Rosemary," Mr. Rossi said, touching his wife's elbow.

She yanked her arm away.

"Yeah mom, y'all go on home," Tina said.

Her mother reluctantly followed her husband outside.

Cheryl hurried to the kitchen for a glass of water, bringing it back along with two graham crackers. Now that they were gone, it was quiet again.

Ricky used both hands to hold the glass, giving it back to Cheryl when he finished. He practically inhaled the graham crackers.

"How does your hand feel now?" Cheryl asked.

He wiggled his fingers and turned his hand this way and that, staring as though it was a robot hand attached to his arm. "Good."

"I don't think you need to rush him to the Emergency Room," Cheryl said to Tina.

"This fingernail hurts," he said, raising his middle finger. "I bit my fingernail and it bleeded."

Tina looked at Cheryl. "Can you fix lunch while I hold the ice pack on his hand? Peggy knows something came up if I'm more than fifteen minutes late."

They had tomato soup, grilled cheese sandwiches, carrot sticks and pickles. Ricky had no problem using both hands.

As they ate, the two women managed to gently ask Ricky enough questions to ferret out what happened. He said when they drove off from the house, he heard the new girlfriend tell his daddy she didn't like parks, that she wanted to go somewhere inside, not outside. He said she sat too close to his daddy and kissed him on the neck. Then she lay down so he couldn't see her and his daddy growled as he drove. When they pulled off the road his daddy told him the park was closed. They went to the bowling alley instead. He said it was stinky and smoky. While his dad got them special shoes, he told Ricky to go find a ball with the number five on it. That's when he smashed his fingers.

"We were gonna have our afternoon of adventure," he said, his mouth quivering.

"Well, you've got to admit," said his mother, "you had a pretty doggone exciting Saturday! You saw that great big helicopter land, and then you got to climb around inside it! That was a pretty cool adventure!"

"Yeah! That was the bestest."

He sat up straight and chomped on a carrot stick.

After he dashed off to brush his teeth, Cheryl couldn't help herself.

"You always say this guy or that guy isn't your type. If you're so particular, how on earth did you ever believe the guy who cleans his ears with his car key was your type?"

Tina rolled her eyes and turned to walk away.

Cheryl persisted. "Really, Tina, why did you get tangled up with a man who takes a plate of food with him to sit on the John?"

Tina whirled around. "I know as well as you do that it was a mistake. But that mistake brought me the most wonderful gift of my life." She gestured toward the sound of Ricky singing a song in the bathroom. "My taste has changed dramatically since high school when I was under pressure on all sides. It's a long story. One that I don't care to delve into right now, if you don't mind."

Cheryl regretted pushing her. She gave her a sympathetic look, trying to make amends.

It was a fast trip to the police department to fill out a report on last night's attempted poisoning. No one seemed the least bit interested, the intended victim being a dog. When Cheryl got home, she fixed herself a glass of tea, spying Ricky playing beneath the big pine tree out back. She took her glass and moseyed onto the porch, sitting down on the top step. On closer inspection she could see he was arranging his collection of army men on a sandy patch of ground.

"What're you up to?"

"It's a battle!"

"Who's fighting?"

"It's America against Australia."

"But America and Australia are friends. Sounds like a tennis match."

He ignored her, engrossed in shifting the little soldiers around. It was at that moment a little boy showed up at the gate. It was Tommy Jordan who lived across the street and three doors down. He was a first grader too.

"Hey, Ricky!"

Ricky looked up, eyes brightening. "Wanna play army men?"

"Sure!" Tommy unlatched the gate.

"Does your mother know you're here, Tommy?" Cheryl said.

"Kind of. She kicks us out after lunch." He marched, soldier style, his arms swinging in great arcs. "She yells at us not to come home unless we're bleeding." He raised an imaginary rifle to his shoulder, pointing it one way, then the other as he scanned his surroundings. He let loose with a barrage of gunfire, making a rat-a-tat sound with his mouth.

She left the boys playing war, glad Ricky had a playmate since his afternoon of adventure turned into an afternoon of disappointment.

Having hung up all her freshly ironed clothes, she put the ironing board and iron away, glad to be done with that odious chore. She went in search of Tina, hoping she wasn't too upset about missing out on her lunch with Peggy.

There were voices coming from the front porch. When she reached the living room, she realized one of them belonged to Allan.

"The caliph of calculus honors us with his presence on a Sunday?" she said, joining them.

In jeans and plaid shirt, he could've passed for a Marlboro man on horseback, but without the horse, the cowboy hat and the cigarette. He was seated on the porch railing, his long legs splayed out in front of him. His normally well-groomed hair was softer today, more natural.

Cheryl snuck a glance at Tina to gauge her reaction. It was blatantly obvious he was a good catch. But she wasn't going to play Cupid. She'd been scolded enough. Message received.

"I was telling Tina my brother Sidney phoned this morning," Allan said. "He lives in Miami. He says military convoys are causing huge traffic snarls down there."

"What's going on?"

"That's the sixty-four thousand dollar question. Sidney recognized some insignia patches. He saw soldiers from the Eighty-second Airborne Division based here at Fort Bragg."

Cheryl thought back to Paul's stunt the day before and what he said about going on some kind of mysterious maneuvers.

"A senator is accusing the Kennedy administration of doing nothing about what's going on in Cuba," Allan went on. "In August and again recently, a New York Senator predicted a confrontation with Castro."

"We can't be going to war with Cuba," Tina said.

"Maybe not. But what country is Cuba's best friend?"

Cheryl exchanged a worried look with Tina.

"The Soviet Union," he said. "Khruschev would love nothing better than to humiliate President Kennedy. So would Castro." He got to his feet. "Kennedy screwed up last year with the Bay of Pigs. Of course, he was following Eisenhower's plan."

"That's a barrel full of speculation," Cheryl said.

He bobbed his head in acknowledgement but stuck to his guns. "If you know anyone based at Fort Bragg who suddenly leaves town, you can bet they're in Florida causing traffic backups."

Allan kept up with the news like other men kept up with sports. Plus, his brother in Miami was a reporter for United Press International. But he had to be wrong. In this day and age, with weapons powerful enough to wipe out whole nations, war was not an option. Besides, wars happened elsewhere, not on America's doorstep. At least not in this century.

"I've lined up five other committee members for the reunion committee," he said, eyes on Cheryl. "Can I tell them you've agreed to be co-chair?"

Cheryl had let it slip her mind.

"One of them is a friend of yours from the old days," he continued. "Gena Barber. She asked about you."

Tina got to her feet. "I need to go check on Ricky. Good to see you, Allan." She took her glass of tea, trotted down the steps and headed around the side of the house.

"It'll be fun working on the reunion," he said.

"Let me think about it a little longer."

"Sure thing. Oh, did you apply for the secretary's job?"

"I did. Got an interview coming up on Wednesday with the principal."

"It would be great if we worked at the same place, wouldn't it?"

"I guess so." Although that hadn't occurred to her.

He looked down the street, taking in a lungful of air. "It's a perfect day for a walk. How about it?"

"Well, sure."

They walked at a moderate pace. The air was crisp but the sun was warm on their shoulders. Walking together brought back her senior year of high school when she and Allan became friends. Which culminated with their prom date. Being calm about dating a boy she wasn't in love with, she enjoyed the night much more than her girlfriends did. They were anxious about what the future would bring. Janie wanted Bill to ask her to marry him. Cindy was afraid Rodney would go off to college and forget her. Celia regretted going to prom with Wayne when she wished she could go with Wyatt who asked Tina. Cheryl had no such anxieties. She and Allan had a blast dancing, sneaking a few drinks and hanging out with friends. No messy entanglements. They'd been good friends since then.

"I had an ulterior motive for suggesting the walk," he said. "I thought it would give me a chance to ask a question."

"About?"

"I wanted to ask if you'd go out to dinner and a movie with me one night."

Which was the last thing she expected.

"You look surprised," he said.

"We've been friends for so long, I didn't think..."

"...that I was attracted to you?"

Dang. Tina was right.

"I've always thought of you as *more* than a friend," he said. "But I could tell you didn't feel the same. So, back then I decided it was enough. Until now, that is. I get a kick out of being around you. I could swear you enjoy our time together too. So I thought..." He hesitated, his eyes fixed on hers. "Tell you what – go out with me once. It'll be like taking a car for a test drive. No commitments. Dinner and a movie one evening. If it doesn't work..." But he didn't finish his thought.

If she'd never met Paul, she might say yes. But she *had* met Paul. Still, she valued Allan's friendship. The last thing she wanted to do was hurt him. She'd been backed into a corner. She didn't want to say no but couldn't say yes.

"Our friendship is too important," she said. "A test drive would screw things up."

"You know, being friends is an important ingredient of a good relationship. Besides, I'm a lot more than the guy who helps you with calculus. Give me a chance to show you."

Her mind raced, searching for a way to soften the blow.

"Think about it," he said. "No rush. I've waited this long."

Should she tell him about Paul? It was all so tentative at this point. Besides, it could make Allan jealous, even a bit competitive. No need to stir the pot.

After supper, Ricky was dying to play with the recorder. The reel-to-reel tape recorder was a little too complicated for a six year old, so an adult had to operate it. Cheryl enjoyed being that adult, thankful her younger sister lost interest and left it at the house when they went to Okinawa.

Ricky watched her push his red rocking horse out of the way before setting the recorder up on the play table in his bedroom. It was housed in a tan case with a removable lid and a handle for carrying. When she finished threading the reel of tape, she gave him the mike. He squirmed in his little blue chair, smacking his lips in anticipation. She pushed the record button and pointed at him.

"Okey-dokey," he said, holding the mike to his mouth, "this is the sound of a army helicopter."

He leaned forward intently, growling through pinched lips, trying hard to recreate the roar of the rotors he heard yesterday. He kept trying different techniques in his quest to mimic a big, loud helicopter. After a few minutes, he stopped.

"I can't do the sound."

"I guess it takes practice."

He twisted his mouth into a sideways knot as he thought it over. Then he held the mike close to his mouth again and released a giant raspberry. It sounded realistic enough to be someone passing gas in a big way. He giggled uncontrollably.

"Can you make the sound of a toot, Cheryl?"

He wasn't allowed to say fart. And when he said toot, she couldn't help but snicker.

"I'll try," she said. "Here's a polite toot." She raised her upper lip on the left side and made the sound of a quiet fart that seemed to come from the other side of the room.

Which succeeded in turning Ricky's giggle box upside down, triggering her own set of giggles.

When they recovered, he announced he was going to make the sound of a rude toot. He made such a loud Bronx cheer, he fell off his chair, laughing until he was breathless.

*

As usual on a Sunday night at nine o'clock, Cheryl and Tina settled in to watch *Bonanza*. The galloping theme song was building to a crescendo when there came a loud crash out front. It was the sound of breaking glass. They both rushed out the front door onto the porch in time to see the tail lights of a large car recede into the darkness. Cheryl hurried down the steps onto the grass but it was too dark to see anything.

"I'll get the flashlight." Tina ducked into the house, returning quickly.

She swung the flashlight from one side of the yard to the other. Then she joined Cheryl at the curb and turned the beam of light toward the cars in the driveway. The split rear window of Cheryl's Volkswagen was shattered, jagged triangles of glass protruding from the window frame.

"Well, damn," Tina said.

Cheryl had felt beleaguered before. Now she felt besieged.

Walking around her car, the rear window seemed to be the only thing damaged. Then she caught a flash of light from inside. She opened the driver's door and folded the seat forward. A soda bottle lay on the floor. She jumped back in alarm. Was it a Molotov cocktail? But there was no rag protruding from it. No liquid. Carefully retrieving the bottle, she spotted a note inside.

Tina slipped her arm through Cheryl's and together they returned to the warm living room. Tina turned the sound down on the TV while Cheryl retrieved a pair of chop sticks. They sat side by side on the couch, as Cheryl used them to extract the note.

It was written on a scrap of paper. The handwriting was barely legible. It said, "I know where you live."

Cheryl wadded the paper up and threw it across the room.

"How about we invite one of those serious men in blue uniform over to chat about what happened tonight?" Tina said. "You could regale him with stories about a red Cadillac following you and a big red clunker dropping by uninvited. I think he'd be interested in what you have to say. Especially when you share that note."

"What proof do I have that Eddie or his cronies had anything to do with this?"

"We've all watched enough *Perry Mason* to know about circumstantial evidence. And that's what you've got!"

"But not one shred of proof! I'd have to tell the police about the ten thousand dollars. I'd also have to tell them what I overheard between Mr. Carlisle and his brother."

"So?"

"Without evidence it would be my word against theirs."

Tina gave her a stern look.

"All right," Cheryl said. "I'll report the bottle through the car window. I can't prove anything beyond that."

This time, Cheryl wasn't asked to come in the next day to file a report. She was told an officer would stop by within the hour. To them, however, it was a still run-of-the-mill case of vandalism.

She didn't want to confess to Tina that she was troubled by what could happen if she spilled the beans. She could only imagine Eddie Carlisle discovering she ratted him out. That's what they said in the cop shows, wasn't it? Then the "rat" usually got... well, she didn't want to dwell on what the rat usually got.

8

The awful ringing of the alarm clock reverberated through her body Monday morning, setting her teeth on edge. She whacked the clock on the nightstand only to realize it wasn't the alarm. It was the telephone jangling loud enough to wake everyone on their street. She almost fell as she staggered into the kitchen. Fumbling the handset, she dropped it on the floor. When she finally put it to her ear, she could only manage a half-whispered hello.

The last thing she expected was an operator announcing that this was a person-to-person call from Norma Donovan for Cheryl Donovan. Not good. Her parents hadn't phoned in the two years they'd been in Okinawa. And with good reason. The cost could equal a month's rent. In addition, the sound quality was said to be awful with no undersea cable in the Pacific like there was in the Atlantic. Her dad told her long distance calls from Okinawa to the States were made using short wave radio signals. Thus, the long transmission delays and the static that could make words too jumbled to understand.

In that instant she came fully awake. Despite her best effort, she failed to keep the tremor out of her voice. "This is she."

"Go ahead, Mrs. Donovan," said the operator, followed by a long pause.

"Cheryl?" Her mother had to speak loudly to be heard over the crackling line. "Can you hear me?"

Another pause.

"Is something wrong, Mom?"

"What?"

Cheryl spoke up. "Is everything okay?"

"I don't think so."

Tina tiptoed into the kitchen holding a sleepy Ricky in her arms, listening intently as Cheryl struggled with her emotions.

The static on the line was the only sound.

"Mom? What's wrong?"

"Your dad..."

Cheryl squeezed her eyes shut as her mother continued.

"...has been reassigned from that training job in Vietnam to some kind of special maneuvers."

Cheryl opened her eyes, relief flooding her body. Her relief quickly turned to irritation.

"You're calling me from Okinawa because Dad's gone on maneuvers?"

Tina carried Ricky to the bathroom.

There was another delay filled with crackling and whooshing.

"I assure you," Mrs. Donovan said, "it's more than maneuvers!"

"Sorry, Mom. It's just that I was about to have a heart attack thinking Dad had been killed!"

"The maneuvers are stateside," Mrs. Donovan said, not hearing Cheryl's words. "He wouldn't tell me anything more. It's top secret." There was a brief flood of static too loud for words to be heard. "… I could tell by the way he acted. There was also the way he kissed me goodbye."

Her mother choked up.

"Aw, don't worry, Mom. He'll be all right."

"What?"

Cheryl raised her voice. "He'll be okay, Mom!"

"I don't know about that."

"Are you still good friends with Mrs. Lopez?"

"What? I can't hear you."

"Are you still friends with Mrs. Lopez?"

"Of course I am."

"Invite her for coffee."

There was a quiet sniffle.

"You know what I think?" Cheryl said.

"What?"

With the crackling getting worse, Cheryl spoke as loudly as she could without yelling.

"I think some kind of specialized training exercise is underway."

"Arthur said it was special maneuvers."

"We better hang up so you don't get a monster-sized phone bill."

"Arthur won't be happy when he…" Her mother's voice faded out as the crackling increased.

"Love you, Mom," Cheryl said, hoping to wrap up the call.

"Love you too, honey."

She was concerned by her mom's behavior. Besides being her first call from overseas, this was also the first time she'd ever phoned without once asking how Cheryl was doing. Which was so unlike her mom. She was truly in a bad way.

"What's going on?" Tina asked, leaning through the doorway as Cheryl hung up.

"I wish I knew."

"Your dad left on secret maneuvers too?"

Cheryl nodded.

"First Paul, now your dad."

*

She left a few minutes early to drop her car off at the auto glass shop to get the two rear windows replaced. After Tina drove Ricky to school, she swung by to give Cheryl a lift to work.

Before heading inside, she noticed a Buick Roadmaster backed into a parking spot like a getaway car. Although only a few years old, the body was dented and scratched. Its dull red paint gave the impression that it was covered in ash.

Removing her sunglasses, she walked over to the huge sedan so she could peek inside. Perched in the center of the bench seat was a pair of large dice, similar to the ones in the car that sped away as she drove home from the shopping center Saturday. She noticed something else as she circled the vehicle – sections of chrome on the toothy front grille were missing, like the car parked down the street from her house Friday night. This had to be the big red bomber.

Turning toward the building, she was blinded by the glass across the front of the realty office that acted as a giant mirror. It was like staring straight into the sun, reflecting the sky behind her so perfectly she could've been facing east, rather than west. She squinted, steeling herself as she marched forward and climbed the steps to the glass doors. Unfortunately, she'd chosen a teal dress with a full skirt and prissy white collar that morning. Catching sight of her reflection, it was clear she was not the least bit intimidating. But here she was, planning to confront the criminal who owned the big Buick.

Although the lobby was empty, she heard men talking somewhere in the building. Salesmen were getting their morning coffee, others were already working the phones. Where was the thug intent on harassing her?

Keeping eyes and ears open, she draped her white sweater on the back of her chair, locked her pocketbook in the bottom drawer and removed the cover from the typewriter. First, she had to check in with the boss. Grabbing her steno pad and pencil, she made a beeline for his office.

She paused at his door, deciding to act like nothing had happened, that everything was normal. If all went well, he would too. After tapping and hearing his "come in," she planted an agreeable look on her face and made her entrance.

"Well, look who we have here, gentlemen!" Mr. Carlisle's arm swept through the air in a grand gesture. "It's none other than Cheryl Donovan, soon to be Carlisle Realty's first woman sales agent."

Her stomach clenched.

Two men sat across the desk from him – Eddie Carlisle and the man she was itching to confront – the driver of that beat-up red car. He was the same man she'd seen with Eddie last week, still as broad-shouldered and scary as the last time she saw him. How naïve to think she could give him a piece of her mind. He would take that piece of her mind, crack some eggs and fry it all up to make brains and eggs.

The office was thick with smoke, reminding her of a scene on *Combat* where the soldiers took a cigarette break during a lull in a firefight.

"Come on in," Mr. Carlisle said. "We were talking about you."

Oh brother.

"Vic, will you get another chair for the lady?" Eddie said, nodding at his bodyguard.

Moving at a leisurely pace, Vic brought a chair from its position along the wall, placing it on the other side of Eddie closer to the door. He sat down again without a word. When Eddie gestured for her to sit down, she did so, maintaining a neutral expression.

Mr. Carlisle took another drag on his Chesterfield, sending him into a coughing fit. When he recovered, he stubbed it out.

"I was explaining how having a woman sales agent would be good publicity for the business," he said. "Eddie agrees, don't you, Eddie?"

Eddie tapped long ashes into an ash tray on the table beside him, looking over at Cheryl with a slippery smile. "Sure I do," he said, giving her a wink his brother couldn't see.

Her plan had been to act normal. But how was she supposed to do that when Eddie and his muscular flunky were sitting in the boss's office gabbing about her?

"I'm sorry I interrupted your meeting, Mr. Carlisle," she said, getting to her feet. "I wanted to see if you have anything for me." She gripped her steno pad and pencil. "If you don't, I've got typing to do."

Reading Mr. Carlisle's expression was a challenge. A parade of feelings seemed to vie for the upper hand – embarrassment, anxiety, frustration, anger.

She nodded at nobody in particular, then headed for the door.

"You and I will go over this later, Cheryl," Mr. C. said, sounding like he needed to convince everyone he was in charge.

A short time later she was surprised when Diane Coleman walked through the door. She was dressed more nicely than when she reported for cleaning duty in the evening. But she still looked like a plump middle-aged woman in a tan shirtwaist dress, brown cardigan, glasses and an old-fashioned brown hat. Cheryl was the only one at the office who knew her secret. She wasn't middle-aged at all. She wasn't plump either. The get-up was designed to avoid unwanted attention. It worked.

"Haven't seen you in a while," Cheryl said.

"Take a gander. I'm applying for a job with the school system. I'm here to ask Mr. Carlisle for a good recommendation when the personnel office contacts him."

"Surely he will. What kind of job?"

"Custodial work. But with the new job I'll be able to work days and take classes in the evening at Fayetteville State Teachers College so I can finish my credits for a teaching degree."

"You're going to be a teacher?"

Diane nodded enthusiastically.

"I didn't know you were going to college. I hope you get the job. Then you won't have to…" and she gestured at the frumpy outfit.

"It's come in handy lately. A couple of strange men have been hanging around on weekends. The boss says they're working on a project. But they make me nervous. They park behind the building, come in through the back door, then play cards and use the phone now and then."

Cheryl was going to ask another question but shifted gears when she heard a couple of salesmen coming.

"Let me see if Mr. Carlisle can see you now."

As Jerry and Roger walked through the lobby on their way to appointments, Cheryl used the intercom to let the boss know Diane was there. He said to send her in.

Diane's arrival coincided with the conclusion of the boss's meeting with Eddie and Vic. They walked out as Diane strolled in. When Cheryl saw them, she leaned down to wipe the toes of her black high heels, hoping they wouldn't notice her. It worked.

Later, she was answering the phone when Diane returned. She mouthed, "good luck." Diane waved.

It was Allan on the phone.

"You hear the news?" he said.

"What news?"

"The president's making a speech tonight on TV."

"About?"

"The announcement said it's an urgent national matter. I'll bet you ten bucks we're going to war with Cuba. Or the U.S.S.R. Or both."

"God, don't say that."

"Will you be watching?"

"You have to ask?"

"How about I come over and watch with you?"

"Is your TV on the fritz?"

"No, I thought..."

"I don't know."

"I'll bring pizza and beer."

He was moving too fast, as Paul was moving too fast. Of course, in Allan's defense, he would make the same kind of call to a buddy of his. Maybe he already had.

"Thanks but I think we'll keep it low key," she said.

"It wouldn't be a date."

"I know. But we can hash it out tomorrow night at Johnny's after class. See you then!"

Funny – if he hadn't come by yesterday and revealed his feelings, she might've said yes. But now she refused to do anything that would encourage him. He'd been a good friend for so long. Becoming a suitor, to use an old-fashioned word, was a major complication.

It was after five when Mr. Carlisle summoned her to his office. He waited until she was seated before he spoke.

"I'm doing my best, Cheryl," he said, his hands folded on his pot belly. "But you're not pulling your weight."

"Pardon?"

"Please don't pretend you don't know what I'm referring to."

"I'm not pretending."

She wasn't going to make it easy for him. He would have to spell it out.

He exhaled slowly.

"Eddie and I are brothers, but we're nothing alike. He's not exactly a caring, gentle soul."

She almost blurted, "And you are?"

"He doesn't mind stepping on toes," he went on. "Or fingers. Or cheekbones."

He studied her for a minute before continuing.

"You need to understand that I don't have any control over him. None whatsoever."

When she said nothing he swiveled around in his chair to gaze out the window. An unforgiving gust of wind sent red leaves fluttering to the ground below a large maple in the distance.

"If you accept my offer," he said, still facing the window, "I might be able to convince him you're on our team. If you don't, all bets are off."

Obviously, he wasn't going to say a word about money laundering. He was being as vague as possible. But it was most definitely a warning.

"Think about it, Cheryl. Think about it carefully. I've tried time and again to reassure him, but he doesn't buy it."

He turned around again, stubbed out his cigarette and gave her a wave of dismissal. As she closed the door behind her, she heard him open the bottom drawer where he kept a bottle of Jack Daniel's.

He couldn't call off the dogs. The harassment would continue unless she agreed to play along and become his first female sales agent. In which case he said he *might* be able to convince Eddie that she wouldn't run to the police. *Might* being the operative word. Which was about as reassuring as a medic in a combat zone whose first aid kit only included Band-Aids.

No way was she going to accept his offer. She had no desire to be a real estate agent. As a matter of fact, she had no desire to continue working at the realty office in any capacity. But she would bide her time. Her interview at Sandhills High School was two days away.

As she finished up one last job for the day, a flash of red caught her eye through the front windows. It was the Caddy careening into the parking lot as if it was trying to outflank the enemy. It came to an abrupt halt, taking up two parking spaces. Eddie Carlisle hopped out and strode toward the entrance as if he owned the place.

It was a good thing nobody was in the lobby when he passed through. He was moving so fast, he would've mowed them down. He scowled at Cheryl as he zoomed by, then charged into his brother's office, slamming the door behind him.

They weren't quite yelling – their voices too muffled to make out – but angry words were lobbed back and forth. Coming on the heels of the boss's warning, she suspected the argument dealt with what to do about the secretary who knew too much.

She covered the typewriter, retrieved her purse and locked her desk. While slipping her sweater on she heard the subtle thump of the safe being closed on the other side of the wall behind her. This was Monday. It was one week to the day since Eddie showed up with ten thousand dollars in cash. She suspected he had brought another envelope of big bills that would be used to buy another house to launder more drug money.

Spotting her taxi out front, she hurried to make her escape before Eddie emerged. She wasn't fast enough. He caught up with her on the front steps.

"You should know, Miss Donovan, that I'm not taken in by my brother's idiotic notion about making you a saleslady. You should also know I've got my eye on you."

She stopped and turned to face him.

"Why?"

"I don't appreciate it when people play dumb with me."

"I'm not playing dumb."

"So you really are dumb."

"My policy is to mind my own business. I would be grateful if you would leave me be."

He examined her closely, then balled up his right hand and punched his open left palm.

"I did some boxing as a young man. I still work out with the punching bag. Vic boxes with me sometimes. Keeps me in shape."

His smile reminded her of a hyena she'd seen on a nature show. Of course, a hyena's smile wasn't a genuine smile at all. The hyena's laugh wasn't real either. Eddie Carlisle was a dangerous hyena.

9

"I'm putting supper on the table," Tina announced as Cheryl stepped through the back door. She lifted a pork chop from the frying pan onto a plate covered with a paper towel. "Can you tell Ricky to wash his hands?"

"Believe I can handle that."

"We're eating a little early so the dishes will be done before the president comes on."

Cheryl whistled for the little guy to come in. While he washed up, she changed into jeans and a shirt. At the table Tina told Ricky he was to play in his room while the adults watched the speech.

"If you don't interrupt us, you can have a bowl of ice cream when we're finished."

"Good golly, Mister Wally!" He clapped his hands with glee. Ice cream was a special treat.

"Can I have some too?" Cheryl said.

"Can Cheryl have some ice cream too, Mommy?"

"If she's a good girl," Tina said, which made Ricky grin.

After speed washing the dishes, Cheryl brushed her teeth and settled in the living room. It was five minutes before seven when she turned on the TV and adjusted the vertical hold to make the image stop rolling. Once she turned up the sound, she sat in her dad's ugly wing chair. Tina joined her after getting Ricky situated.

"I'm nervous," Tina said, plopping down on the sofa.

"Me too."

That's when the rhythmic sound of Ricky riding fast on his rocking horse filled their ears. Tina jumped up to close his bedroom door.

A sounder played for the president's live address. After a few seconds, President Kennedy looked into the camera and began to speak.

"Good evening, my fellow citizens." He was all business.

Over the course of the next eighteen minutes the president stunned the nation as he announced American U-2 spy planes had discovered Soviet missile bases in Cuba which would provide the Soviet Union with nuclear strike capability against the entire Western Hemisphere.

Kennedy accused the Soviets of lying to the US. He called it a "provocative threat" to world peace and insisted that military action by the US would remain an option. He said America's goal was to prevent the use of those missiles and to secure their withdrawal or elimination. While saying the United States would not prematurely risk the cost of nuclear war, neither would the US shrink from that risk.

"We won't shrink from nuclear war?" Cheryl said.

The president laid out steps he was ordering, including a blockade of Cuba. He didn't use the word blockade, choosing instead to characterize it as a quarantine. But it meant the same thing. America would stop Soviet ships from bringing any more weapons to the island. Close surveillance would continue. He had ordered the American military to prepare for *any* eventuality.

Cheryl closed her eyes thinking of Paul and her father.

Kennedy said any missile launched from Cuba targeting any nation in the Western Hemisphere would be viewed as an attack by the Soviet Union against the United States. He said that would require a full, retaliatory response against the Soviet Union.

"Good God!" Tina said.

He went on to say the United Nations was being asked to convene an emergency meeting of the Security Council to take action against this latest Soviet threat to world peace. He said a US resolution would call for the prompt dismantling and withdrawal of all offensive weapons in Cuba under the supervision of UN observers before the quarantine could be lifted. And he pressed Soviet leader Nikita Khruschev to abandon the course of world domination and join in the effort to end the world arms race. He said Khrushchev had the opportunity to move the world back from "the abyss of destruction."

"The abyss of destruction," Cheryl repeated.

When he looked into the camera and said, "Thank you and goodnight," the women sat in a daze. None of the chitchat at work or the news broadcasts announcing the speech had prepared them for the extreme gravity of the situation. The world was teetering on the brink of nuclear war.

Shivers ran down Cheryl's spine. "I can't believe it. Allan was right."

Tina crossed the room to turn off the television. "God help us."

"We need to stock the fallout shelter," Cheryl said, remembering how people made fun of her dad when he built it in the basement after they bought the house.

Ricky rushed into the living room. "Is the president over?"

"Yes he is, sweetie," Tina said, lifting him in her arms and holding him tight.

He grinned, having no idea his mother was upset.

"Can I have my ice cream now, Mommy?"

"Of course! As a matter of fact, I think I'll have some with you. Let's sit at the kitchen table together."

"Oh boy! Want some ice cream, Cheryl?"

Cheryl's eyes were unfocused, her mind far away.

"I'll fix her a bowl," Tina said.

"Come on, Cheryl!" Ricky cried.

She forced a smile and followed them to the kitchen, sitting in her usual spot across from Ricky as Tina scooped chocolate ice cream into green Melmac bowls.

"Good gooly, Mister Fooly!" He bounced in his chair. "Did you hear that, Cheryl? Good gooly, Mister Fooly!"

She faked good cheer, wishing she too could be blissfully unaware. But terror gnawed at her insides. She couldn't stomach the thought that this precious little boy she loved so much might not have a chance to grow up.

"Here you go!" Tina said, setting three bowls of ice cream on the table with a flourish, then taking her seat.

"Thank you, Mommy," Ricky said, his mouth full to overflowing. "This is the bestest ice cream I've ever had!" He quickly developed a halo of chocolate around his lips, oblivious to the women's distress.

When the black wall phone rang, neither Cheryl nor Tina made a move to answer it. It seemed rather ominous now in the cheerful yellow kitchen.

Ricky looked at them, a question in his eyes.

Cheryl finally did the honors.

"It's even worse than I thought." It was Allan. "I think Kennedy is fixated on ousting Castro. He screwed up last year with the Bay of Pigs. Now he's loaded for bear."

"No offense, Allan, but if you want to talk politics, include me out."

"Sorry. I'm pissed, that's all."

"Tomorrow night would be better."

As soon as she put the receiver back on the cradle, the phone rang again, sending a tiny vibration through her hand.

This time there was a woman on the other end of the line.

"Hi Cheryl, this is Peggy. Is Tina there?"

"Hold on."

Cheryl put her hand over the mouthpiece and pointed at Tina.

Tina talked less than a minute, saying yes, no, and okay, then hung up. "Peggy's coming over."

Cheryl nodded, understanding why Peggy would want to leave the house. From all she'd heard, Peggy's parents were about as congenial as Tina's mom and dad.

When the ice cream was gone, Tina herded Ricky out of the kitchen to get him in the tub. He was chattering up a storm about having an ice cream cone when they were at the beach. He went on and on about playing in the waves and floating on a raft. As Cheryl cleaned up the kitchen, the president's carefully chosen words supplanted Ricky's words in her head – while the United States wouldn't fire the first nuclear missile, it wouldn't shy away from firing the second. The expression he used, "the abyss of destruction," kept replaying over and over. He said Khrushchev was the one who could save the world from the abyss of destruction. God. How did they get to this point?

She needed to sit in the dark on the front porch and soak up the quiet of the evening. But before she could hang the dish towel on the rack, there was another unwelcome phone call, the ringing insistent, pushy. When she answered, she didn't mean to sound impatient. But there was such a thing as being telephoned out. An operator announced a person-to-person call for Cheryl Donovan. She identified herself and the operator gave the go ahead.

For a couple of seconds all she could hear was static. Then there was a huge sob followed by anguished weeping.

"Oh Mom, don't cry." Cheryl's eyes watered. "You'll make *me* cry." She stretched the spiral cord as far as it would go to reach the napkin holder, using a napkin to blot her eyes. "Dad will be safe and sound, Mom."

"Did you watch the president?"

"Yes, I..."

"It's Armageddon!" Her mother blew her nose.

"It's not Armageddon. Please don't cry. It won't do any good."

"I cried when they shipped your father off to World War Two. I cried when they sent him to fight in the Korean War. Now that they've sent him off to an atomic war, I'll cry if I see fit. At least he stood a chance of surviving before. He doesn't stand a snowball's chance in hell now!"

"Dad isn't in any more danger than the rest of us. We're all on the front line if it comes to nuclear war. But I don't believe it'll come to that. The president doesn't want that. Khruschev and Castro don't want that, even if they're psychotic imbeciles. This is a bunch of posturing, you know, like a cat arching her back so she'll look big to scare a growling dog."

Her mother's weeping resumed.

"Mom! Please calm down."

She boo-hooed for another minute, the line dropping out for a few seconds, then returning. Then she sniffed several times before apparently holding a tissue to her nose that muffled her words.

"You're saying I should worry as much about my four children, my daughter-in-law and my two little grandsons as I worry about your father! You're no comfort at all!"

"Mom, please! Dad would tell you not to worry."

"And I would ignore him as I always do. And, for your information, it's not only your dad! I tried to reach Mike. I was told he shipped out."

"I thought he got back a few weeks ago. He was at sea for nine months."

"It can't be a coincidence that his ship left port today of all days."

That threw Cheryl for a loop. She should've guessed that her Navy brother would be directly impacted by what was going on.

"Try not to fret, Mom."

"Wait till you're a wife and mother. Then try telling yourself that! My husband and my son…" Her voice cracked.

Cheryl gave her a moment. She didn't know why she was trying to convince her mother not to worry. She might as well tell her to stop loving Dad.

"Listen Mom, at this rate, you'll have to get a job to pay your phone bill."

"If we all die, there won't be a bill."

"We're not going to die. Which means there *will* be a bill! And it'll be the size of Texas!"

"What do you know? You're twenty-six years old. I've got spools of thread older than you!"

"Why don't you ring Mrs. Lopez? You two can get together. She still lives a couple of streets over, doesn't she?"

There was sniffling on the other end, then static.

"Mom?"

Silence.

"Are you there, Mom?"

The static ended. A loud dial tone replaced it.

Cheryl hung up.

"Is your mother losing it?" Tina said.

Cheryl threw her head back, closed her eyes and took a deep breath. "It seems her husband *and* her son have been deployed. The way she's weeping, you'd think they've already been incinerated."

"Mike too?"

"She phoned the base and they told her his ship set sail today." She almost repeated what she said to her mother, that they were all on the front line in this kind of war. She stopped herself. No sense terrorizing anyone else with that horrible thought. She could kick herself for saying it to her mom.

The look on Tina's face betrayed the panic growing in her gut. She was on the verge of saying something but was interrupted by a knock at the door.

"That's Peggy." Tina hurried to get it.

Cheryl lowered her chin, shaking her head. She hoped Mrs. Lopez would be a good shoulder to cry on.

On her way down the hallway she said hello to Peggy as she and Tina sat down in the living room. The two had been friends since twelfth grade. Cheryl liked her but Tina had always kept that friendship separate. Tonight it was clear they preferred a private tête-à-tête.

Cheryl put a sweater on and grabbed a blanket. She stopped in the kitchen for a bottle of wine and a juice glass before making her way to the front porch. Wrapping herself in the blanket, she sat on the porch swing and poured herself a little wine. With the porch light off, she was hidden from view. She filled her lungs with fresh evening air, swinging gently to and fro.

It wasn't until she'd settled in that she noticed she wasn't alone after all. Some of the neighbors were clustered under the streetlight several doors down in coats and sweaters. Occasionally their words carried far enough to reach her ears. "Asleep at the wheel," one man said. Another said, "What did you expect after Kennedy botched the invasion?" Someone said, "Khrushchev can't be trusted." A woman said, "This is the end times."

Cheryl didn't begrudge them the neighborhood parley, but wished she couldn't hear them. Quiet is what she needed. She took a sip of wine and closed her eyes, wanting to hold off the dread percolating through her veins, hoping to avoid that abyss of destruction the president alluded to.

She was about to go inside when she realized the neighbors were heading to their homes in ones and twos. It was sprinkling, the raindrops barely visible against the streetlight. The pavement glistened as a hush descended.

She gave a little push with her toes to keep the swing moving, the muscles in her body relaxing. She imagined how she must look sitting on the swing wrapped in a blanket.

The ringing of the telephone, easily heard on the porch, put an end to the fleeting tranquility. The darkness was replaced by an intense glare from the porch light, followed by the door opening and Tina's face looking out through the screen.

"Long distance for you."

Cheryl took a deep breath as she rose, leaving the rumpled blanket on the swing like a discarded chrysalis.

When she reached the kitchen, she used the cord to haul the receiver up from where it lay on the floor. She wasn't surprised when the operator spoke.

"Is this Cheryl Donovan?"

"Yes?"

"I have a collect call for Cheryl Donovan from Paul McIntyre. Will you accept charges?"

"Of course."

"Go ahead, sir."

"Cheryl! I'm sorry I'm calling collect. I don't have any cash on me. And I only have a minute or two."

"Is there an emergency?"

"I'm fine. But I had to speak with you." He took a deep breath. "I realize we only met a week ago but I already know you're the woman I want to spend the rest of my life with. I believe our souls are connected and we were put on this earth to find each other. I can feel it. I apologize for whatever I said that made you angry. I'll make it up to you. I wouldn't rush into this but with all that's happening, I don't know how much time we've got. So I'm getting down on one knee here in the phone booth."

She listened to him shuffle around.

"Cheryl, will you marry me?"

She slid a kitchen chair closer so she could sit down, her head spinning. Memories of their short time together flashed through her mind: talking and joking at the Sakura Restaurant; their moonlight stroll and the passionate kisses at Hope Mills Lake; him landing his helicopter – against Army regulations – to say goodbye; and that goodbye kiss. It was true, she had never experienced such intensity of emotion with another man.

It was also true that in the few days since they'd met, he'd shown he was a nineteen-fifties kind of guy. All those things that had given her pause before he left, *still* gave her pause. Could he change? She remembered one bit of advice her mother gave her: don't marry a man and expect to change him. She said that would lead to heartache. While hurting Paul was the last thing she wanted to do, it was better to put the brakes on now than to cause a train wreck down the line. She couldn't let a looming war, nuclear or otherwise, pressure her into compromising who she was.

Then it hit her that proposing marriage now was kind of irrational.

"Paul, if missiles are fired and we all go to hell in a giant handbasket, there wouldn't be time for a wedding. And if we get through this nightmare alive, there'll be plenty of time later."

"On my way!" he shouted to someone in the distance. "Cheryl?"

"I'm still here."

"My ride is leaving. I've got to get back before they discover I'm gone. I get what you're saying. But I want you to know how serious I am, how committed I am. I'd like you to say yes, that you'll marry me as soon as possible. Just think about it, okay? And know I love you. I'll call again when I can."

There was a clunk followed by a dial tone.

10

Tina and Peggy were making up the couch as a bed when Cheryl stopped in the living room to say goodnight. Peggy had changed into Tina's green plaid pajamas. Tina was in her terry bathrobe.

"Peggy and her parents got into a raging argument after the president's speech." That was Tina's succinct explanation about why her friend came over. But her eyes said, 'I hope I haven't overstepped my bounds.'

Cheryl nodded.

Peggy's dark eyes were swollen and rimmed with red. Her cheeks were flushed, in contrast to her pale skin and long black hair. "Thank you, Cheryl," she said, her sincerity palpable.

Cheryl nodded. "I'll be out of the shower in two shakes."

She took a high speed shower to avoid monopolizing the bathroom. Drying off, she heard people talking loudly. She put her flannel robe on and wrapped a towel around her hair, then hurried to the living room to shush them. It was a bad sign if Tina and Peggy were already having a heated argument.

It wasn't Tina and Peggy. It was Tina's overbearing parents. Mrs. Rossi was decked out in a pink full-length robe and matching slippers, a hairnet covering her teased hair. Standing behind her, Mr. Rossi wore a deep green robe over striped pajamas and brown leather slippers. He listened as his wife launched into yet another harangue belittling their daughter.

"By the time I was your age I was married with two children. I wasn't a divorcee who ended her marriage, then refused to find another husband. You'll turn to dust if you wait for Mister Perfect. There is no Mister Perfect!"

"Please keep it down," Tina pleaded. "You know Ricky's asleep."

"Why is Peggy here? You already live with one girlfriend. You don't need another one hanging around."

"Shh!" It was hard to shush someone with your teeth gritted, but Tina managed to do it.

"You need to pay attention to what I'm saying rather than trying to shut me up!"

Sudden bawling erupted from the back of the house. Tina stomped from the room but it didn't slow her mother down.

"Setting a horrible example for your son!" she called out.

By the tension in Peggy's shoulders, it appeared she wanted badly to tell Mrs. Rossi to go jump in the cone of an active volcano. But she kept her mouth shut, no doubt realizing that saying something would only make things worse.

Tina returned with a crying Ricky in her arms, his head on her shoulder, eyes squinting in the light.

"Mom, Dad, please leave." she said, rubbing Ricky's back.

"There's our little grandson," Mrs. Rossi cooed, crossing the room, arms outstretched. "Come to Grandma."

Tina turned away, whisking her little boy back to his room. A click could be heard as she locked his door.

Cheryl had had enough. "Mrs. Rossi, if I didn't know better I'd say you *wanted* to wake him up!"

She didn't reveal what she was really thinking at that moment – that the insufferable woman probably had children just so she'd have someone to browbeat.

"This is none of your business," Mrs. Rossi said, then headed for the hallway.

Cheryl stepped in her path. "Tina can get him to calm down and go back to sleep if we all shush."

Mrs. Rossi tried to sidestep around her but Cheryl was faster. "This is my parents' house. They rent it to me. As the legal resident I'm asking you nicely to leave."

If Mrs. Rossi didn't understand the unspoken threat, her husband, the retired policeman, did. As his wife puffed up, ready to make more trouble, Mr. Rossi moved to her side.

"Let's go, honey," he said.

"She can't boss me around!"

She attempted to get around Cheryl again but her husband grabbed her arm.

"Let me go, Frank!"

"We're going home, Rosemary. Now!"

He avoided looking at Cheryl and Peggy as he led his wife outside, leaving the door wide open, cold air rushing in through the screen door. Cheryl closed and locked it, twisting the deadbolt into place that her father added. A peephole had also been installed. They would have to start using both.

When Tina peeked into the living room from the hallway to see if it was safe to return, Peggy had an 'I'm sorry' look on her face.

"It wasn't your fault," Tina said. Then she turned to Cheryl. "Thank you. I've been trying not to provoke my mother. She keeps Ricky for free, you know. I've got to find someone else to babysit after school. My mom is a horrible influence."

No wonder Tina tiptoed around her mother. This was a serious financial issue. Free babysitting weekday afternoons helped keep her afloat.

That's the night sleep became a battleground. Cheryl awoke to the least little sound. Worse, she had a dreadful dream. Eddie Carlisle was driving across a barren landscape in his Cadillac, slamming into anyone in his path, bodies bouncing off the hood of his car.

She awoke in a sweat, gasping for breath, her rollers askew on her head, mumbling something she couldn't quite hold onto.

*

Despite the president's startling speech the night before, Tuesday morning seemed pretty normal. Cars passed by the house, more leaves fell in the yard, and Max was as silly as ever, wagging his tail while Ricky filled his food dish.

Arriving at work, she had to scoot across the lobby to answer the ringing telephone, her purse still on her arm.

"Carlisle Realty, may I help you?"

"You can get that asshole brother of mine on the line, pronto!"

Such a cheerful way to start the day.

Putting him on hold, she decided not to use the intercom in case the boss had someone with him. Instead, she dashed to his door, knocked, then opened it a crack.

"Mr. Carlisle?"

"I'm busy."

Ignoring the brush-off, she entered anyway. "Your brother is cussing on line two. He demands you pick up."

He waved her away like a pesky gnat.

Back at her desk, she ignored the lights on the phone figuring if Mr. C. didn't pick up, Eddie would call back. He didn't call back.

Jerry Inman arrived wearing casual slacks and a cardigan sweater. Odd, he wasn't on the vacation schedule. Instead of heading for his office, he ambled across the lobby to her desk.

"Cheryl, hope all is well with you this morning."

How peculiar that he would do more than mutter 'Morning' as he hurried by.

"I wanted you to know I'm moving my family to Virginia so we can be with my parents. Yesterday was my last day. I'm here to pick up a few of my things."

"I'm sorry to see you go."

"A piece of advice before I leave – I urge you not to accept that sales job. I suspect they would set some land mines in your path. I believe it could only benefit Mr. Carlisle."

"I appreciate the advice. If you don't mind my asking, why are you leaving?"

"If our days are numbered, I don't want to spend them selling houses. I need more time with my family."

She wished him well as he continued on his way to the sales offices. How many people were making similar decisions this morning?

As she finished typing a couple of offers, Mr. Carlisle asked her to come to his office. She closed the door when she walked in, taking her usual seat across the big desk from him. She opened her steno pad, pencil at the ready.

"I need you to call Jay Corbett and reschedule the Barclay Avenue closing for a week from today. Same location, same time we had on the books for today. Got it?"

"Got it." She scratched a quick note to herself.

"One other thing. Jerry quit on me a few minutes ago. The president's speech caused him some kind of mental problem. Which means I'm short one agent. I want your answer to my offer by closing time tomorrow. Say yes and I'll increase your salary immediately by fifty percent while you learn the ropes. One way or another, I'll need you to place an ad in the newspaper, either for the secretary position or a sales agent position, depending on your decision. Time waits for no man *or* woman."

Her mind was racing. But he misunderstood her hesitation.

"You're not going to quit on me too, are you?" he said.

"Unlike Jerry, I can't afford to."

"That's comforting to hear."

Sitting at her desk afterward, another wave of anxiety swept over her. She had her interview tomorrow morning at Sandhills High School, but she wouldn't know if she got the job for some time. She'd still be in limbo by close of business tomorrow. She'd hoped to delay responding as long as possible, fearing the ugly persecution would get even worse when she declined.

For some reason, her mother's comment last night came back to her. "If we all die, there won't be a phone bill." It was true. If the politicians failed to reach a compromise, there would be no bills of any kind for her mom and dad to pay. Or anyone else, for that matter. For Cheryl, there would be no more big red cars tailing her, no more threats to keep quiet about Eddie's drug operation. People would be blown to smithereens, or whatever nuclear bombs did to the human body, something she didn't care to visualize. Ironically, if rationality prevailed, Eddie and Vic would go on terrorizing her.

She flipped through the rolodex looking for Mr. Corbett's number. Squealing tires drew her attention to the front when Eddie Carlisle's car sped into the lot. She braced herself as he stormed into the building as though leading a charge on the field of battle. He blew by her and barged into his brother's office, slamming the door so hard it made her jump. That's when the shouting began.

"The seller cannot back out!" Eddie's angry words bled through the wall.

Mr. Carlisle's reaction was muffled.

"Threaten him with a lawsuit!" Eddie snarled. "I need to get this money in the bank!"

More muted words from Mr. C.

"Dammit, Harry! I'm not waiting a whole week!"

Cheryl strained to hear her boss's words but he was speaking too softly.

"You tell that lawyer to demand the seller get his ass into the office so we can close the deal!"

With that, the door flew open and Eddie stalked through the lobby. Mr. Carlisle raced after him in his shirt sleeves, struggling to catch up. Eddie cranked his car as his brother jumped in. Eddie paid no attention, backing out fast, causing

Mr. C. to hit the dash. Cheryl feared he'd fall out of the open door and be run over. The Cadillac raced toward the street as Mr. Carlisle pulled his door closed before Eddie peeled a wheel accelerating onto the highway. The Caddy nearly slammed into another car, which swerved in time to avoid a smashup that would've spread body parts across the roadway.

Cheryl decided Eddie must've been born with a pair of horns on his head. It's just that his hair was thick enough to hide them.

She phoned Jay Corbett, the real estate attorney, telling him Mr. Carlisle wanted the closing on the house Eddie was buying to be rescheduled for the following Tuesday. The message could be out of date after Eddie's angry rant, but she did what she'd been ordered to do.

There was a call from a man who had previously made an offer on a new house in the Garden Hills subdivision but changed his mind. Now he wanted a house with a basement so he could set up a fallout shelter down there. His sales agent was Jerry Inman who was moving to Virginia. So she transferred the call to Roger.

When this strange Tuesday at the office was over, Cheryl headed for A&P to buy cubed steaks. It was her night to cook and Ricky loved cubed steaks with mashed potatoes and *graybee*.

She grabbed a shopping cart and pushed it toward the meat section, but was stunned when she cut through the paper products aisle to see empty shelves. She stopped in her tracks and stared at the spaces where packages of bathroom tissue were normally stacked high. A middle-aged woman grabbed two packages of tissue, giving Cheryl a challenging look as she scooted around the end of the display.

Cheryl took the last package and continued to the canned goods aisle, finding half-empty shelves. She tossed cans of tuna and dried beef in the basket. Moving slowly along the aisle, she chose cans of vegetables, soup and fruit. She added two bags of dried beans to her basket, two bags of rice and a couple of boxes of noodles. Then she sped to the meat department, grabbing a package of cubed steaks before getting in line.

Ricky and Tina were in the back yard when she got home. She left the groceries in the car except for the meat. Then she rushed into the house and tied her mother's yellow gingham apron on to keep her dress from being spattered. Getting busy in her faster-than-a-speeding-bullet mode, she had supper on the table in a jiffy.

Once the three of them sat down together, it was plain that something was troubling Ricky. And something – likely the same something – was troubling his mom as well. Tina cut Ricky's cubed steak for him and let him pour his own gravy over the meat and mashed potatoes.

"He had a bad experience at school today," she said.

Ricky dragged a piece of meat through the puddle of gravy, sliding it into his mouth while his mother did the talking.

"Miss Dunn took it upon herself to present a film teaching the kids about duck and cover." She looked at Ricky to gauge whether she should continue. "They had to practice it – how many times was it, sweetie?"

"Five times," he said, without looking up from his plate.

"What exactly did you have to do?"

"I got on my knees under my desk and put my head on the floor with my hands on my neck. And then we went into the hallway and did it again. I didn't like it."

"I don't blame you," his mother said. "Why did you have to learn to duck and cover?"

"Miss Dunn said a big bomb is pointed at our school. We're s'posed to duck and cover if we see a big flash."

Tina gave Cheryl a testy look.

"Did the film have a turtle in it?" Cheryl asked.

"Yeah. His name was Bert. Bert was nice. He was scared. I was scared too."

"Scared of what?" Cheryl asked.

"The big flash and the wind and the windows getting broke. Bert hid inside his shell."

"I think it's the same film they showed to kids when we were in high school," Cheryl said to Tina. "It was made for children but we saw it too. Remember?"

"Now that you mention it, I remember the turtle. And I remember we had to practice even though we were too big to get under our desks."

"Can I have some more graybee?"

"Of course you can." Cheryl poured more gravy over his meat and potatoes. "I'm sorry that old movie upset you. But don't be afraid."

"Cheryl is right," Tina said. "Don't worry sweetie. I'll take care of you."

"Grandma says everybody's gonna die." His face was pinched.

Fury burned in Tina's eyes.

"Grandma has a habit of expecting the worst when something happens. If it rains, she doesn't say that the rain will help the flowers and the trees get a drink of water. She says it's going to flood. If it's hot, she doesn't suggest playing in the sprinkler. She says you can't go outside, that you'll die of heatstroke. I guess she can't help it. Her mama could've been that way, I don't know. But you have to remember that when she says something, she can't help it when she predicts terrible things will happen."

She had his undivided attention.

"Just so you'll know, I don't believe for a minute that everyone's going to die. And you shouldn't believe it either. You can't trust that all adults know what they're talking about." She leaned over and gave him a hug.

Normally, Cheryl would eat and run in time to get to her Tuesday night class, but she wanted to watch a network "Report on Cuba." If she was late, so be it. She had to know what was going on. Tina took Ricky for a walk before it got dark so he wouldn't hear the TV.

The report hammered home the magnitude of the situation. The blockade of Soviet ships headed for Cuba would begin at ten o'clock Wednesday morning. An Assistant Secretary of State said if the Soviet Union was not prevented from deploying missiles in Cuba, it would try to put them elsewhere. Soviet leaders said the United States was playing with fire and Castro labeled Kennedy a pirate. A war of words which could easily develop into a war beyond anyone's imagination.

The most unsettling part of the report was film of nuclear testing in the 1950s, including horrific scenes of an atomic blast with a monstrous mushroom cloud billowing high into the sky. Just as horrifying was footage of the shock wave slamming into abandoned buildings that were obliterated in an instant. The bright flash that school kids were warned about was so much scarier when you could see how blindingly intense the bright light really was. The footage left her shaken.

Accounting class was half over by the time she got there. Many of the desks were empty. A discussion raged about whether President Kennedy knew what he was doing and whether a conflagration was imminent. Allan motioned her to sit at the desk next to his.

"He says any force necessary," A man near the front said. "Kennedy is threatening to fire atomic weapons."

"In defense!" another man said. "Not a first strike!"

"Kennedy's the one doing the escalating!" the first man insisted.

Cheryl leaned closer to Allan. "Has this been going on the whole time?"

He nodded.

She stood, picked up her things and headed back toward the door.

Mr. Klein, the instructor, watched her, his fingers tangled in string that he was using for another game of Cat's Cradle, or whatever his latest creation was. "Miss Donovan, you've only been here a couple of minutes."

"I was under the mistaken impression that we were having accounting class tonight."

"I think it's educational – the kind of thing all good CPAs need to keep up with."

She didn't bother to hide her skepticism, leaving the classroom behind. Before she got to the end of the hallway Allan caught up with her.

"Want to have one last study session at Johnny's?"

"Yeah. I have one problem I want to ask you about."

They both drove their own cars, meeting up in the parking lot and walking in together. The bar was even louder than the classroom, with the same kind of heated arguments going on.

"It's awfully noisy for calculus," she said.

"Let's get the corner table."

He pointed to a high table with two stools. She claimed it and pulled her calculus notebook out while Allan threaded his way between tables to the bar.

"You didn't seem to have any patience for the guys in class," he said returning with two steins.

"It reminded me of listening to sports fanatics who think they're smarter than the players and coaches. If Kennedy messed up, I think the truth will come out. Voters can decide whether he gets another term two years from now."

"If the United States still exists two years from now."

"I get depressed if I think about an apocalypse. But are we supposed to sit idly by and let Khruschev have his way with the world?"

"You know, it's ironic Kennedy said last year at the UN that we're all living under 'a nuclear sword of Damocles' that's hanging by a thread which could be cut at any time by 'accident, miscalculation or madness.'"

"And look at him now."

She sipped her beer, then opened her notebook, pencil in hand.

"Let's do calculus, shall we?"

Catching on more quickly than she expected, they were finished in short order.

"I think I'll do okay on the exam, thanks to you."

"Glad to help."

She reached for her purse, hoping to avoid any uncomfortable questions.

"Before you go, I wanted to tell you my brother Sidney – you know the one who lives in Miami – he called me last night after Kennedy spoke." He paused to collect himself. "He called to say goodbye. He feels it in his bones that annihilation is unavoidable. He says living so close to Cuba, his family will be among the first to die."

"Oh, Allan."

"I almost told him the president would probably be the first to go since the missiles would target Washington. But I thought better of it when it hit me he was dead serious. Sidney says he considered packing up the family and driving north. His kids are little, only seven and four years old. But he says once it starts, it won't matter where they are – no one will stand a chance. He thinks it would be better to die right away."

"That's gotta be tough. But I don't believe Kennedy and Khruschev will let it happen."

Allan fell into a silent reverie, staring at his half empty beer stein.

Cheryl touched his hand, then rose to leave.

11

When Cheryl got home, she smelled popcorn as she turned the key. She found Tina lounging on the couch, sock feet on the coffee table, watching *The Red Skelton Show*. The big bowl in her lap was nearly empty.

"Couldn't take another minute of your riveting class?" Tina said, sounding smug.

"The future number crunchers were too busy having a verbal sparring match about Cuba to focus on accounting. Allan and I went to Johnny's so I could ask him one final question to prep for the calculus exam. It was even noisier there. Who would've guessed the bar would be packed with geopolitical experts sharing expert opinions about who's to blame for bringing us to the abyss of destruction." She took her sweater off and collapsed in the chair, running a hand through her hair. "The world has gone mad."

"You know, if you'd told me in high school that one day you'd get a degree in accounting I would've laughed out loud. You know why? You would've been joking, that's why! What happened to the girl I used to know who spent her free time doing creative stuff? Snapping the strangest photos ever seen by human eyeballs. Taping flattened cereal boxes together to make a tablecloth for a picnic table. Writing a screenplay for a movie about twin sisters who solve crimes. What happened to her?"

Cheryl got her dander up for a moment, then took a deep breath.

"Well, she became an adult. Which means working boring jobs to pay for an education that will guarantee a decent income."

"Did you have to choose accounting?"

"I had to be realistic, Tina. It was a degree I could do part time. Classes were available right here in Fayetteville. Plus, when I finish my classes I can get a job as a CPA and earn good money."

"You get a blue ribbon in Practicality one-oh-one, but did you have to flush all your creativity down the toilet?"

Cheryl made a dopey face. "I can still do *this*!" She went into nasal mode to chant, "nanny nanny boo boo!"

"And now you're thinking of co-chairing the class reunion committee," Tina said. "Wasting your time looking backward instead of forward! If you keep doing that, you're gonna turn around and – abracadabra! – you'll be forty years old. And then – abracadabra! – you'll be fifty. Then, guess what! – abracadabra! – you'll be sixty, wondering what the hell happened to all the exciting opportunities you ignored when you were young. And then…"

"I get it, I get it! Abracadabra! – I'll be a grey-haired seventy-year-old, dreaming of what might've been." Cheryl threw the challenge back at her. "I don't want to be rude, but don't forget, you trained to become a keypunch operator."

"Big difference. I'm a mommy."

Cheryl knew Tina had a point but found herself feeling a little prickly, so she changed the subject. "How was Ricky tonight?"

"We played *Chutes and Ladders*. He won. Which made him happy. I read *Half Magic* at bedtime – it's his favorite story lately – and he went to sleep."

"Poor little fella. Glad he calmed down." Cheryl didn't usually give Tina parenting advice. This time she broke her own rule. "I know you're trying to protect him, but the other kids can't help but talk about the crisis. I wonder if it would be better to discuss it with him so he won't be frightened at school."

"Funny you should mention that. I've been thinking about it all day." Her head nodded ever so slightly, more for herself than for Cheryl. "I've decided to talk with him once I figure out what to say."

Cheryl was pleased.

Later, as Tina was about to take a shower, she cleared her throat, saying she had a favor to ask.

"Peggy needs a place to stay. She checked with some friends but no one has room for her."

Tina plainly felt uncomfortable.

"I thought she was going to live with her parents a while longer," Cheryl said.

"It's gotten way beyond awful. They don't say a word to her. Plus, they've doubled her rent."

"I feel for her, I do. But Ricky's already having problems. You wouldn't want to move him out his bedroom."

"Absolutely not. Peggy could sleep on the couch or bed down in my room with me."

Cheryl bristled and wondered why. She preferred things the way they were. But Peggy was Tina's good friend.

"Do you mean a few nights?"

"She's already scanning the paper for apartments to share."

Cheryl rolled her head around, stretching her neck. "When does she finish school?"

"Not until May."

"Oh." Cheryl was sorry Peggy had such a difficult relationship with her parents but, honestly, she didn't want her to move in. She was concerned her presence could change things. Now was a terrible time to make such a drastic change. They were all on edge.

She met Tina's waiting eyes, ready to make it plain that this was too much to ask. But in the three seconds before she opened her mouth, she saw that Tina was having a hard time maintaining her composure.

"She's on her way over," Tina said. "I told her she could stay tonight."

Cheryl absolutely could not make Tina cry. Letting Peggy stay was obviously a huge deal.

"She has to pay a third of the rent and utilities. Can she afford it?"

Tina's shoulders relaxed. "I think so."

"She has to pitch in with the workload."

"That's fair."

"And she should move out as soon as she can."

Tina replied with a nod.

"I don't want to spend time coming up with a list of house rules, but she has to fit in. No smoking, no staying up late or sleeping late. Stuff like that."

"I know you don't want another roommate. I deeply appreciate your kindness."

She leaned over and gave Cheryl a quick hug.

Before taking her turn in the bathroom, Cheryl brought the groceries in that she'd left in the car, hauling them downstairs to the fallout shelter. She rolled her hair and was in bed by the time their new roommate arrived. She heard Peggy and Tina talking in the living room. Eventually she closed her eyes and drifted off to the Land of Nod.

What seemed like moments later, screaming roused her. She struggled to untangle her feet from the covers that were now wrapped around her legs. When she freed herself, she jumped out of bed and darted into the hallway. Following the terrified cries, she hurried to Ricky's room behind Tina. Looking small in his twin bed, he sat up, eyes closed, face contorted, his cheeks wet with tears.

Tina sat on the bed and pulled him onto her lap. Wrapping her arms around him, she rocked him slowly, rubbing his back as she murmured softly in his ear.

"Mommy's here, sweetheart. Mommy's here."

His body gradually relaxed in her arms and his cries quieted.

Cheryl hugged herself, trying to keep warm in her nightgown.

"Mommy?" he said, almost too soft to hear.

"Yes, honey?"

"The bomb burned all the houses and the trees and the cars. I had to run and run. But Bert the turtle wouldn't let me hide in his shell."

"It was a bad dream. You're safe here with me and Cheryl."

He looked up into his mother's face as though making sure she was real, then glanced at Cheryl for good measure. They thought he would calm down but his face fell, his eyes filling.

"Everybody died, Mommy."

Tina pulled him closer and kissed his forehead. "No one has died, sweetie. Everything is fine. I love you."

His little body shuddered and his nose began to drip. Cheryl found the tissue box, setting it on the bed beside them. Tina wiped his nose and kissed him again.

"Tell you what," she said. "How about I sleep with you tonight?"

He nodded.

"First let's go tinkle. Then I'll get my pillow and we'll climb into bed."

He buried his face in her bosom.

As Tina carried him to the bathroom, Cheryl returned to her bedroom, catching a glimpse of Peggy peeking into the hallway from the living room. Thankfully, she had the sense to lay low.

*

By Wednesday morning Tina had transformed herself from the tender mother feline nurturing her baby into a lioness ready to fight to the death to defend her cub.

It was a chilly morning in the upper forties so they put coats on before leaving the house. Cheryl followed Tina to school to meet with Ricky's teacher. She had taken the morning off for her job interview at Sandhills High School. But she had time to go with them first. On the one hand, she wanted to make sure Tina didn't slap Miss Dunn cross-eyed. On the other hand, Cheryl was just as angry as Tina that teachers were allowed to frighten first graders with a film that led them to believe bombs were on the way.

Oscar C. Richards Elementary was a one-story school with three wings and connecting hallways. Like a lot of schools built to accommodate expanding enrollment, it was designed for function only. There was nothing about it that was pleasing to the eye. The exterior was made of pale orange bricks with white trim. The sandy ground was covered by sparse weeds with a few small scrub oaks and pines close to the street.

As the three of them walked through the entrance, Ricky was tense. He knew this wasn't a normal occurrence. Tina said goodbye to him in the hallway before he hurried into his classroom.

The room could've been in a prison with its bare cinder block walls and long straight rows of desks. Standing at the front was a forbidding woman who glowered at the children. Her arms were folded across an ample bosom that appeared to be encased in steel. Her hair was blue grey, no doubt a result of the blue rinse so popular with old ladies. A *lot* of blue rinse. Her brown dress reached midcalf over skinny ankles and small feet in black orthopedic shoes.

When she caught sight of Cheryl and Tina, she moved rapidly in their direction like a soldier on guard duty spotting an intruder.

"Mrs. Armstrong?" she said without a trace of warmth.

"I'm Ricky's mother, Tina Rossi. This is my friend, Cheryl Donovan."

"Why are you here?"

"The film you showed the children yesterday caused my son to have a nightmare."

Miss Dunn looked over her shoulder at the clock above the blackboard.

"It's eight twenty-nine, Mrs. Armstrong. School starts in one minute."

Tina was uncowed.

"Ricky is convinced an atomic bomb is going to wipe out all of humanity. I would've preferred he not see the film."

"Mrs. Armstrong, the teachers do not consult with parents about what teaching materials to use in class. I expose my students to a number of filmstrips, chosen by me, not the parents. With the current situation, I'm surprised a mother wouldn't want her child to be safe. We have fire drills regularly so students know how to safely evacuate the building in case of fire. Now that we're facing the possibility of nuclear missiles being fired at Fort Bragg and vicinity, we'll do our best to prepare them in the event that happens."

The bell rang loudly, echoing through the hallway.

"Please excuse me." And without further ado, Miss Dunn stepped back into the room and closed the door.

Tina seethed, her hands balled into fists at her sides. "I'm tempted to walk in there and say my piece in front of her class."

"I doubt that would accomplish anything other than making Ricky's life miserable."

Tina barreled back down the hallway. Cheryl had to hustle to keep up.

*

When she was ushered into Mr. Swaney's office a couple of minutes after ten, Cheryl felt confident of her credentials and experience. She was also comfortable about her look. She'd chosen a quiet tan dress that didn't hug her body or accentuate her waist and she'd pulled her hair back in a French twist. She didn't want to attract any attention from high school boys.

Unlike her current boss, Mr. Swaney was polite, welcoming, professional and had already familiarized himself with her resume and application before she sat down across the desk from him.

"Miss Donovan, tell me why you want to work at Sandhills High School."

"To be honest, I'd prefer to work with the school district knowing it would be a stable job with good benefits. As for why I chose this school, it has a good reputation for academics and it has a good reputation as a work place. I believe I'd be treated with respect in the front office. I can imagine staying a long time."

He nodded slowly, giving her a look that seemed to say he approved.

They discussed a variety of things, including how the person in this position would also be required to help out with projects, events and unexpected crises that had nothing to do with being a secretary. She let him know she enjoyed that kind of team work.

When she exited the building, her step was lighter. Mr. Swaney assured her he would be in touch within a week. There was real hope now.

As quickly as hope swelled, it scuttled away like a chipmunk fleeing a wily cat on the prowl. She wished she could be more optimistic about the outcome of the crisis. Perhaps it would help if she better understood what was happening, including the back and forth between Kennedy and Khruschev.

If only civilization survived. If only some drunken Russian soldier didn't misinterpret his superior's order and fire a warhead at the White House.

She headed to Point News, a Fayetteville landmark. It was a shop where you could buy all kinds of newspapers and magazines.

Hay Street was downtown Fayetteville's main street. Businesses began at the bottom of Haymount Hill. The street ended at the historic Market House, a red brick building featuring arches on all four sides and a cupola with large clocks facing each direction. It was ringed by a traffic circle. Tawdry bars were the big draw on the first block. Railroad tracks crossed the street at the end of the seedy area, with trains blocking traffic as they passed through town. Once you crossed the tracks, you reached the respectable section, with department stores, movie theaters and other businesses.

Ordinarily it took fifteen minutes to reach her destination, but traffic came to a halt on Hay Street as she reached the Prince Charles Hotel. She had already made it across the train tracks so the backup was caused by something else. Refusing to sit there and wait, she eased over far enough that she could make a U-turn to zigzag along side streets to come up behind the news shop, parking on Old Street.

The building was constructed on a slim pie-shaped lot that came to a sharp point where Hay Street and Old Street formed a narrow V intersection, thus the building's shape – a narrow triangle – and its name, Point News.

While feeding the parking meter, she heard something happening on the other side of the store. Walking rapidly, she bypassed the Old Street entrance of the news shop and rounded the sharp front corner to find a crowd of protesters in the middle of Hay Street, the sun shining down on them as if they were the anointed ones.

Many of them carried signs. One said, "No War Over Cuba." Another read, "Disarmament now." They were chanting, "Peace or perish!" It looked like the leaders of the group were beatniks. The girl wore tight black pants and a grey jacket, her long brown hair draped over her shoulders. The guy was dressed all in black with dark shaggy hair. Police officers encircled the group, preventing them from marching. A newspaper reporter moved among them, interviewing people. A photographer followed, snapping pictures.

Cheryl felt compelled to witness the demonstration. More than that, she had an urge to join in. Maybe she wouldn't feel so helpless if she took action. Even if it was only chanting "peace or perish!" on the main street of little old Fayetteville, North Carolina – far from Moscow, far from Havana and far from Washington DC.

As she watched, two police cars pulled onto Hay Street from Old Street. Two other patrol cars parked on the far side of the street. Eight newly arrived officers joined the circle around the demonstrators. The policeman in charge raised a bullhorn, ordering protesters to stop chanting and listen up.

"Because you're blocking traffic and you don't have a permit, we can arrest you and book you into jail. We don't want to do that. We'd rather let all of you leave peaceably. If you want to organize another demonstration, I'll tell you how to apply for a permit and where you can find out what the rules are. Right now we have to reopen Hay Street to traffic. A lot of people trapped in their cars have business to take care of. And the merchants and businessmen along Hay Street need their customers."

The protesters traded glances, some of them looking to the beatnik couple for guidance. After a long moment, the couple lowered their signs and the long-haired man addressed the group. "Let's move off the street. Write your name and number on a piece of paper and give it to me and Lulu before you go. That way we can let you know when the next protest will be."

With that, he and the girl strolled over to the sidewalk near Cheryl. The demonstrators stopped by to give him their numbers. When they dispersed, police let traffic resume.

Cheryl found a piece of paper in her handbag and used it to write her name and number down. She stepped forward to give the man her slip of paper.

"Thank you," he said before walking with his girlfriend toward the Sears building.

She watched them go, feeling a surge of optimism. Did it make any sense to feel this way? Nothing had changed. Regardless, she was relieved to feel optimism twice in one day. But she still wanted to check out the newspapers and magazines.

It only took a few minutes to pick up several papers, paying the man behind the counter. Her self-education project began over a sandwich when she got home.

*

The realty office no longer felt like a trap when she reported for work that afternoon. She was already counting the days until she could say goodbye to the lecherous Mr. Carlisle, his crime boss brother and the chauvinist salesmen who believed a woman's role in life was to serve her man, be it in the bedroom or the kitchen.

There was a scribbled note on her desk from the boss. "Headed to hospital. Don't know if I'll be back."

That's all he said. She walked down the hall peeking into the sales offices. The only agent she could find was Dan O'Keefe. He was working at his desk, a transistor radio beside him.

"About time you got here," he said. "I'm tired of handling penny-ante phone calls."

"The boss left for the hospital? Any idea what's up?"

"Something to do with his son." He shrugged, his attention returning to the papers in front of him.

The boss didn't get back by five-thirty. Thus, it was her responsibility to lock up. She waited for the sales agents to trickle out and was in the process of covering her typewriter when she heard a car in the parking lot. She cursed under her breath when she saw it was once again Eddie's Devilmobile. The red paint and chrome reflected shafts of evening sunlight, making it appear the Cadillac was on fire.

Hopefully, he wouldn't have a wad of bills on him and he'd be on his way as soon as she told him his brother was out.

"Where's that bastard's Lincoln?" he roared, plowing through the front door. "Tell me his car is at the shop and my brilliant brother is in his office."

Reluctantly, she shook her head.

"Goddammit! That moron doesn't listen to a word I say. I tell him, 'I'll be there at five-thirty.' He says, 'see you then.' So here I am at five-thirty and where the hell is he?"

"At the hospital. Something to do with his son."

"Harry thinks his boy's gonna be an NFL star one day. But that's only gonna happen when hell freezes over. He's too small and too slow. Now, I've gotta put money in the safe."

What if the police walked in on them? Would she be arrested as an accessory? If the authorities found out about the money laundering, would Eddie implicate her? What was she supposed to say? 'I'm sorry, Eddie, but I don't want to participate in your criminal activity.'

He told her to count the money. There was seven thousand dollars in a manila envelope.

She removed the dust cover from the typewriter and typed up a receipt. Once both of them signed it, she unlocked Mr. Carlisle's office and they walked across the room to the safe. She opened it and Eddie placed the envelope inside. Once it was locked, he gave her a cagey look.

"Thanks for your assistance, Miss Donovan."

If she were paranoid, she would suspect Eddie knew his brother wouldn't be here and engineered this whole encounter, including having her help him stash money in the safe. If she were paranoid, that is.

"Harry swears you'll keep your trap shut." His gaze was unnerving.

She struggled not to let her anxiety show. Or her hatred. Her new job couldn't come soon enough.

Her mother's reasoning about the phone bill never coming due if a nuclear war happened, weaseled its way into her consciousness. If Eddie was setting her up as an accessory, it would be a moot point if warheads rained down from the sky. Worrying about Eddie doing her harm would cease. It would be a minuscule silver lining to the most ominous cloud imaginable.

12

That evening, Cheryl sensed the usually cheery kitchen was anything but.

Ricky kept his eyes on his plate. Dishing food into serving bowls, Tina was somber too, giving off an aura of barely contained rage. For the second day in a row, something had apparently happened at school.

Tina gave her a brief, unsatisfying explanation. "The school held a big drill after lunch." Glancing at her son, she clammed up.

He slowly ate around the edge of his hamburger, nibbling on the French fries. This was one of his favorite meals but you would've thought he was being forced to eat liver and onions.

They filled their stomachs in a businesslike manner and moved on.

Cheryl was intent on watching the news, so Tina took Ricky out back to spend time with Max and Pinky.

The broadcast showed Acting United Nations Secretary-General U Thant telling delegates he sent appeals to President Kennedy and Premier Khruschev to voluntarily delay any actions that could lead to war, namely that Kennedy should hold off on the blockade of ships and Khruschev should halt sending ships to Cuba. Thant said that would give the UN time to find a peaceful way out. But a reporter said American sources indicated his appeal was not taken seriously by the Kennedy administration.

It was getting dark when she turned off the TV and walked to the back door. She let Ricky know she was about to bake some cookies, asking if he wanted to help.

He mumbled something under his breath.

"I'm making peanut butter cookies!" she said.

He looked at her, thinking it over. Then he headed toward the porch ready to come in, his mother behind him.

An hour later, they had three dozen warm peanut butter cookies arranged on sheets of waxed paper spread across the table. He sat in his chair, savoring his all-time favorite cookies with a glass of milk. Cheryl was pleased he was able to put the day's unpleasantness out of his mind, at least for a few minutes.

Once Tina tucked him in bed, she sat down with Cheryl in the living room to describe what Ricky had been through.

"After lunch a special bell rang and students had to hurry into the hallway. Ricky said there was lots of shouting by Miss Dunn and the other teachers making the kids hurry up, telling them how to do the duck and cover, ordering them to keep their heads down. They crouched on all fours and put their heads on the floor, covering their heads with their hands. He said they had to stay in that position a long time, waiting for the principal. But he didn't have time to use the bathroom after lunch and needed to pee. He raised his hand, waiting for Miss Dunn to notice. But she wasn't paying attention. So he lifted his head and saw her with another teacher further down the hallway. He said he didn't dare get up so he called out to her. She rushed down the hallway telling him to shut his mouth and put his head back on the floor. He told her he had to use the bathroom but she wouldn't let him get up."

Tina paused, her jaw tightening.

"So he peed in his pants. Of course, that made him cry. Miss Dunn came over to tell him to be quiet. She saw the puddle and yelled at him so the other kids could hear, telling him he was a bad boy for wetting himself and causing a mess."

"She yelled at him? Good God!"

"The kids teased him the rest of the day and Miss Dunn did nothing to help other than sending him to the restroom to change into a pair of dry pants she keeps in a drawer."

"She's the reincarnation of Attila the Hun!"

"Ricky says he never wants to go back to school." Tina sat silently for a moment before continuing. "Needless to say, I'll be meeting with Mr. Hackett in the morning."

"I'm going with you."

"What a horrible first year of school he's having. Why couldn't he get a kind, loving teacher? That should be a requirement to teach first grade! *Liking* children."

Cheryl suggested they watch some TV.

"Might do you some good to take your mind off everything. Why don't we watch *The Dick Van Dyke Show?*"

Tina nodded listlessly.

A knock at the door interrupted them. She peered through the peephole, deciding that if it was Mr. and Mrs. Rossi, she would tell them Tina was asleep and send them on their way. But it was Allan.

He had an uncertain look on his face.

"You look tired," he said when she opened the door.

"Tired of bullies."

He looked wounded.

"Not you," she said, waving him in.

Tina was ready to clear out so they could have the living room, but Cheryl said they'd sit in the kitchen, inviting her to join them if she wanted. Tina opted for relaxing in front of the TV.

"It's your lucky night," she said as Allan took a seat at the kitchen table. "Ricky and I baked cookies. He won't mind if you have a couple."

She chose several from a large plate covered with Saran wrap, arranging them on a dessert plate that she set on the table.

"Milk?" she asked.

"Perfecto."

She poured them each half a glass and sat across from him.

He popped one in his mouth, closing his eyes as he chewed. "Mm!"

"What's up?" she said.

"I'm thinking you need a fallout shelter. I can build one for you."

"You'll be glad to hear we already have one."

"I didn't know that."

"It's in the basement. Dad built it."

"He must've had a crystal ball."

"There's only one room down there, no windows. Dad added a stronger door at the bottom of the stairs and shelving along the walls. It's stocked with all kinds of stuff."

"That's a load off my mind."

"Yeah, but I'd rather take action than wait for the worst to happen. I'm joining a group demonstrating for peace. Maybe if we speak out, the president will listen."

"But will Khrushchev listen?"

"We can only hope."

"When's the next protest?"

"I'm waiting for someone to let me know."

"I'm interested. When you get word, call me."

She nodded as Tina strolled in.

She sat down in her chair at the end of the table, helping herself to a cookie. "What's this about a protest group?"

Cheryl related how she watched the protest on Hay Street, mentioning she gave her phone number to the organizers.

"Count me in too. Ricky can tag along."

"You're kidding!"

"I think it would be good for him to do something to help stop a war. We had a chat this evening." She looked at Cheryl. "You were right. He needs to know on a first grade level. I explained to him that the principal and teachers are trying to help the kids be ready if there's a nuclear blast. But I told him we don't think it's going to happen. You know what he asked me?"

"What?"

"He wanted to know if 'that *Kooschef* guy' is a bully."

"And you said?"

"I told him I think so. But I said there's more than one bully."

"The Soviet Union is a bully nation," Allan said. "Then again, so is the good old US of A."

When Allan left, Cheryl tackled some reading on her bed. Leaning on a couple of pillows, she opened a special edition of a news magazine dated last fall. There was an opinion piece she was interested in about the Bay of Pigs.

The longer she read, the more worried she became about Paul, her father and her brother. Which was illogical. As she pointed out to her mother, the front line was everywhere in this kind of conflict. But there was still a chance of old-fashioned bombs and weapons fire.

She hoped to finish one more article before turning out the light, but nodded off, a newspaper on her lap.

Loud, anguished cries awakened her. She leapt from bed still in her clothes. Hurrying into the hallway, she nearly collided with Tina. Ricky was having another nightmare. Tina rushed into his room, pulling him into her arms. His tear-stained face was twisted with fear. Tina stroked his back gently, rocking him on her lap, telling him she loved him and that she would take care of him.

"Oh dear," She glanced up at Cheryl. "He wet the bed."

Cheryl found clean pajamas in his drawer and helped remove the wet ones and put the dry ones on. Poor kid. This was something new. Tina strolled through the house with Ricky's head resting on her shoulder, a sweater draped over his back. Cheryl hurried to the linen closet. Working fast, she removed the wet sheets and blanket and completely remade his bed, including using an old quilt as a dry mattress pad and a new blanket on top. When Tina tucked him in, he was sound asleep.

*

Before they sat down for breakfast the next morning Cheryl got Tina's permission to let Ricky see the fallout shelter, hoping it would help him feel safe. He had seen the room before but had no idea back then that it was anything other than a cramped, dark basement where things were stored. When she revealed its purpose, he saw it with new eyes, studying with interest the shelves of canned goods and the jugs of water. When he spotted a game of Monopoly on a high shelf he was intrigued.

"Can you teach me how to play?" he said.

"I'll be happy to."

"But where do we sleep?"

Cheryl pointed to two tall tubes covered with canvas tarp in the corner. "Those are big mattresses that we would put on the floor for us to sleep on. We've got blankets and pillows too." She pointed to a big cardboard box.

"But what if it's dark?"

"We have candles and flashlights with lots of batteries." She pointed to another shelf.

"Come on, you two, we need to eat breakfast," Tina called down the stairs. "You can ask questions anytime you want."

Throughout breakfast he kept thinking of more. Could he bring his toys with him? A few. Could they bring the tape recorder? That was a great idea. How long would they have to stay down there? They didn't know.

Thankfully, he didn't ask about Max and Pinky. Cheryl and Tina didn't have a good answer to that question.

As before, Cheryl followed Tina and Ricky to school. Tina had convinced her son that attending school was very important and that he should tell her if he was bullied.

Cheryl listened to the news on the way, learning that some Soviet ships had turned back rather than continue to Cuba. She wanted to believe it was a good sign. But there was no way of knowing.

She parked behind Tina along the curb, watching as she kissed Ricky goodbye, understanding it should be done out of sight of the other kids. The two women stopped in the office where Tina told the secretary she needed to see Mr. Hackett. The secretary glanced at the clock – it was eight twenty-one – and told Tina to wait a moment. She slipped into the principal's office, returning quickly.

"He can spare five minutes." She ushered them in.

Mr. Hackett was a tall man in brown slacks, white short-sleeved shirt and tie. He was about forty with glasses and hairy forearms.

"Good morning, ladies. I don't have much time so please be brief."

"Mr. Hackett, this is my friend Cheryl Donovan. I'm Tina Rossi – Ricky Armstrong's mother. He's in Miss Dunn's first grade class. Ricky's been traumatized two days in a row – first by a film his teacher showed the class about what to do if a missile is launched, then by yesterday's drill."

The welcoming expression on the principal's face vanished.

"While I want my son to know what to do in case a missile heads our way, he should be treated with respect and care. After lunch yesterday his class was in such a rush to get ready for a big drill that he didn't get a chance to go to the bathroom. During the drill, he needed to relieve himself and called out to Miss Dunn, telling her he needed to pee. She told him to be quiet. He had to remain on the floor for so long, he wet his pants. Miss Dunn then humiliated him in front of the other kids, telling him in her big loud voice that he was a bad boy for making a puddle on the floor. The little bullies followed the lead of their big bully teacher and picked on him the rest of the day. I can only imagine he'll be picked on today and tomorrow, and probably the rest of the school year."

Mr. Hackett opened his mouth to speak but Tina rushed ahead.

"The day before yesterday, Miss Dunn showed the class a film about what to do if there's a big flash, telling them how to duck and cover. He came home frightened, not understanding what was going on. Twice he's had nightmares about people dying, including those he loves. I feel strongly that parents should be communicated with *before* such dramatic measures are taken at school. That way parents can help guide their kids through these anxious times. Ricky now says he doesn't want to go back to school. He claimed to have a tummy ache this morning, trying to get out of class. I had to give him a pep talk to calm him down."

"I'm sorry your son is agitated by what's going on, Mrs. Armstrong. If we had more staff and more time, we would've told parents before ordering this important safety measure. A letter was prepared by the superintendent's office that all students in the school system will take home this afternoon. Such drills and films could save student lives. As for your accusation concerning Miss Dunn, I'll talk with her about it."

"That may sound logical to you, Mr. Hackett, but I wouldn't be surprised if she retaliates. She doesn't like children, you know. What an awful way for kids to begin twelve years of school, with a teacher whose idea of education is keeping her students quiet and shaking in their sneakers from eight-thirty to three. And she's been making children hate school for decades."

The stony look on his face suggested he didn't appreciate what could be construed as Tina's indictment of his effectiveness as principal. He checked his watch. "Thank you,

Mrs. Armstrong." He opened his door, leaving the office and the women behind.

The bell rang as Cheryl and Tina passed through the main entrance to the portico.

"Mrs. Armstrong," Cheryl said, imitating the principal and the humorless teacher, using the name they both insisted on calling Tina, a last name she dumped as part of her divorce.

"It's deliberate, you know." Tina growled.

"You're right. By the way, good job back there. You crammed a lot into a couple of minutes, and you managed not to tell him he's full of camel caca."

"I understand what they're trying to do. But I can't let Miss Nineteenth Century Dunn get away with being a blue-haired bully. I think she enjoys tormenting children. I wrote a letter last night to the school superintendent. I'm mimeographing copies today so I can mail them to school board members as well."

"You're smarter than you look."

"And you're still as much of a smartass as *you* look."

*

Cheryl made it to work in the nick of time. As she walked in, Mr. Carlisle boomed over the intercom.

"Cheryl, need you in here!"

She stowed her purse, grabbed her steno pad and pencil, and hurried to his office.

"I'm leaving in a few minutes to return to the hospital," he said. "Call Mr. Corbett. Cancel our meeting for this afternoon. Call my brother and tell him I need to see him tonight in my office. Nine o'clock. When he starts to ask you questions, say I told you to hang up. Then hang up. Type up this letter I dictated to Perry Odom." He handed her the Dictaphone as he continued his instructions. "When you're finished typing it, leave the letter and the Dictaphone in the safe. That's important. It's confidential. Don't reveal the contents to anyone." He gave her a stern look. "I'll sign it tonight and mail it myself. Got it?"

She finished scribbling her notes. "Got it. One thing though."

"What's that?"

"He'll be furious if I hang up on him."

"I can't help that."

"But..."

"You can go now."

"He'll call back," she said.

"Let him."

He restacked some papers and put them in his inbox. "Lock up tonight."

"But..."

Using his thumb, he pointed at the door.

She thought to ask how his son was doing but he was in no mood.

Shortly after he left, Roger walked through the lobby on his way out.

"Roger, how is Mr. Carlisle's son? Do you know?"

He slowed his step.

"Haven't you heard? His son's in a coma."

"From a football injury?"

"Don't think it was football." He raised his eyebrows for emphasis.

That poor kid. She hoped things were not as bleak as Roger made out.

A few minutes after ten she braced herself and dialed Carlisle's on the River, Eddie's most la-di-da restaurant with a view of the Cape Fear River. Hard to believe that such a low-class guy owned such a high-class restaurant. She was surprised by how professional the secretary sounded. Even more amazed when a man picked up and said, "This is Eddie Carlisle." He sounded as smooth and friendly as *Dr. Kildare*, TV's handsomest doctor.

"Mr. Carlisle?"

"Yes, how can I help you?"

"This is Cheryl Donovan. Your brother asked me to tell you he needs to see you tonight in his office at nine o'clock. He told me to hang up once I relayed his message to you."

"Don't you dare!" Now he was back to the Eddie Carlisle she knew and detested.

"I'm sorry, Mr. Carlisle, but Mr. Carlisle – I mean my boss – ordered me to…"

"No one hangs up on Eddie Carlisle!"

"Please don't take it personally. I would never hang up on you or anyone else if I had any say-so. But Mr. Carlisle ordered me. So I have to do it or possibly face getting fired."

"Miss Donovan…"

She set the receiver on the cradle as gently as possible, knowing what would happen next.

Try as she might, it was impossible to ignore the loud ringing. Dan yelled from his office for her to answer the damn phone. She shot right back that the boss told her not to.

Eddie gave up after five tries and the quiet day in the office got quiet once more. There were two last-minute cancellations of showings as potential buyers got cold feet about even *looking* at a house with the end of the world hanging over them.

It was during this period of calm that she used her earpiece so she could listen discreetly to the letter her boss dictated. In the letter he told his prospective partner that he would let Odom Realty's accountant look over Carlisle Realty's books late next week. Mr. C. said his own accountant, Harland Peavy, would be available at that time to share the ledgers.

Up until a couple of weeks ago she wouldn't have given the letter a second thought. But knowing what she did about the money laundering, it came across as a delay tactic. Mr. Carlisle could be worried about illegal activity being obvious to a good CPA. She guessed postponement would give him time to make sure nobody learned he'd been cooking the books. Mr. C. wanted the merger to happen. Perhaps he *needed* the merger to happen. Was that why he got involved with his brother's money laundering in the first place? He needed the money?

By the end of the day Cheryl and Dan were the only ones in the building. She walked back to his office and asked him if he would leave a few minutes early so she could go ahead and lock up. She didn't tell him why.

As soon as he was out the door, she rushed to follow him, afraid Eddie would show up any moment. Once she was safely on Raeford Road she looked in the rearview as a red car pulled into Carlisle Realty's parking lot. It was too far away to be positive, but it had to be Eddie. Nervous about being spotted, she turned off the highway a couple of streets early.

Food was on the table and Tina and Ricky were just sitting down when Cheryl arrived. She kissed Ricky on top of the head before washing her hands.

"Thank you for a fine meal, Tina," she said, serving herself a slice of meatloaf.

"Yeah, Mommy."

Tina pushed an envelope toward her. It was from Paul.

In spite of feeling a thrum in her chest, Cheryl set the letter aside, asking Ricky how school was.

"I didn't drink till it was over," he said. "When we finished, I drank lots."

"So the drill went okay?"

"The principal said we did good. Can I have some peanut butter cookies for dessert, Mommy?"

"You can have cookies while you're watching *Mister Ed*."

He smiled, which warmed Cheryl's heart.

After clearing the table, she took a few minutes to change clothes before tackling the dishes. In her room, she sat down on the bed and opened Paul's letter.

"My darling Cheryl,

"Unlike a lot of guys here I don't think the world is about to end. I think sanity will prevail. The timing of my deployment couldn't have been worse. Well, I suppose it could've been worse. If I had shipped out last Monday I would never have met you. But the maneuvers came at a terrible time – precisely when I needed to convince you of the depth of my love. I needed more time to demonstrate my passion and my commitment. I'm not as good at writing letters as I am at kissing your lips. I wish I was a poet, so I could create an acceptable substitute for lying down with you on a grassy slope and touching your smooth skin and tasting the nectar of your soul.

"I'll be home first chance I get. Suddenly you are my home. You are the hearth where my fire burns hot. You are the sweetness of a warm bed on a cold night.

"Please wait for me. I'm desperate to be with you, to share the air you breathe. If you're not in a hurry to get married, I can wait. You're worth waiting for."

"My heart beats for you with the intensity of the sun.

"Paul"

The sensation in her chest was like two butterflies flitting after each other in a field of wildflowers. He claimed not to be a poet but she begged to differ.

His words left her breathless, making her question her own principles.

13

Waiting for the evening news to begin, Cheryl drummed her fingers. Tina rocked forward and backward on the couch. When the sounder played for the broadcast, they both leaned forward.

Dramatic film of American warships sweeping across the high seas in staggered formation filled her with dread. Pictures of gun emplacements on the Cuban shoreline and missile sites in the trees made her muscles tighten. She groaned as they watched US marines unload from airplanes at America's naval depot at Guantanamo Base, Cuba. And the sight of gun emplacements on Florida beaches was shocking.

The anchor reported there had been some tense moments as a Soviet tanker approached the quarantine zone. Two American warships made ready to intercept, but the tanker was allowed through when they determined it was carrying oil. The U.S. Navy expected more challenging interactions with Soviet ships in the next forty-eight hours.

"I don't think I can take it," Cheryl said out loud.

It was hard to know if any progress had been made to de-escalate the confrontation. President Kennedy had agreed to talks with Acting UN Secretary-General U Thant over his proposal for a two to three week pause on both sides. Khruschev agreed as well. But the blockade would not end and neither would the movement of Soviet ships headed for Cuba.

"Damn," Tina whispered.

Three days after Kennedy's address to the nation, tension was like a fiend from hell invading Cheryl's dreams and filling her subconscious with bright flashes and mushroom clouds.

As soon as the anchor signed off, Ricky breezed into the living room. He was already bathed and in his pajamas, ready to watch *Mister Ed*.

Cheryl relocated to the kitchen, Tina behind her.

"I'm having a glass of wine," Cheryl said. "You?"

Tina nodded. "I think my pulse is racing."

"Mine too."

Tina placed two peanut butter cookies on a plate and fixed a small glass of milk while Cheryl poured wine into two orange juice glasses.

"I was thinking of Dad, Mike and Paul the whole time we were watching," said Cheryl.

Tina took Ricky his snack, placing it on the coffee table so he could sit on the floor and watch the program with the talking horse.

"Was there any news in Paul's letter?" she said, returning.

"It was obvious he was ordered not to say a word about the crisis or his location. Which is understandable."

"Well, what did he say?"

"There was no news."

"It was a love letter." Tina accentuated the word *love*.

Cheryl fought to keep a self-conscious look from her face, but Tina gave her a sly grin.

When the telephone rang, Tina grabbed it.

"Sure. Why don't you come over tomorrow evening after supper? You can hang out with him in the yard until it's time for his bath. That gives you about an hour or so."

There was a momentary pause.

"But your visitation was last weekend."

Another pause.

"Don't tell me you've forgotten that you asked for every other weekend. You told the judge every weekend was too much. Remember?"

Cheryl could hear Wyatt holding forth on the other end of the line, using all the bad words he knew. And he knew quite a few. Tina stared at the ceiling as she waited for him to run out of gas.

"I'll either see you tomorrow evening about six-thirty or I won't," she said. "Your choice."

She hung up, giving Cheryl the lowdown.

"Because he's broken his promise for two years in a row to take his son to the beach, he wants to take him now before Armageddon arrives."

"In October?"

"His brain is the size of a pistachio."

Cheryl grabbed her things. She was late for class. To tell the truth, it was hard to focus on figures when the fate of humanity hung in the balance. She stood at the door, dithering.

"To hell with it." She put her things away, settling in for a quiet evening at home.

Once Ricky was in bed, Cheryl and Tina read for a while. Cheryl was reading an Agatha Christie novel when the protest guy rang her. Stu Levy said the next protest would be

Saturday at noon along Hay Street, saying this time they wouldn't block traffic. He asked her to bring a homemade sign and spread the word.

She phoned Allan, blurting out the information about the protest before she'd properly said hello, not wanting him to jump to the wrong conclusion.

When Peggy got home, she brought two large suitcases that she stored in Tina's room. The period of the boarder had begun.

*

Before the president's speech, Cheryl went to bed at night expecting to wake up the next morning. But it was no longer a given. There was a chance a nuclear warhead could be launched, and then another and another, making it impossible to assume her eyes would ever open again.

So when she awoke Friday morning, she was thankful to be alive. She lay still for a moment listening to Max bark while Tina filled his bowl, telling him to hush. A neighbor cranked his car. Someone flushed the toilet. The sounds of normality.

After a breakfast of pancakes and bacon, Tina and Ricky headed for school. Cheryl finished dressing and took off for work while Peggy cleaned up the kitchen. In fact, Peggy offered to do the dishes every day, saying it would be easy for her to take care of the morning dishes, having a later work day than theirs. Definitely a good sign. The transition from having three in the house to having four was simpler than Cheryl expected.

Cheryl had chosen her red suit so she'd look good in the lobby. It was a gesture of good will toward Mr. Carlisle and the missus. And on the day Mr. Carlisle demanded she give thumbs up or thumbs down to his job offer, she hoped it would also be a subliminal message that she viewed herself as part of the team, even if she declined. Nobody seemed to notice.

Sitting down at her desk, she found a list on a sheet of paper ripped from a legal pad. It was written in the boss's nearly illegible handwriting. Six chores for her to take care of. He said he'd be at the hospital. Which meant his son was still in a coma.

Her phone rang before she had time to prioritize the list. Oddly, it was Diane Coleman, the cleaning woman who wasn't really middle-aged.

"Cheryl, I've got more to tell you. But I'd prefer to do it in person. Can you meet me at noon?"

"Sure."

"How about Point News? Lots of folks gather there to catch buses."

*

Waiting with the crowd at the downtown bus stop, she noticed a pretty Black woman walking in her direction. When the young woman waved at her, Cheryl was amazed. Even though she knew Diane's secret, and even though she was waiting for her to arrive, it took her a moment to understand this was the real Diane Coleman. The real Diane could easily be a fashion model with her trim figure, beautiful face, striking eyes and short, soft black hair. She could've been on her way to a magazine photo shoot in a pleated tan skirt and cream turtleneck.

"Wow! I see now why you disguise yourself at work," Cheryl said, sliding her shades to the top of her head.

Diane gave her a self-conscious look.

They crossed the street, heading east toward the Market House, strolling along the wide sidewalk, close to the diagonal parking spaces and parking meters.

They could've been two friends shopping together. Except that a white woman and a Black woman walking together was an uncommon sight. They ignored the stares.

"So," Cheryl said, "what's going on?"

Diane took a quick look around.

"I usually work Friday night but I have to do something else tonight, so the boss told me I could do the cleaning last night. I got off the bus and saw Mr. Carlisle's car and his brother's car out front. I walked around to the back door to let myself in like I always do. I figured they'd be in his office. And they were, but the door was open. You remember those shifty men I told you about coming in on the weekend? Now I know what they've been doing."

"Drugs?"

"You *know?*"

"The Carlisle brothers have a bad habit of leaving the door open."

"Right away, I decided I'd better announce myself so they could close the door. I took two steps toward the office when I heard Mr. Carlisle say, 'I'm not washing your drug money anymore, that's the end of it!' Then his brother says, 'You're in too deep to back out now.' And Mr. C. says, 'Like it or not, that's exactly what I'm doing.' At that point I decided if I let them know I was there, I'd get myself killed. I backed away, desperate to get out of there before they saw me. They would've known I heard every word."

Diane looked around again before continuing.

"I heard the boss's brother tell Mr. Carlisle he couldn't leave him high and dry. Mr. Carlisle told him he could go to hell. I was about to slip out the back door when I heard Eddie tell Mr. Carlisle to meet him Monday night. Eddie said, 'You've got till then to accept the rules. If you're not here, I'll tell Vic to tan your hide till it's ready to be used for shoe leather.'"

When they reached the Market House traffic circle, they crossed, then walked back along the other side of Hay Street. With a wink, Diane suggested Cheryl do a little shopping at The Capitol Department Store.

"I appreciate you filling me in," Cheryl said.

"I figured somebody ought to know. I can't go to the police and report what I heard. They wouldn't believe a Black cleaning woman. My body would likely end up floating face down in the Cape Fear River."

"I overheard a conversation too. Eddie's been trying to scare me ever since. And succeeding. It's a good thing you got out of there when you did."

When they reached The Capitol, they said their goodbyes, having agreed it would be best for them not to return together.

"My number is on this piece of paper." Diane handed Cheryl two slips of paper and a pencil. "If you write your number on the other one, then I can reach you at home if I need to."

With their phone numbers exchanged, Diane headed on down the sidewalk while Cheryl strolled into The Capitol as if she was ready to go on a shopping spree.

*

The afternoon started out slow. Cheryl wondered if people were stocking up at the grocery store or saying their long distance goodbyes with loved ones as Allan's brother did.

If she had run out of jobs to do on a slow day a few weeks ago, she would've reorganized her desk drawers. Now that she was gearing up for a job change, she wasn't motivated to do busy work. Instead, she would type her mother a letter.

As she was about to begin, the day went from quiet to noisy in a flash. Mr. Carlisle snuck in the back door, motioning Cheryl to come to his office.

"I parked behind the building so no one knows I'm here. I've got to make an urgent call to my estate lawyer and I don't want to be interrupted. If anyone asks, I had to go somewhere for an important meeting. That includes my brother. And my wife. Got it?"

"Got it."

"Whatever you do, don't tell Eddie or Margie I'm here. Understand?"

She nodded.

"If anyone gets pushy, tell them you lost your key."

"May I ask…"

"No, you may not. Now go back to your desk and hide your key. I'm locking my door. I've got to get this done right now. Zero interruptions."

When she got to her desk, she grabbed the key from the drawer, ducked into the ladies room and tucked it inside her bra. This was too weird, she thought, feeling the cold metal on her skin. When she returned, line three was lit up.

Why was a call to his estate lawyer so important that he had to hide in his office and refuse to see anyone? Peculiar behavior, to say the least.

She didn't have to wait long for fireworks. Mrs. Carlisle flew into the lobby like a fighter jet ready to shoot down the enemy. Normally she said a few words to Cheryl. Not today. The relationship between them was mowed down by the rumor mill that day in Belk's when she accused Cheryl of sleeping with her husband. Which would've been laughable if it weren't so infuriating. Today she headed straight for her husband's office.

When she found it locked, she pounded on the door, shouting for him to open up. When that didn't produce results, she returned to Cheryl's desk, her angry stride at odds with her delicate ankles.

"Where is he?"

"He's not here," Cheryl replied.

Mrs. Carlisle rolled her head around. Rolling her eyes apparently wasn't nearly enough to express her skepticism.

"Let me see. The only reason you'd lie is that Harry ordered you to."

Cheryl held Mrs. C.'s gaze but with great difficulty.

"I happen to know he's here. I saw his car pull in. Which means it's parked out back."

Cheryl was incensed that the boss put her in this position. But there was nothing she could do about it at the moment.

"Give me the extra key to Harry's office. I know you have one."

"He took it back the other day. I wondered then if he no longer trusts me." Which was a pretty believable lie, actually.

"Fiddlesticks!" Said in a booming voice.

Mrs. Carlisle barreled around the corner of the desk and grabbed the back of Cheryl's chair, giving it a forceful shove. Cheryl careened across the lobby, crashing into one of the

Danish modern sofas. She shrieked as she tumbled from the chair to the floor.

Mrs. Carlisle ignored her, rifling through the desk drawers. When she found Cheryl's purse she searched that too.

"Hey!" Cheryl got to her feet.

She took a few steps toward her desk but stopped, deciding it was safer not to interfere.

Mrs. Carlisle turned the purse upside down, shaking the contents into the bottom drawer. When she was satisfied the key wasn't there, she stormed back across the lobby to her husband's office, her high heels tapping out a warning.

"I'll flush him out," she said.

Instead of knocking, she reached into her handbag and withdrew a small black pistol.

Cheryl gasped and darted behind one of her file cabinets, peering over the top.

"Harry!" Mrs. Carlisle bellowed. "I know you're in there! I saw your Lincoln pull in." She pointed her gun at the door and without a moment's hesitation, pulled the trigger.

A sharp report stabbed the air, followed by Mr. Carlisle's muffled shouts from behind the door.

"Dammit, Margie! Put that gun away!"

The door swung open. Husband and wife came face to face.

Roger and Dan, the only salesmen in the building, peeked through the doorway from the break room. Only their heads were visible.

"Margie..." Mr. Carlisle said.

"You know what they found in his system?"

"I..."

"Heroin! That's what put him in a coma, an overdose of heroin!"

He was silent.

"Wonder where he got it?" she said. "Who would *you* buy from if *you* wanted a little bag of heroin?"

Still he said nothing.

"If you think I don't know what you..."

"You're distraught, Margie. Calm down."

"Calm down? Calm down?" she cried, eyes bulging.

"Listen, Margie..."

"Listen? I think not, you skirt-chasing, phoney-baloney jackass!"

"Now, sweetheart..."

"Don't you *sweetheart* me! I've got the business card of my sister's divorce lawyer in my purse." She pulled the card out of the side pocket of her handbag, waving it at her husband as she continued. "And I'm not afraid to use it. No more telling me what I can and cannot do. Things are about to change, Harry. At the moment, I have to get back to the hospital."

Stuffing the pistol back in her purse, she hurried out of the building, slid behind the wheel of her pink Grand Prix and whipped out of the parking lot, tires squealing. Cheryl's impression of Mrs. C. as a prim and proper Junior Leaguer was shattered.

Mr. Carlisle studied the bullet hole in his door, turning to face Roger and Dan as they edged into the lobby.

"No need to call police. She fired it accidentally. I was in my office with the door closed when the gun went off." He pointed at the damage to the door.

When the two men made themselves scarce, Mr. Carlisle turned to Cheryl.

"She fired it accidentally, you know. She would never shoot me."

"I'm sure you're right, Mr. Carlisle."

When he returned to his office, she retrieved the business card Mrs. Carlisle dropped on the floor in her rush to leave.

14

The scene replayed in Cheryl's head on her drive home. She'd been terrified Mrs. Carlisle would kill her husband. Judging by what she said, Mrs. C. knew about the money laundering and knew exactly where the dirty money came from. She had put her foot down. Hard. She wasn't going to be a party to Mr. Carlisle's deal with the devil. The fact that their son could die from a heroin overdose while Mr. Carlisle was helping launder the proceeds from Eddie's heroin business could very well prove to be the undoing of the Carlisles' marriage.

She had to shift gears emotionally when she got home. It was her night to cook. Fortunately she'd planned an easy fix supper. Within twenty minutes of walking through the door she had food on the table – chili and rice, applesauce, pickles and Saltines. Ricky loved it. Especially when she grated cheese on top and proclaimed it gourmet dining.

He was scraping the last of the applesauce from his bowl when they heard a knock. Cheryl answered it to find Wyatt slouching on the porch in his oil-stained coveralls, an Amoco emblem on his shirt pocket. Clinging to his arm, his girlfriend Ramona had the look of someone who had just crawled out of bed, blonde hair in disarray, mascara and eyeliner smeared below her eyes.

"Here to visit my son." It sounded like his mouth was full of marbles.

She left them at the door while she went for Tina. "It's your ex and his girlfriend." Then she silently mouthed, "He's drunk," for Tina's eyes only.

Tina grunted softly, instructing Ricky to go brush his teeth. Then she put a jacket on and led Wyatt and Ramona around the house and through the gate to the back yard. Cheryl ran hot water in the sink for the dishes, keeping watch on the yard through the open curtains.

Ricky brushed his teeth in record time, running full speed through the kitchen and out the back door, almost knocking his mother down on the porch.

"Daddy!"

Tina stood there for a moment, hands in her pockets. Then she came inside, closing the door behind her.

"I'll have to keep an eye on them," she said to Cheryl. "First I have to get his jacket."

Cheryl pulled the curtains open wider. Not so she'd have a better view – she wanted the nosepicker to notice she was watching. He did, his bloodshot eyes darting toward the window twice.

Once Tina delivered the jacket and helped Ricky put it on, she came back inside, telling Cheryl she was ready to take over doing dishes. That was the deal – whoever cooked didn't have to clean up.

"I'll do them while you sit on the porch," Cheryl suggested. "I don't mind at all."

"No need. I can keep watch through the window."

Cheryl passed her apron to Tina and headed down the hallway. Changing out of her suit, she had time to spare before the news came on.

When she returned to the kitchen a short time later the dishes were stacked in the dish drain, the sinks were empty and the table and countertops had been wiped clean. Figuring Tina had gone outside to check on things, she stepped onto the back stoop. The yard was empty. Had they all gone around front? It was possible Max had made a nuisance of himself.

Then she heard Tina scream Ricky's name. Cheryl ran around to the front in time to see Tina collapse onto her knees on the lawn.

"They're gone!" she screamed.

Wyatt's car was no longer behind theirs in the driveway.

"I've got to call the police," Tina said, getting to her feet, and charging up the steps.

Cheryl followed. "Maybe they went for ice cream?"

"I told him in no uncertain terms that he couldn't take Ricky anywhere."

Reaching the telephone, Tina dialed the number on the emergency card on the wall.

Cheryl hurried to Ricky's bedroom thinking he slipped in somehow and was in there pouting after his father left early. She checked all the rooms. No Ricky.

In the kitchen Tina said an officer was en route. "But Wyatt's getting too big of a head start! I've gotta go after him!"

"You don't know where he went."

Tina steepled her hands in front of her face, eyes unfocused.

"The beach," she said with conviction.

"But which one?"

"Wrightsville Beach! His buddy owns a trailer down there. He lets Wyatt stay for free. I went with him once. I know exactly where it is."

She dashed into her room.

"What are you doing?" Cheryl trailed after her.

"I'm driving to Wrightsville Beach."

"But..." Cheryl stopped herself from objecting. Tina wouldn't listen. And maybe she shouldn't listen.

"I could go with you," Cheryl said.

"I need you to be here when the police officer comes. And in case Wyatt brings him back. I'll stop at a payphone to check in with you." She pulled the door open, then paused. "Whatever you do, don't let my parents know what's going on."

Cheryl watched Tina back out and drive away. She wasn't normally a speed demon. Tonight was different.

When the officer showed up, Cheryl was near tears. She did her best not to cry as she answered all of his questions. She also gave him descriptions of Wyatt, Ramona and Ricky. He said they would post a statewide bulletin and alert authorities in New Hanover County.

She paced through the house after he left. Somehow the officer's visit made her even more anxious, making the abduction all the more real. Ricky was in danger. His dad was drunk. The girlfriend couldn't care less about her half-witted boyfriend's son and wouldn't look out for him. Ricky knew how to dial his home number, but he didn't know how to do it when it was long distance. Had Tina ever taught him how to dial the operator? She needed to do something besides pace.

Retrieving the feather duster and a dust cloth, she busied herself dusting furniture, tidying up as she went. She had finished the living room when the phone rang. Rushing to get it, she stubbed her little toe on the leg of the coffee table. Any other time she would've wailed. Not now.

"Hello?"

"This is Diane Coleman. May I speak with Cheryl please?"

"Diane, this is Cheryl."

"I remembered more of what I heard."

"I definitely want to hear about it, but we've got a family crisis here at my house. I need to hang up. I'm expecting a call."

"Of course. I understand."

They both hung up. Cheryl took some slow, deep breaths, her hand on her chest. She'd hoped it was Tina saying she had Ricky. Sitting down in a kitchen chair, she rubbed her throbbing little toe, hoping it wasn't broken. But that was the least of her worries.

She dusted and tidied the dining room, her bedroom, Ricky's room and was about to do Tina's bedroom when the phone rang again. This time, she hurried but didn't run.

"Hello? Tina?"

"This is the operator. I have a collect call for Cheryl Donovan from Paul McIntyre. Will you accept charges?"

"No, I can't. I'm waiting for an urgent call. I'm sorry."

She hung up rather than allow any further discussion and then felt guilty. Did he have some news? She couldn't afford to dwell on it.

"God, what a horrible night!" she muttered. "Please let it be over. Please let Ricky come home."

She stomped her foot. Unfortunately, it was the one with the throbbing toe and she instantly regretted it.

It was after nine-thirty when a car parked in the driveway. She raced to the front window. It was Peggy, not Tina. She'd forgotten Peggy would be arriving. Cheryl filled her in as succinctly as possible. Peggy was shaken by the news.

"What can I do?" she said.

"Pray maybe."

The night dragged on. When she ran out of dusting and tidying to do, she used a Brillo pad on the bottoms of several old pots and pans. There was no way she could sleep. She decided to clean the exterior of the appliances. Using a sponge, she did the Frigidaire and was ready to move on to the stove when the phone rang again. It was going on midnight.

"Hello?"

Peggy showed up in the doorway, anxious to hear.

An operator asked if she would accept a collect call from Tina Rossi.

"Yes, yes! Tina?"

"Cheryl?"

"I'm here. Did you find him?"

"Yes, thank God. He's okay."

Cheryl was silent, unable to form words, a lump in her throat.

Peggy stepped closer, waiting. When Cheryl gave her a nod, Peggy closed her eyes.

"We're on our way home. Did the police come?"

"Yes," Cheryl croaked.

"Well, do me a favor. Tell the police I've got him and that we're headed home. Give them this address for the trailer. You got a pencil?"

Cheryl grabbed the pencil hanging from a string on the wall. "Ready."

Tina read her the address and told her she'd be home in about an hour. Cheryl had a million questions but they could wait. Tina had her little boy back. He was safe.

Seated at the table listening, Peggy looked to Cheryl for news.

"She says they'll be here in about an hour. That's all she said."

Then she called the police department. The officer said Tina should come in tomorrow if she wanted to file charges.

An hour and a half later, Cheryl and Peggy were sitting in the living room, after the TV stations had signed off for the night. They were half reading, half dozing when Tina let herself in. Ricky was sound asleep on her shoulder, his body limp in her arms. Cheryl dashed ahead of her to pull his covers down, wiping tears from her face with the backs of her hands.

Tina told her friends she was too exhausted to talk. She made a pallet on the floor in Ricky's room and bedded down beside him. She wasn't letting him out of her sight.

*

In the morning, Cheryl was first in the kitchen, determined to make a big breakfast. She did all the prep work. When she heard the others stirring, she turned on the oven and the stovetop and got busy. She made bacon and scrambled eggs, grits, biscuits and butter gravy. As she set the food on the table, Tina wandered in, holding Ricky in her arms, his legs dangling. She was in her robe and he was in his pajamas topped by a blue flannel robe.

Cheryl wiped her hands on her apron and approached the two of them, hugging her favorite little boy and kissing him on the cheek three times. He didn't resist.

She forced her eyes not to mist over, but it wasn't easy.

"I made biscuits and gravy," she said. "Or you can have biscuits with jelly. We've got apple jelly, grape jelly and strawberry jam."

Ricky nodded, clinging to his mother. He had gravy on one half of a biscuit and grape jelly on the other half, two pieces of bacon and a helping of scrambled eggs. When he'd eaten his fill, he didn't run into the living room to watch Saturday morning cartoons as he usually did.

"Mommy, want to watch Mighty Mouse with me?" he asked.

She said yes without hesitation, understanding how unsettled he was.

Peggy volunteered to wash dishes, allowing Cheryl and Tina to join Ricky in the living room. Lying on the floor, he relaxed once Mighty Mouse began saving the day. Cheryl and Tina sat on the couch together on the far side of the room.

"Are you going to file a complaint?" Cheryl asked, keeping her volume down.

"Yes, but I don't want to take him with me. And he doesn't know Peggy yet."

"He can stay with me."

"You've got calculus class this morning. And there's that protest at noon."

"I'll skip class. And you'll be home in plenty of time for the protest."

Tina gazed at her little boy. "Okay. I owe you one."

"No you don't."

That's when Tina told her what happened the night before, speaking quietly so Ricky couldn't hear her over the noisy cartoons.

"I was watching through the window doing dishes. Ricky was having a good time. Then Pinky came meowing into the kitchen. I opened a can of cat food and dished it into her bowl. It only took a minute. When I looked out the window to check on them, the yard was empty. Ricky said Wyatt told him they were playing a war game where they had to be quiet to sneak through enemy lines.

"Then he told Ricky they were going to the beach, that I had given my permission. When they'd been driving a long time he said he started crying. That good-for-nothing told him to shut up. When they arrived at that filthy trailer, Ramona said she wanted to go to a bar. Wyatt left Ricky alone in the trailer while he took his girlfriend out drinking. I broke a window, climbed inside and found him on the dirty couch where he had cried himself to sleep."

Cheryl wrapped her arm around her friend and gave her a squeeze.

Once Tina left for the police station, Cheryl and Ricky watched one last cartoon, then put on coats to go outside. Winter seemed to have suddenly arrived, rather than fall. She'd worn a sundress last week and was now bundling up. Cheryl raked leaves and Ricky played with his army men. When his tummy told him it was snack time, they sat together on the top step of the porch having cookies and milk that Peggy brought them. They talked about whatever he wanted to talk about – why Max had a white crest on his chest; how the earth turned around and around; how tall Cheryl thought he would be when he grew up; and why God created ants and mosquitoes.

He was all smiles when Tina returned.

"Mommy, guess what! Cheryl says God didn't create ants and mosquitoes. She says they..." and he paused to look at Cheryl for the word.

"...evolved," she said.

"...they ee-balled all by themselves. She says we ee-balled too, that we used to be monkeys and gorillas."

"*We* didn't used to be monkeys and gorillas," Cheryl said. "Our ancestors millions of years ago were like monkeys and gorillas."

"Yeah," he replied as if that's exactly what he had just said.

Max joined them, wagging his tail. Even the hoity toity Pinky strolled over to tell Ricky she loved him. Cheryl left mother, son, snooty cat and comical dog out back while she went inside. She suggested to Peggy that she join them. Peggy gladly did so, throwing her coat on. This gave Cheryl the privacy she needed to return Diane Coleman's call from the night before.

"What else did they say the other night?" Cheryl asked Diane.

"Mr. Carlisle told his brother that 'she didn't hear anything.' I didn't know who 'she' was at the time. Then Eddie says, 'I've been making sure she understands to keep her trap shut.' Then Mr. Carlisle says, 'If you touch one hair on Cheryl Donovan's head, I'll...' but Eddie didn't let him finish. That's when I knew they were talking about you. Then Eddie said, 'It's not a good idea to threaten Eddie Carlisle, even if your name is Carlisle.' It reminded me of Cain and Abel."

Cheryl had twisted the cord around and around her fingers until it was all knotted up. Why she'd shrugged off something this serious was baffling. Back in high school, she would've contacted police without delay. What had changed? Now she thought of herself as an adult capable of handling the challenges thrown in her path. But did that include threats to her life?

"You still there?" Diane said.

"Sorry. I was lost in thought."

"I would be too."

"Diane, with what you heard and what I heard, we could go together to…"

"I can't go to police. It would be my word against the word of two successful *white* businessmen. Even if we went together. Plus, Eddie Carlisle is a dangerous man. He scares me. I'm sorry."

15

"No nuclear war! We want peace! No nuclear war! We want peace!"

They heard the chant before they saw the protesters. When Cheryl pulled into the large parking lot behind the Sears building, people were milling about, practicing chants. Tina sat beside her. Ricky was in the back seat, bouncing up and down with excitement.

As they got out of her Beetle, Tina gave Ricky last-minute instructions.

"Remember what I said now. I'm going to hold your hand the whole time. Don't try to pull away."

"Do we march like soldiers, Mommy?"

"No, this is a different kind of march. We walk normally but we walk in a line."

"Oh."

Wearing black pants and a cable knit sweater, Cheryl adjusted her sunglasses. What a relief they had sunshine. With her hand-lettered sign that said "Peace" propped on her shoulder, she led them to where the protest leaders had gathered.

Stu Levy got everyone's attention to give them their marching orders.

"I visited the proper city office this week and found out we can demonstrate as long as we stay on public property – in this case the sidewalk – and we don't block traffic, either car traffic or foot traffic. And – this is important, listen up! – we can hold our protest as long as we don't incite violence or threaten anyone, as long as we don't get wild and cause a ruckus. Remember, if police tell us to leave, we leave. If you have any questions during the protest about what a police officer says or does, check with me. Don't say or do anything rude to him. Or to anyone else. We're marching for peace. We need to demonstrate what peace looks like. Remember, the other people on the sidewalk and in their cars are not the enemy. Neither are the police officers. We're all in the same ark. Lulu, Marlon and I will take the lead." He gestured at the woman by his side and the young Black man standing with them. "Don't forget, we're walking single file. Even if you came in a group, don't walk side by side. Maintain single file. You'll have plenty of time to talk afterwards.

"Some of the organizers will walk up and down the line from time to time to lead us in a different chant or give assistance," Stu continued. "All right, folks, let's march peacefully!"

A big cheer went up as a line formed behind him and his co-leaders. Then they slowly moved forward.

"Are we marching, Mommy?" Ricky asked.

"Yes we are."

"Like in a battle?"

"Not exactly. This is a march for peace. We don't want to go to war."

"We don't?"

"No, war hurts people. Peace is much better."

"What is peace?"

"That's when people and countries get along and don't fight."

"Oh."

They walked in front of Cheryl, Tina holding Ricky's hand.

"I wish Peggy could've gotten off work so she could be here," Tina said.

"Yeah, that would've been nice."

"What happened to Allan? I thought he was coming."

"I don't know." Cheryl was as surprised as Tina was. He'd seemed genuinely enthusiastic.

When they reached Hay Street, they turned left, heading toward the Market House. Some of the leaders made their way up and down the line, reminding folks to stay to the right and always allow pedestrians to pass between them. Then the organizer named Marlon led them in the chant they'd heard when they drove up.

"No nuclear war! We want peace! No nuclear war! We want peace!"

They chanted as they walked with purpose, some of them waving signs above their heads. There were lots of stares, some of them curious, others suspicious.

Ricky threw himself into chanting with the others. Meantime, Tina beamed at Cheryl, thrilled to be taking part. Cheryl gave her a thumbs up. It was invigorating to step up and be counted. People needed to speak out for peace, to convince leaders who had their fingers on the button not to touch that button.

Thankfully, Cheryl had brought her camera. She asked the older woman walking ahead of them if she could take a couple of pictures of her, Tina and Ricky as they marched. In exchange, Cheryl did the same for her and her sister.

As they approached the Market House, organizers walked down the line explaining that they were going to cross Hay Street in small groups so they didn't block traffic. That was accomplished without a hitch and they continued on the other side of the street back toward their starting point.

There were a few critics along the way. The burly guy coming out of the Kress store. "Bomb the Commies!" he shouted. A man standing in front of a shoe store had his say. "It's Kennedy's fault! Remember that in sixty-four!" But you could see it in the eyes of most people – they didn't want annihilation. They wanted life for themselves and their families.

When they arrived once more in the Sears parking lot, the demonstrators clumped together in groups, all abuzz with what they'd seen and how they felt. Stu whistled to get their attention.

"We're working on another protest for next week. If we don't already have your name and number, write it down on a piece of paper and give it to me or one of the other organizers. We'll let you know the when and the where. A reporter and photographer from the paper were here. So look for a story and a picture or two. Pass the word along to friends when we let you know about the next demonstration. Thanks to all of you for sending an important message!"

A cheer went up.

As they threaded their way through the parking lot to her car, Cheryl spotted Allan leaning against it, arms folded over his chest.

"Sorry I didn't make it. Something came up."

"We marched!" Ricky sang out.

Tina looked down adoringly, still holding his hand. "We marched for peace, didn't we?"

He nodded happily.

"My stomach is growling something fierce," Cheryl said. "Is anyone else's tummy growling?"

Ricky put his hand on his tummy and concentrated for a second. "I think mine is."

"Me too," Tina said.

"Me three," said Allan.

"Well, it's my treat – hamburgers, French fries and milk shakes!"

"Oh boy!"

Allan followed Cheryl's car to a nearby burger joint where they chowed down while telling him all about their first protest. Ricky performed his favorite chant. Some nearby diners were amused, others weren't.

"I know we're average people in an average North Carolina town," Tina said, "but every little bit helps. At least, I hope so. Kennedy and Khruschev need to remember they're not in a spitting contest. No one should be proving his manhood here."

"Wish I could've marched with you," Allan said.

"There's another protest next week," said Cheryl.

"You really dig it, don't you?"

"As Tina said, adding my voice could help turn the tide. If not, at least I wasn't a worthless store mannequin with no brain and no mouth."

Allan followed them home, saying he wanted to give Cheryl something. She hoped it wasn't anything romantic.

At the house, she asked him about the mystery gift first thing.

Tina grasped the situation immediately.

"Come on, Ricky! Let's go get your wagon out of the shed and play out back."

Together they walked along the side of the house and through the gate.

"Okay, what gives?" Cheryl said.

"It's in my truck."

Nervously, she watched as he lifted a sapling with a large root ball wrapped in burlap from the back of his pickup.

"I saw a brilliant yellow maple one day that made me think of you," he said, flushing. "So I went by the nursery and bought this sapling. I brought a shovel so I can plant it."

This was a special present from someone who viewed her as more than a friend. She wanted to ask him why now? Instead, she told him what a cool gift it was and thanked him.

"I know you won't live here for long," he said, "but I'm guessing your parents will. When you come to visit in the fall you can enjoy it. Where shall I plant it?"

She studied the lawn. There was an established oak on the left side of the yard.

"Here!" she said, pointing to a spot on the right side. If her parents objected, it could be moved without much trouble after they returned next summer.

With his work gloves on and his shovel in hand, he made quick work of setting the little tree in the ground. He spread a little pine straw around the base afterwards and watered it.

"I better go now," he said, putting the shovel back in the truck bed. "But before I do, I have a bit of news. You know I'm in the Air Force Reserve."

"Yeah." Her shoulders tensed.

"Well, I've been called up for active duty. I have to report tomorrow morning."

She was speechless. She knew he'd served in the Air Force and that he was in the Reserves, but she thought there would be no need for the Reserves. Turning away, she walked toward the house. Every man she cared about would be in the danger zone. Her father, her brother, Paul, and now Allan. Ready or not, tears were coming.

"Cheryl?" he said.

She stopped, tears spilling down her cheeks, but did not turn around. The sapling was a going-away present, something to remember him by. Only it was him leaving, not her.

"That's why I had to come over," he said, still standing by his truck. "To say goodbye."

She could say goodbye without looking him in the eye, then flee to her bedroom. But that would be cowardly and cruel. Or she could turn around and let him see how emotional she was. After Tina, he was her best friend.

Pulling her shirttail out of her pants, she used it to wipe her cheeks, eyes and nose. She tucked it back in, folding the sweater down to cover her waist. Only then did she face him.

"I don't like your news one bit." Her voice quivered, in spite of her best effort to keep it steady.

In an instant he closed the distance between them and wrapped his arms around her. It was an embrace overflowing with tender affection.

"I'll continue protesting for peace," she said, gently disentangling herself.

In one swift motion, he leaned down and kissed her on the lips.

"I had to do that in case this is the end," he said, then walked away.

She touched her mouth, trying to interpret the kiss and her reaction to it. Definitely not the kiss of a man who was just a friend.

Refusing to watch him drive away, she escaped to her room.

Allan's news punctured the ballooning hope she'd latched onto following the peace march.

After supper, she secluded herself in her room, downhearted. She lay on her bed, hoping to distract herself reading. She didn't realize she'd fallen asleep until tapping at her door startled her awake. Peggy peeked in.

"You have a long distance call."

Sitting up, she saw it was almost nine. Before picking up the receiver, she took a sip of water, then said hello.

"Cheryl, it's Paul. I was worried when you couldn't talk last night. Are things back to normal?"

"Yes, thank goodness. It's a long story. I'll tell you sometime when there's no long distance charge."

"What a relief. Did you get my letter?"

"I did."

"And?"

"You say you aren't a poet, but you are."

"You inspire me. I don't even have a picture of you in my wallet but your features are imprinted on my soul, especially your eyes. They're a golden brown. I could gaze at them all night."

"Paul…"

"I'm not through."

"That's so old-fashioned," she said, doing her best to keep the irritation out of her voice.

"You don't want me to say these things to you?"

She hesitated. "What if a woman gushed about how handsome you are – and you're definitely a handsome man. But what if she went on and on about your eyes, your eyelashes, your hair, your face, your physique, pouring out her affection for you by describing your appearance?"

"I'd be flattered."

"So you believe a relationship should be based on mutual flattery?"

She heard him swallow as he shuffled around in the phone booth.

"If it's a pretty face that draws you in," she continued, "then the next pretty face might cause you to abandon the last pretty face."

"It's not just your face I love."

The operator broke in at that point, directing Paul to deposit more coins.

She could hear five coins drop into the payphone with a loud clunk, one at a time. Then the operator said, "Go ahead."

"God, Cheryl, you mean the world to me! You're funny, you're smart, you fascinate me. You're the only woman I've ever met who I can imagine coming home to for the rest of my life! But, damn, it's a nice bonus that you're beautiful too.

It's not just the color of your eyes, though. It's what I see deep inside them. How's that?"

"How's that? I'm not fishing for compliments."

She could hear his grin.

"I almost snuck out of my tent last night while the others were asleep. I figured I could hitchhike to Fayetteville in twenty-four hours. I was desperate to hold you close. I got dressed and stood by my cot for a long time, agonizing about whether it was worth being court-martialed."

"God, I can't believe you considered it!"

She heard a distant squeal through the phone line. "My ride is ready to go. Write me a letter and put this address on it." He read off his service number and APO number and told her how to format the address. "I'll get it eventually."

She heard a man in the distance.

"I've gotta go," he said. "Oops!"

There was a loud thud and the line went dead.

16

Sunday morning Cheryl drove downtown, parking her car on Old Street. Walking the short distance to Point News, she was anxious to buy some newspapers with coverage of the crisis. The shop wasn't open, but they had more newspaper vending boxes out front than anywhere in town. She dropped a quarter and a nickel in and pulled out the *New York Times*. The top headline was worrying.

"US Gets Soviet Offer to End Cuba Bases, Rejects Bid to Link it to Those in Turkey." She skimmed the article right away. It said Khruschev made the offer, then withdrew it. President Kennedy sent the Soviet premier a letter asking him to stand by the proposal to remove Soviet missiles. Then there was this headline: "U-2 Lost on Patrol, Other Craft Fired On." She had a sinking feeling. This was exactly the kind of incident that could provoke the launch of a warhead.

Back in her car, she stared up at the sky. What would a big flash be like in person? She'd seen footage of those nuclear tests in the 1950s that made the flash look so bright you couldn't keep your eyes open. She never wanted to experience that.

At home she plopped down in the wing chair to peruse the papers. There it was: a report on the American U-2 reconnaissance plane lost over Cuban air space. Such distressing news. There were reports about Air Force Reservists like Allan being called up, more than fourteen thousand of them.

What was her father doing this morning? Where was he? Was he preparing for a jump onto Cuban soil? Would he be with an invasion force? Not fair. He'd fought in World War II and the Korean War. Now he was on the front line again, if you could call it that. He'd done his duty. He'd put himself in harm's way. He had the scars to prove it.

What about Mike? Her brother's ship, the *USS Newport News*, was the flagship of the Atlantic Fleet – truly in harm's way. The fleet was enforcing the blockade, challenging any Soviet ship bound for Cuba.

Being a pilot, she didn't know exactly what Paul would be doing. Besides flying helicopters, he also flew planes. What role would he play if a conflict occurred? It was possible he could fly rescue missions to transport wounded soldiers. It was also possible he would transport soldiers *to* the action.

And now there was Allan. He was an Air Force reservist. It's not something he talked about, so she had no way of knowing what he would do if his unit was involved.

She worried about all four of them, along with all the military personnel preparing for the worst while hoping for the best. Ironically, she worried even more for all the civilians at home who could lose their lives, including Tina and Ricky and her own family. All the children in their classrooms on any school day, the families all across the country and around the world. The death toll from this war – if it came – would make the death tolls from past wars pale in comparison. She had read that a nuclear conflagration would kill hundreds of millions, first by the blasts, then radiation and eventually from starvation.

Fixing herself a glass of iced tea, she strolled out back. There was Ricky playing in the yard, Max bounding in circles around him. Tina sat on the porch in a baggy blue sweater, Peggy on her right in a jacket, Pinky on her left basking in the sun.

"About time you came out of that Cuban cave," Tina said.

Pinky meowed in agreement, rubbing against Cheryl's leg. She leaned down to stroke the cat's arched back.

"Perfect day for a backyard picnic," she said.

By one o'clock the picnic table was ready. Covered with a red and white checked tablecloth, four large paper plates had been arranged, loaded with sandwiches, potato chips, pickle spears and apple slices. In the center was a package of waffle cream cookies for dessert.

Ricky was first to sit down, excited about eating outside on a sunny autumn day. Tina put Max on a leash and hooked it to the clothesline so he could get some exercise without driving them crazy.

"He has no table manners," Tina said, winking at Ricky.

Their relaxing lunch began with him announcing what he'd been playing in the yard.

"Me and my army men, we marched around the big tree for peace."

Which made the women smile.

Any semblance of a peaceful afternoon evaporated, however, when they heard the gate rattle. Tina's mother strolled into the yard dressed in tan tweed, followed by her husband in his brown suit.

"Grandma and Grandpa are here!" she sang out, eyeing her grandson. "We've come to find out if you're safe and sound."

A grimace replaced the smile on Tina's face.

Ricky kept his eyes on his food, refusing to look at anyone.

"I'll take him to the bathroom," Cheryl said.

He didn't resist, leaving his sandwich on the plate with two bites missing.

Tina thanked her with a glance then addressed her parents.

"Mom, Dad, we're in the middle of a nice little picnic, hoping for a restful Sunday afternoon. No offense, but you have a tendency to say unkind things and ruin our day when you show up uninvited."

"All I ever say is the truth! And we're never invited! Our own daughter says we're not welcome at her home, Frank."

"That's because you always want to stir up trouble," Tina said.

Cheryl ushered Ricky through the back door, suggesting he play in his bedroom. She remained by the open kitchen door, listening.

"It's my obligation," Mrs. Rossi said, "to see that our grandson is brought up correctly. I'm concerned he's not getting proper guidance. He needs good Christian role models like your father and I."

"Please leave. I don't want to get into a loud argument with you today."

"We came to see that you're taking care of your son properly. Yesterday afternoon your father stopped by the police department to shoot the breeze with some of his former co-workers. He took a look-see at the police blotter and, lo and behold, he saw a complaint filed by Tina Rossi accusing her ex-husband of abducting her son Friday night and taking him all the way to the beach! Lord! A good mother would not allow that to happen. A good mother would keep her child safe from harm at all times!"

Tina glanced at Peggy, seated with her back to the Rossis, sending her a message with her eyes.

"Your father and I feel strongly that our grandson may be living in an unsafe environment. I looked up the number for the office where you report abusive or neglectful parents. I'm beginning to think you're not fit to be his guardian. We could definitely provide him a safe, wholesome home where abduction would never be a possibility."

Tina hurried toward the house, Peggy behind her. Cheryl stepped aside as they entered the kitchen. Then she shut and locked the door. Tina closed the curtains above the sink. Then she hurried to the front door, locked it and pulled the cord on the drapes.

She checked on Ricky before returning to the kitchen. Sitting down at the table, she listened as her parents made their way along the driveway to the street where their car was parked. When she heard them drive away, she spoke quietly so the boy with big ears wouldn't hear.

"How do you divorce your parents?"

Peggy took the chair beside her. "Your parents are bullies."

"You don't truly believe she'd try to take him away from you?" Cheryl asked.

"Oh yes I do. In fact, I've known it was coming."

"You're a terrific mother. Everybody knows that."

"Your parents know it too," Peggy said, wrapping her arm around her friend from the side, giving her a little hug.

"They're not taking my son."

"I don't remember your mother being so mean when you and I first became friends," Cheryl said. "She seemed mostly normal back then. When did she change?"

"There was some ugliness when I was in ninth grade. That's when my brother moved out, telling Mom and Dad he didn't want to see them for the rest of his life. He was in eleventh grade. He's been true to his word, which means I have no idea where he is." She paused to compose herself. "Once Nick was gone, Mom only had one child to torment – me. It got worse year by year. She eased off when I went to the prom with Wyatt. But after I graduated, she wanted me to hurry up and get married. She went on and on about it."

Cheryl felt a twinge of guilt, thinking about all the times she'd pushed her friend to go on a blind date.

"So when you married him…" Cheryl said.

"She treated me nice for the first time in years."

"When did it turn sour?"

"When I told her I was filing for divorce. She ranted and raved about a woman letting her marriage fail. She said I'd always be labeled a divorcee, which is a dirty word in her book. She nagged me about Ricky needing a father in the home. She hasn't let up."

"It amazes me you held your tongue this long," Peggy said.

The phone rang at that point. Cheryl grabbed it, on high alert for bad news. An operator announced another person-to-person call for Cheryl Donovan.

"Cheryl? Are you there?"

It was her mother, the connection worse than usual.

"Mom! Is everything good?"

There was a delay, followed by garbled words.

… shot down an American spy plane, for heaven's sake! I expect a bomb to land in our back yard any moment now!"

"Mom, calm down. There's no sign that…"

Tina and Peggy cleared out so Cheryl could have some privacy.

"Don't tell me to calm down!" Mrs. Donovan said. "Arthur and Mike are in the thick of things. They'll be the first ones turned to dust! Even if me and Vicky and Wayne survive, we won't have your father or your big brother with us anymore. And you're not exactly in the best location yourself, being so close to Fort Bragg!"

She sobbed so loudly that Cheryl had to wait a moment for her to lose steam.

"Mom, I think we're likely to get some good news pretty soon."

"You're just saying that and we both know it! The end of the world is upon us!"

"I hope you don't say that to Vicky and Wayne."

"It's my job to prepare them for the worst."

"Oh, Mom. I think it's your job to reassure them. To hold them when they're frightened. That's what we do with Ricky."

"He's a first grader! Vicky and Wayne are in high school. They're practically grown. Vicky's decided not to apply for college. She doesn't think she'll live long enough to go. And she and her boyfriend, Brad, want to get married right away."

"Good God! She needs hope, Mom! Making important decisions like that when she thinks the world is coming to an end could ruin her life! Did you try to talk some sense into her? They're both way too young."

Her mom was quiet.

"I don't mean to sound harsh, Mom. We're all worried. But we need to hold on to hope."

"It's hard for me to do that when your father is gone."

"You did it during World War Two."

"I had to."

"And during the Korean War, you always told us not to give up hope."

"Mm."

"We'll make it through this. And before you know it, you and Dad and Vicky and Wayne will all be here in Fayetteville again and Dad will be getting out of the Army!"

Her mother sighed. "I guess I'll ask the kids to remind me to hold onto hope."

"And you'll talk with Vicky?"

"I'll talk with Vicky."

"Tell her I love her. And tell Wayne. Oh, and Mom, I love you too."

After she hung up, Tina told her she was taking Ricky to the Prayer Service for Peace at Rowan Street Park. She'd seen a sign as they were marching along Hay Street the day before. Peggy and Cheryl thought it was a great idea.

They donned their coats and piled into Tina's car. She found a parking spot a couple of blocks from the park, which straddled a little stream with a wooden foot bridge over it. There was a kidney-shaped wading pool, swings and jungle gyms, and a concrete whale painted blue with a smiling face. There was also a meadow shaped like a natural amphitheater where people could spread blankets to sit on the grass for concerts. That's where the prayer service was being held.

A church, it wasn't. But the several hundred folks in attendance had something important bringing them together to form an unusual congregation – a desire for peace. There were white people and Black people. There were families with young children and there were grey-haired retirees. There were those wearing their best church attire and those dressed in jeans and turtlenecks. No one cared about their differences. Not today.

Sitting in folding lawn chairs at the front was a Catholic priest, a Protestant pastor and a Jewish rabbi, all of them wearing coats on this chilly day. Each of the clergymen spoke of peace and love, leading the congregants in prayer. They prayed for leaders to listen to God and remember that peace is what all people needed around the world. Then two men and two women sang a lovely song about peace in four part harmony.

Afterwards, Cheryl spotted Mr. Swaney, the principal at Sandhills High School where she was anxious to be hired. She didn't want to seem pushy so she chatted with her friends as she folded her blanket, hoping he'd look her way. He did.

The look on his face said she looked familiar but he couldn't place her. So she swung into action.

"Mr. Swaney!" She gave him a friendly wave. "I'm Cheryl Donovan, an applicant for the secretary job."

"Miss Donovan. Of course." He turned to the woman by his side and they walked in Cheryl's direction.

"Good to see you," he said as they strolled by.

"Same here."

Once he was gone, she joined her friends to make the trek back to Tina's Fairlane.

"You didn't honestly expect him to stop and chat, did you?" Tina said.

"I just wanted him to see me at this event. It means we have something in common."

"I'll bet the last thing he wants to be reminded of on a Sunday afternoon is his job. And you represent work."

"Insulting me, are you?"

"Every chance I get."

Peggy was amused by their banter.

"I don't understand why you haven't gone after other positions," Tina said. "You've put all your eggs in the Sandhills High School basket. Applying for as many job openings as possible would increase the odds of getting hired somewhere."

"He wants to hire me. I can feel it."

"You know what you'd tell me if I was doing what you're doing? 'Cover your bases, Tina!'"

"No, I'd be telling you to cover your ass!"

Peggy giggled but Tina pointed at Ricky walking between them. "No wordy durds," she said.

"What's a wordy durd, Mommy?" he said, not missing a beat.

"It's a rude word."

The three women chortled.

Once they were in the car headed home, Tina turned the radio on. "Let's find something fun to listen to."

She twisted the knob to find a station, scrolling past a newscast in her search for music.

"Wait!" Cheryl pleaded. "Go back."

"We want music, Cheryl. Not more droning on and on about you know what."

"Go back!"

Tina reluctantly turned the knob back to the left until she found the news.

"...that President Kennedy has accepted Soviet Premier Khruschev's decision. Khruschev released an open letter broadcast on Soviet radio stations stating that construction of missile bases in Cuba is being halted, and existing missiles are being dismantled and transported back to the Soviet Union."

"It's over!" Peggy clapped her hands.

"Shh," Cheryl said.

"In his telegram to the Soviet Premier, President Kennedy said, quote, 'I think that you and I, with our heavy responsibilities for the maintenance of peace, were aware that developments were approaching a point where events could have become unmanageable. So I welcome this message and consider it an important contribution to peace.' Kennedy said the Cuban blockade would end, promising that the United States would not invade the island nation."

"You're right, Peggy," Cheryl said. "Sounds like it's over."

"Thank God," Tina said, her voice cracking.

As tears began to fall, she pulled onto the shoulder of the road and rummaged through her purse for a tissue.

"What's the matter, Mommy?" Ricky said.

Tina blew her nose.

"She's happy," Cheryl explained.

"She's crying," Ricky said.

"They're tears of joy," Tina said, leaning over to where her little boy sat in the front passenger seat to kiss him on the cheek.

"But you're crying."

"Sometimes we cry because we're happy. And right now I'm very happy there's not going to be a war."

"Well, that's cuz it worked!" he said.

"What worked, sweetie?"

"We marched and then we prayed. And it worked!"

"That's right. We did our part."

The first thing Tina did when they got home was pull out a half gallon of ice cream and dish it into bowls. Ricky clapped his hands.

They sat down together to celebrate peace with chocolate ice cream and a glass of wine for the ladies, apple juice for the very underage first grader. After Ricky inhaled his snack, he ran outside to play with Max.

"I hope the agreement doesn't fall apart," Tina said. "You think the president has things under control, but a front-line soldier on either side could still do something stupid."

"Oh, ye of little faith," Cheryl said.

Peggy patted Tina's arm. "Cheryl's right. Have faith."

They watched the news after supper. The broadcast reported that Americans greeted the news with caution, especially in light of an incident in which an American U-2 spy plane flew over Soviet airspace in the far east. President Kennedy apologized, saying it was caused by a navigational error. But it made them wonder if retaliation could happen without American or Soviet leaders' knowledge. The danger wasn't over. They wondered if the danger would ever be over.

Still, everyone was calmer than they'd been since the president's address. Tina said Ricky drifted off to sleep almost as soon as she opened the book to read him a bedtime story. Cheryl dozed off during *Candid Camera*, waking up as Tina and Peggy turned off the TV to go to bed.

She yawned, then turned off the lamps, ready to hit the sack herself. But as she turned toward the hallway, the phone rang. Dashing to catch it, she cut it too close through the kitchen door, banging her shoulder on the door facing. She stifled a groan, taking a deep breath as she lifted the receiver.

"Hello."

Another operator. Another collect call from Lieutenant McIntyre.

"Cheryl, darling, isn't it wonderful?"

She opened her mouth to reply but didn't get a chance.

"No word yet on when we go home, but it better be sooner rather than later. I really need to hold your intelligent body close and kiss your wise-cracking lips."

She chuckled at that.

"I've gotta see you as soon as I get home. Day or night. So you'll have to forgive me if I come knocking at your door at three in the morning."

"Call first. I keep a baseball bat under my bed."

"Yes, ma'am!"

"Goodnight, Paul."

"I love your voice. Your intellectual voice. I'll dream of you as usual tonight and all of the interesting things we'll do together once I get home."

His sly tone didn't escape her notice. But she didn't fall for the ploy, hanging up before he could say anything else.

Leaning against the refrigerator, she rubbed her left shoulder. She couldn't deny she was anxious to see him. Recalling how his kiss stirred her that night at the lake, she touched her lips and imagined their reunion.

Flipping off the kitchen light, she padded in her sock feet down the hallway. As she passed the doorway to the living room, a huge crash brought the evening to an explosive end. It was so sudden and so loud, she instinctively threw herself to the floor, covering her head, waiting for the blast to turn her to cinders.

But there was no fiery wind. There was no wind at all. Cheryl raised her head, peering into the darkened living room.

Tina opened her door, her bedroom lamp casting a column of light into the hallway. "What happened?" Peggy stood shoulder to shoulder with her, both of them in plaid pajamas.

Cheryl retrieved a flashlight. Pointing it into the living room, she was staggered by the sight. The large pane of glass in the picture window had been smashed into a thousand pieces. Lying in the middle of the room was a four-way tire iron.

She was shellshocked.

17

Cheryl had hoped for a good night's sleep after Sunday's glorious news about the missiles being withdrawn from Cuba. But she was bleary-eyed Monday morning. After the window bashing and a discouraging visit by a police officer who said there wasn't much they could do, she'd had bad dreams about being chased. She remembered the last one. She was riding a merry-go-round. Bullies were running along its edge, pushing it faster and faster. She woke up in a fright as she lost her grip and was thrown off, landing on the ground so hard, her back was broken. The bullies' laughter still rang in her ears as she opened her eyes.

She dressed in jeans and an old sweater over a flannel shirt. Cleanup of the living room would be a bear of a job. But the window had to be replaced immediately. There was no time to waste.

They had closed the drapes over the broken picture window after the officer left last night, then taped a shower curtain over it and hung a blanket over that. They were trying to keep the cold out with the temperature dipping down to freezing overnight.

They had also closed the doors to the living room and dining room, placing blankets along the bottom to try to keep the cold from the back of the house.

As the others went about their usual routine, she put on winter boots and her old car coat, tying the drawstring of the hood to keep her head warm. She pulled on work gloves before entering the living room. It felt like a deep freeze in there.

After removing the makeshift window coverings and opening the drapes, morning sunshine streamed through the window revealing the true extent of the damage. Tiny points of light sparkled all over the couch. On closer inspection she discovered shards of glass protruding from the cushions, reflecting the sun's rays. It was the same with her dad's chair. The oval rug was dotted with bits of glass too.

It looked like a war zone, as if she was under attack. In truth, she *was* under attack. What next? Being run off the road at night? Being kidnapped? What if Eddie's enforcer hurt Tina or Ricky? She had to do something.

Right now, though, there were phone calls to make and the dangerous mess in the living room to clean up.

First, she called the office to let them know she'd be late. Then she found her parents' home insurance policy. She had a bowl of cereal in her bedroom, studying the policy while the others ate breakfast in the kitchen.

When nine o'clock rolled around, she called to request a claims adjuster. She was told to take pictures, then proceed with cleanup. An adjuster would arrive after three. The second call was to arrange for a new pane of glass to be installed, which would be done that afternoon as well.

With a roll of film already in her camera, she snapped photos of the damage, getting shots with bits of glass reflecting the light. Then she and Peggy got busy, work gloves protecting their hands.

"It's a good thing you weren't sleeping on the couch last night," Cheryl said as they picked up large pieces of glass, depositing them in a metal trash can that reeked of garbage.

"That's the first thing that popped into my head."

The next step was sweeping. Because that much glass would kill the vacuum cleaner, they swept until their backs ached, depositing dustpans filled with small pieces of glass into the trash can.

Peggy helped haul the rug outside. They laid it flat on a big tarp in the yard so they could set the damaged furniture on it, hoping to avoid spreading shards of glass. They managed to carry everything but the couch.

*

Nobody seemed to notice when she walked into the lobby at eleven forty-five. Mr. Carlisle's white Lincoln was in the parking lot so he must be in his office. She thought back to two weeks ago when her biggest concern was dodging his wandering hands. His hands didn't wander anymore. The challenge now was the unnerving intimidation by his drug lord brother. She wished she could stand up to him. All she needed was a platoon of armed soldiers to back her up.

She hung up her coat and grabbed her steno pad and pencil, heading for the boss's office. Finding his door open, she knocked on the door frame before entering.

He looked up from paperwork, tapping his fountain pen on the desk as he studied her.

"Are you positive you don't want to give sales a try?" he said.

"A hundred percent."

"I wish you'd reconsider."

"Is there anything you need me to do this morning?"

"I'll let you know."

She walked quickly to the door, but came to an abrupt stop as she nearly ran into his wife.

"Why don't you stay, Miss Donovan? I could use a witness."

Mrs. Carlisle refused to step aside, forcing Cheryl back into the office, tugging her along as she walked toward the desk.

"I talked with my lawyer," she said. "I'm filing for divorce. You'll be served with papers this week."

Mr. C. jumped to his feet. "Why, Margie, why?"

"I've made it crystal clear how I feel, Harry."

"Margie, I love you. Before you do something rash, we've got to talk."

"No more talking. You don't listen anyway."

"I'm listening now."

"I said what I came to say. I've got to get back to the hospital. I can't leave Dean alone more than a few minutes."

"I'm coming over to sit with him at lunchtime."

"Good. I need to run some errands while you're there."

She let go of Cheryl's arm and marched out. Cheryl trailed after her. She had to give it to Mrs. Carlisle. She wasn't going to put up with her husband's involvement in Eddie's business.

But there was a loud crash behind her. Turning, she saw Mr. Carlisle standing at his desk which was now bare. His intercom, inbox, reference books, calendar, ash tray and a full mug of coffee now littered the floor, a brown stain already showing on the rug.

As much as she didn't want to clean it up, she went to the break room to get cleaning supplies and returned to tackle the mess. She took the opportunity to tell him she needed to leave early to be there for the claims adjuster and the glass man.

"But you took the morning off."

"So I could clean up the mess. I also had to make calls to set up this afternoon's appointments."

"You said a tire iron was thrown through the window."

"As we were going to bed. They must've been watching and saw when we turned out the lights."

He didn't look overly surprised.

*

The insurance adjuster examined the jagged pieces of glass protruding from the window frame, the furniture and the rug. He also studied the tire iron, commenting that he hadn't heard of a tire iron being thrown through the window of a house. A car, yes, but not a house. He said he'd turn in his report right away. His reimbursement recommendation was disappointing. It would be enough to buy a new couch and pay for the window pane. But drapes, a new rug and a replacement for her dad's beloved chair would have to come out of her paycheck.

The truck from Bishop Glass arrived a few minutes later. The two men knew what they were doing. A new pane of glass was installed in the picture window in under an hour. Cheryl wrote a check, cringing when she subtracted the amount from her already strained balance. God, she hoped the insurance payout didn't take long. A part of her imagined presenting a bill to Eddie Carlisle.

Leaving the front door open, she listened for neighbors coming home from work, hoping for help hauling the sofa out. She hit the jackpot when Mr. Jowers across the street arrived. He was on the lower end of middle age, with enough strength and experience to walk the sofa through the front door using work gloves she provided. Then he guided it down the porch steps before she helped him carry it to the rug. She thanked him profusely and promised a banana nut bread and a plate of peanut butter cookies.

She spent the rest of the afternoon cleaning the coffee table and lamp tables and moving them into the dining room. After she re-swept the floor, she vacuumed thoroughly, putting a new bag and filter in. Then she cleaned the walls.

When Tina and Ricky arrived, Cheryl was so stiff she could hardly move. But the front room was clean and usable. Sort of. At least they could watch TV if they brought chairs to sit on.

Tina made spaghetti for supper, using extra sauce from two weeks ago that she'd frozen. She was smart that way. Afterwards, she did dishes even though it was Cheryl's turn.

Ricky decided it was a good night to play with the tape recorder.

"I think Cheryl is tired, sweetie. And she wants to watch the news."

"I'm not too tired for the tape recorder," Cheryl said, looking at her watch. "We've got time."

"Oh boy!"

"Besides, the living room isn't exactly a comfortable place to relax."

"But we still want to watch the news," Tina said, "even if we're sitting in a straight-back chair. So you have fifteen minutes."

They set up on the play table in his room. He happily babbled into the microphone saying whatever popped into his head.

"Good golly, Miss Molly! Good golly, Miss Jolly! Good gooly, Miss Dooley! Good dooly, Miss Fooly!" And on and on. When he heard his mother walking down the hallway, he sang out to her, "How much time do I have now, Mommy?"

She stopped at the door, checking her watch. "You have about... eight minutes."

"Eight minutes?"

"Yes, eight minutes."

As his mom continued on her way, he asked Cheryl to rewind the tape so he could listen. She rewound, then pressed 'play.'

He grinned, listening to himself say silly things. When the tape reached the interchange with his mother, he grew still.

"Mommy! Come here!"

"What do you need, honey?"

"You have to come. I want to show you!"

He asked Cheryl to back up the tape.

When Tina appeared in the doorway, Cheryl hit the play button. Tina cringed in mock agony listening to herself.

"I didn't know you were secretly recording me! That's not how I sound! That's a southern belle!"

"I tricked you, Mommy!"

"Yes you did, you little rascal!" She rushed in, giving him a hug and a little tickle.

The fun-loving relationship between them made Cheryl smile to herself.

As she watched them, Tina's words ran through her mind again – *I didn't know you were secretly recording me.* Of course! She'd had the means all along to get evidence against Eddie Carlisle – her tape recorder! Amazing that the credit for her epiphany went to a six-year-old boy. If he could secretly record his mother, then she could secretly record the Carlisle brothers. It was time to put a stop to the threats. She was tired of being under siege.

As Tina stood up, Cheryl leaned over to kiss her best little buddy on the forehead. "Thank you for the ammo," she whispered, then zipped out of the room, leaving him with a confused look on his face. She dashed to the kitchen, found Diane's number and dialed. Diane had told her Eddie demanded a meeting with Mr. Carlisle tonight. But what time? It rang and rang. No answer. Now what?

Shifting into high gear, she slipped her shoes on and packed up the recorder as Ricky climbed on his rocking horse for a wild gallop.

"You going somewhere?" Tina said from the living room. "I thought you wanted to watch the news."

"Going over to Diane's house," she lied. "I forgot about it."

"Diane?"

"Diane from work. We've become friends." She pulled a jacket on as she reached for the keys in her handbag.

"I don't remember hearing about Diane."

"I'll fill you in tomorrow. Don't wait up for me!"

Although it was dark, she exceeded the speed limit all the way to the office, rolling through stop signs and charging through stoplights as they blinked from yellow to red. Time was of the essence. Still, she didn't turn into the Carlisle Realty parking lot when she reached it. She had to reconnoiter, scoping out the parking lot as she drove by. No cars. She turned around at a church and headed back toward her destination. She passed the building a second time, then made a U-turn. This time, she pulled off the highway into the driveway of a small auto repair shop next door to the realty office. She parked in back, out of sight.

There was a stand of trees between the repair shop and the realty office. She was about to dash to the wooded area when it occurred to her that she didn't have to go through with this. But it's not like she was going to confront anyone. She was just going to hide so she could record them talking. She was determined to get the ammunition she needed to put Eddie behind bars. Making her way into the patch of woods, she checked to see if cars were parked in the rear. No cars. Darting through the shadows to the back door, she turned off the burglar alarm, unlocked the door, stepped inside and reset the alarm.

She hurried to Mr. Carlisle's office. There was only one place to hide and covertly record them – the small closet where Mr. C. hung his coat, stored an extra suit, a pair of shoes, a few office supplies and half a dozen bottles of whiskey. The space was smaller than she remembered. There was no way to conceal herself if one of them opened the door. If that happened, she was a goner.

Did she want to gamble her life doing this? Vic, Eddie's burly bodyguard, probably had more tire irons in the trunk of his Buick. She winced thinking about it. What she needed was an injection of guts. Taking a deep breath, she steeled herself and eased inside.

Sitting down cross-legged on the floor, she placed the recorder in front of her. With no electrical outlet available, she inserted eight batteries, then threaded the reel of tape, securing it to the take-up reel. She plugged the small microphone in and set it by the louvers along the bottom of the door. Lucky for her, the louvers admitted a little light as well as providing ventilation. She tested the machine, saying, "one, two, three," then listened back. It was good to go.

Now all she had to do was wait. Wait and try to keep her nerves from frazzling. She'd always known she couldn't walk into police headquarters and make wild accusations against Eddie Carlisle. And *wild accusations* is exactly what police would label them if Cheryl had no proof. But now that she was ready to carry out what she thought was a brilliant plan forty-five minutes ago, she was terrified.

Still, she closed the door, carefully positioning herself so she wouldn't touch anything. She hoped the brothers would arrive soon. But the evening dragged on. Eight-thirty came and went. Nine o'clock went by. Then ten o'clock. Cheryl's body hurt from being cramped in one position after doing all that sweeping of glass. She scrambled out so she could take a few laps around the office to get the blood flowing and relieve her aching body. As she returned to the closet and pulled the door closed, she heard a car engine, then the sound of the back door being opened. At which point, she pushed the 'record' button on the tape recorder. She held her breath as someone entered the office.

He walked to the desk and sat down. There was the sound of him opening a drawer and removing something, then setting it on the desk. When she heard the clink of glass, she knew it was a bottle of bourbon from his bottom drawer and a tumbler. She listened as he poured and took a swallow. Next he lit a cigarette. Then nothing, except the random squeak, squeak of the chair as he swiveled one way, then the other. Definitely Mr. Carlisle.

She should turn the tape recorder off and wait till Eddie got there. She studied it on the floor in front of her, realizing she couldn't push the 'stop' button. If she did, he would hear the noisy click. She hadn't foreseen this problem.

Mr. Carlisle dialed the phone.

"Where are you?"

A pause.

"You said ten-thirty. I've got better things to do than sit and wait."

Another pause.

"Get over here now or I'm going home."

He slammed the receiver down.

It was another half hour before Eddie showed up. Of course he had to settle in, wait for Mr. C. to pour him a drink, light a cigarette. Her armpits were wet with sweat.

Glancing at the recorder, she noticed she'd already used half the reel of tape. Her pulse raced. She had to calm down. It should be enough. All she had to do was be still and stay quiet.

Mr. Carlisle got the ball rolling. "I'm officially giving you my notice – one month. I'll continue to process your cash through the end of November. Starting in December, you need to be ready to wash your money elsewhere."

Slats of light passing through the louvers allowed her to see what she was doing. She checked the VU meter, noticing the volume was a little low so she increased the gain. It didn't have to be great audio, but the level had to be high enough that police could understand the words and who was saying what.

"It's not as simple as that, Harry."

"It *is* as simple as that. I'm not going to be your partner in crime anymore. My son might not make it. If he does, well, we have no assurance he'll ever be normal again. I spoke with my estate attorney about providing for his care if I die. That's become a major concern of mine since I've gotten involved with your money laundering scheme. Knowing it was heroin that did this to him, there's no way I can continue."

"You don't walk away from my business."

"I won't go to the cops. But I have to wash my hands of it. Not only because of Dean. Margie contacted a lawyer about getting a divorce. I can't let her do that."

"Why not? You'd be free to…"

"I don't want to be free to tomcat around. In the last couple of weeks I realized how important my family is. It dawned on me when I was faced with losing everything. I love Margie. She loves me. I need to remind her of that. But if I don't remove myself from your drug operation, she'll never forgive me. And I won't be able to forgive myself."

Eddie responded with a disdainful snort. "Turning down easy money? You're a fool, Harry."

"Another thing," Mr. Carlisle said. "In case you've forgotten, you can make good money without selling drugs. You can use your business savvy for something honest. If you keep on doing what you're doing, someone's bound to tip off the police. It won't be me. It'll be one of your own dealers or someone cooperating with the DA. Or you could get yourself killed. A kingpin doesn't last forever. He's like the king lion, always being challenged by young upstarts who want to take over."

There was a loud thud that made Cheryl jump, almost knocking the microphone over. She held her breath, slowly moving her left toe so it wasn't anywhere near the mike.

"I'm not interested in all your bullshit, Harry! We have an agreement! You help me launder the money, I give you a percentage to make up for your pitiful sales. You don't back out of a deal with Eddie Carlisle."

"I have to. You can buy some laundromats. Then you won't have to split the proceeds with anybody. Least of all your older brother."

"I need a refill. Make it a double." Eddie came off as a rich oil tycoon accustomed to ordering servants around. "I knocked my drink over."

"That's what you get for pounding the table like a spoiled brat."

"You're walking on thin ice, Harry."

There was a clinking sound, followed by the opening and closing of a drawer.

"I'll have to get another bottle," Mr. Carlisle said, his chair squeaking as he stood up.

There were quiet footsteps on the Persian rug.

Cheryl froze, her fingernails digging into her palms. Her boss was about to open the closet door. There was nowhere to hide. Her only options were to sit still and hope he changed his mind or make a run for it. But Eddie would be on top of her before she could get the back door open. She held her breath, petrified.

The handle jiggled. The door opened.

Cheryl's hand flew to her mouth.

Mr. Carlisle leaned forward to reach for a bottle of bourbon on a shelf behind her. He stopped like he'd discovered a bomb.

18

Mr. Carlisle froze. The look of alarm in his eyes changed to one of terror. He said nothing, taking in the microphone and tape recorder with the reel of tape going round and round.

His eyes locked on Cheryl's eyes for a long moment. She waited for the inevitable.

"Don't tell me you don't have another bottle!" Eddie barked.

Mr. Carlisle hesitated.

Cheryl forced herself not to scream.

"Deciding which one I want!" Mr. C.'s voice wobbled slightly as he answered his brother.

That's when he signaled with his hand for her to lean to her right so he could reach the liquor. She did so, careful not to touch the mike or the recorder. He grabbed a bottle of Jack Daniel's. Straightening up, he gave her a hand gesture that she translated as 'stay put if you value your life.'

She did value her life. Although now there was a distinct possibility she might not live much longer. She felt like a thirteen-year old girl who still believed in Santa and the tooth fairy, even though she should know better. Why did she think she'd be immune from danger hiding in the closet?

Mr. Carlisle's reaction was so unexpected. She assumed he would alert Eddie. If he'd done that, Eddie would've rushed over, pulled his gun and pointed it at her. Then he would've tied her up, gagged her and tossed her in the trunk of his car for a trip to the concrete plant.

But it didn't happen that way. Mr. C. protected her from his nefarious brother. Diane said Mr. Carlisle told Eddie to leave Cheryl alone. Now she knew he did, in fact, want to shield her. In that moment when he realized what she was up to, he decided not to let his brother know. That way, she would live to see another day. All he had to do once Eddie left was to confiscate the reel of tape and tell her to vamoose. She'd be alive but he would destroy the evidence.

As the men resumed arguing, Cheryl tried to calm her nerves so she could pay attention. But it was hard to stop shaking.

Although they weren't discussing specifics of the drug operation, she listened closely. Even if Mr. C. confiscated the tape, she would remember what they said. Mostly. Which could come in handy to pass along to police at some point. After she moved to a fishing village in Newfoundland where nobody could track her down.

"I've already found four laundromats that are bustling day and night," Mr. Carlisle said. "Taking large amounts of cash to the bank isn't suspicious if it's a cash-based business. Perfect for money laundering, same as your restaurants."

"I can't let you do this, Harry. It would set a bad precedent."

"How many people know about you buying houses? Besides Vic, that is."

There was silence.

"Is Vic trustworthy?" Mr. C. asked.

"Is John Wayne a movie star?"

"Tell Vic I was sloppy. Whatever you want. Tell him you told me to get lost."

"Can't do that."

"I'm not asking your permission. I'm through with the drug business as of November thirtieth. That's final."

"Pour me another double."

There was the clink of bottle on glass. Then another, followed by Eddie taking a gulp and exhaling sharply as the liquor burned his throat.

"I'm not gonna sit here all night, Harry. I'm telling you how it is. You're part of my operation and will continue to be part of my operation. I'm gonna keep on buying and selling houses to clean up my dough. And you're gonna help me. 'No' is not acceptable."

Cheryl shook her head in frustration. They kept repeating the same thing. Mr. Carlisle wasn't going to give in. Neither was Eddie. They had reached a stalemate. She wondered how long they would keep repeating themselves. They were engaged in a verbal battle. It was thrust and parry, evade, intercept, and deflect. No one was willing to raise the white flag.

Glancing at the recorder, she saw there was fifteen or twenty minutes left on the tape. It dawned on her that when it reached the end, she would either have to push the stop button or it would continue turning until the tape ran out, leaving the reel to whirl around and around with the dangling tape making a racket as it flapped and flapped until it stopped. That wouldn't do. Despite Mr. Carlisle's effort to protect her, the noise would give her away. She imagined Eddie hearing it and pulling his gun as he approached the closet.

Time slipped away. She lost track of the back and forth between them, beads of sweat forming on her upper lip. The remaining tape on the supply reel was running out much faster than she expected. If she were using electric power, she could ease the plug out of the socket so the two reels would gradually slow to a halt without making a sound. But there was no way she could extract the batteries. That would mean turning the recorder over and removing the cover, making even more noise. The only way to shut it off was to push the 'stop' button. When they heard the click, her goose would not only be cooked, it would be carved and served on a silver platter.

She watched the tape unspool. She had to do something! But what? Then the last length of tape unwound from the reel. At the very instant it started to flap, flap, flap, she used her mouth in desperation, lifting the corner of her upper lip, to make her polite toot noise that caused Ricky to laugh so hard. As she did so, she set her left hand down on the supply reel, forcing it to stop. Fearing she wasn't making enough camouflage noise to disguise what came next, she increased the volume on the polite toot so that it wasn't quite as polite. With her right hand, she snatched the uptake reel from the recorder so the flapping was over before it got going. She held her breath, as still as a stop sign.

"Jesus, Eddie. You haven't changed a bit," Mr. Carlisle deadpanned.

"You're the one who's always been the gas bag."

"Wasn't me."

"Mm-hm."

Her hands were shaking so badly, she was on the verge of dropping both reels. Very slowly she pulled her hands toward her until the reels were pinned against her chest. There was a whooshing sound in her ears.

One of the men yawned loudly.

"I've gotta go," Mr. Carlisle said. "I'm heading to the hospital to sit with Dean till Margie comes in the morning."

"We're not finished."

"I'm finished."

"Don't tempt me, Harry."

The boss's chair squeaked as he got to his feet. There was shuffling and the sound of a drawer opening and closing. He must be putting the bottle of bourbon away.

"We aren't done," Eddie complained.

Keys jangled and there were footsteps coming closer.

"Have to lock the closet." He turned the key, which actually locked it, then turned it a second time to unlock it.

She watched a small piece of folded paper drop through the louvers, landing on the floor near the mike. Then there were retreating footsteps.

"Now wait a minute, Harry! I said we're not finished!"

"I have to go. Walk out with me."

"Goddammit!"

There was more shuffling and keys jangling, another set of receding footsteps accompanied by low grumbling. The light was switched off before the door closed, which meant there was no light coming in through the louvers. She sat quietly in pitch blackness. The deadbolt lock turned. Their words became more and more distant as they walked to the back entrance. The outer door slammed shut, followed by silence.

She waited. In the distance she heard a car engine. Then another. Still she waited, listening to her own breathing, aware of her heart beating rapidly. Her mouth was dry. She slowly returned the reels of tape to the spindles on the recorder by feel. Then she carefully put the mike into its small compartment, also by feel. She paused to listen before gently setting the cover in place and securing the clamps, all in complete darkness.

Before moving, she searched the carpet with her fingers for the piece of paper Mr. C. dropped.

Cautiously she got to her feet, the blood draining from her head from sitting so long. She held on to the door frame, waiting for the dizziness to ease. When it passed, she tucked the folded piece of paper in her pocket, easing the door open an inch. No voices. No footsteps. No car engines. She pushed it all the way.

Accustomed to the dark, the bit of ambient light from the window was enough for her to see. She lifted the recorder. Then she closed the closet door, stole across the room, going behind Mr. Carlisle's desk. Reaching the door to the lobby, she used the same careful technique, listening each step of the way, locking the door behind her. She turned the burglar alarm off and exited the building, resetting the alarm before dashing through the wooded area to the car repair shop.

When she made it to her car, she fumbled the keys unlocking the door. As soon as she was inside, she locked the door and started the car. Rushing, she took her foot off the clutch too quickly and the engine died. Her limbs weren't functioning properly. She scanned her surroundings as she turned the key again, sliding the gear shift into first and racing out of the parking lot. She was scared witless that Eddie would appear behind her any second. It was a miracle she wasn't stopped for reckless driving on her way home.

Of course, everyone was asleep when she let herself in the back door, recorder in hand. She was weak in the knees. Her first priority was reading what was written on that piece of paper. She tip-toed to her bedroom and sat on the edge of the bed to open it.

"Take tape to police chief only. E. has friends on force."

Mr. Carlisle took a big risk writing the note. If he hadn't, she would've handed the tape over to whoever was on the desk when she walked into police headquarters. Then all her efforts to get proof would've been for naught and she, herself, would've been in greater danger.

She didn't like this clandestine stuff at all. Tonight marked her debut *and* retirement from a brief and clumsy career as a private eye.

*

She called in sick Tuesday, which she rarely did. She had something else to do.

But first, Tina pressed her for an explanation about where she went last night. It was tough pulling the wool over her eyes. Once Ricky sat down at the table, Tina asked Peggy to keep him company while she trimmed Cheryl's hair a little. The two of them went into the bathroom for the phony haircut and closed the door.

"Well?" Tina said.

"Remember last night when Ricky recorded you without letting you in on it?"

Tina nodded.

"That's when it hit me that I could get evidence against Eddie. All I had to do was secretly record him."

She related the whole story, which caused Tina's eyes to grow wider and wider. When she got to the part where Mr. Carlisle opened the closet door and discovered her, Tina squeezed her eyes shut. When the story was over, Tina shook her head.

"God, Cheryl. You could've gotten yourself killed."

"But I didn't. This morning I'm delivering the tape to the police chief."

Which prompted a confession from Tina.

"I thought you were exaggerating the danger. I didn't understand how serious it was. That you managed to survive last night to tell the tale is nothing short of a miracle."

When Cheryl walked into police headquarters in her blue suit and black heels, she had the look of a woman to be taken seriously. Reporting directly to the police chief's office, she presented herself to a middle-aged secretary whose nameplate said Mrs. Vera Hoke.

"Do you have an appointment?" she asked, studying a sheet in front of her that was probably the chief's schedule.

"No. But it's a matter of urgency. I have evidence I need to deliver to him personally."

"I can direct you to the appropriate…"

"I have to deliver it to the chief."

"He's a busy man, Miss…"

"Cheryl Donovan. I understand. But this is extremely important."

"Miss Donovan, Chief Girard prefers you make an appointment."

"If it wasn't so urgent, I'd do just that. I only need five minutes. Please."

The older woman looked at her watch, then consulted the paper in front of her once more.

"Have a seat." She pointed to a waiting area with several upholstered chairs.

While Mrs. Hoke slipped into the chief's office, Cheryl remained on her feet. She was too jumpy to sit. Mrs. Hoke returned saying the chief would see her, but to be brief.

Chief Girard looked up from his desk when she entered. He appeared to be in his fifties with short greying hair, glasses and a physical presence that said he knew how to handle himself. He didn't invite her to sit down.

"What can I do for you, Miss Donovan?"

Cheryl pulled the reel of tape from her pocketbook, concentrating on keeping her hand from shaking.

"I recently became aware that my boss's brother, Eddie Carlisle, is running a drug operation in Fayetteville."

His bored expression wasn't encouraging, but she plowed ahead anyway.

"He's been laundering some of his drug money buying houses through my boss's realty company, Carlisle Realty. But my boss, Harold Carlisle, told Eddie he's through laundering his money. I didn't have proof about any of this until last night. I hid in the closet in my boss's office and recorded the two of them. This is the recording."

"Why did you insist on handing it to me?"

"My boss tipped me off that Eddie Carlisle has friends on the police force. He said I shouldn't take it to anybody else."

"I see."

What if Mr. Carlisle had set her up? Maybe the chief himself was one of Eddie's friends on the force. She couldn't make heads or tails of his reaction. Would he dismiss her accusation and not bother listening to the tape? She pondered whether she should've taken it to the district attorney instead. She held it tightly, debating whether or not to hand it over.

Using his intercom, he asked Mrs. Hoke to have Lieutenant Malone report to his office.

"But what if this Lieutenant Malone is one of Eddie Carlisle's friends?" she said.

"No need to worry. I trust Lieutenant Malone with my life."

The lieutenant was a large man whose blue shirt strained across a muscular chest. He looked able to tackle and cuff two violent criminals at once without any assistance. But he had a friendly face and gave her a warm nod.

"Miss Donovan, this is Lieutenant Harvey Malone. Would you please tell him what you told me?"

She took a deep breath, hoping she was doing the right thing, then repeated her short spiel. When she finished, the two men exchanged a look.

"So you think it's possible Harold Carlisle may be willing to talk with us about his brother's operation?" Malone said.

"I don't know. He said he won't go to police, but he wants to break free of Eddie's drug business. His son is in a coma after a heroin overdose. My boss thinks he probably bought the drug from one of Eddie's dealers."

There was another meaningful look between the two.

"Miss Donovan," the chief said, "I need for you to sit with Lieutenant Malone and listen to the tape. He may have some questions about who's who. We need you to make a statement telling us how you learned about the drug operation and Eddie Carlisle's involvement."

She nodded.

"Harve, I want you to handle this personally. Miss Donovan says her boss warned her to bring the tape directly to me because Eddie Carlisle has friends on the force." He raised his eyebrows as if they both knew who those *friends* were. "Only Gail should take notes. Tell her this is top secret."

"Check."

The lieutenant led Cheryl to his office. A stenographer joined them. He loaded the tape onto a big reel-to-reel machine and they sat down to listen. The stenographer took notes. When they finished, Malone asked a lot of questions as the stenographer continued writing everything down in shorthand. When she left to type up her notes, the lieutenant had deli sandwiches brought in.

"Will you arrest Eddie Carlisle?" Cheryl asked.

"Gotta take care of some preliminaries first." He took a big bite of a ham sandwich.

"If he knows about me coming to you with this tape, my life is in danger. As well as the lives of my roommates, including my friend's little boy."

"He won't find out," he said, his mouth full.

"And if you question Harold Carlisle, his brother could kill him."

The lieutenant continued chewing.

"In fact," she continued, "he might kill my boss anyway if he quits the drug operation."

He wiped his mouth with a napkin. "We'll see what he says about it. Harold Carlisle said on the tape that he wouldn't go to police. He hasn't done that. *You* came to us. It's possible he's willing to let us come to *him* rather than the other way around."

"There's one other thing. I said it in my statement. Vic Acosta is a dangerous man. I've heard the term *enforcer* on TV. I think that's what he is. Which means I may need protection."

"We'll be picking him up too."

Once her statement was typed, she signed it and was free to go. Now it was in police hands. All she had to do was lay low until they had those guys in custody.

The house was empty when she got home. She changed into pants and a sweater and fixed herself a cup of tea. She put her coat on and took her tea to sit on the back porch so Pinky and Max could keep her company. Pinky sat next to her in the chilly sunshine watching Max gambol around the yard. Cheryl stroked her fur, more for her own benefit than the cat's enjoyment.

Her muscles had been tight for days as she dreaded news that the pessimists were right and nuclear war was underway. Word of an agreement had been so comforting. But stress over Eddie Carlisle had intensified. Hiding in the closet had drained her. She hoped all of that was coming to an end.

Max barked, rushing to the gate.

Cheryl went through the house to take a look out front. A knock at the door made her jump. Deciding to take a peek first, she stopped when she reached the door between the kitchen and dining room. From there, she could see out the picture window. There in the driveway behind her Volkswagen was a big red Caddy.

19

What the hell? Eddie Carlisle shouldn't be knocking on her door. He should be behind bars! The whole mess was supposed to be over and done with. Just like those nuclear warheads.

Had she fallen into a trap delivering the tape to the police chief? Was he Eddie's friend on the force? Did he call him up right away to alert him that she ratted him out? Had Eddie listened to the tape?

Instinctively, she moved toward the wall phone to call police. "Moron!" she muttered to herself. Just her luck, the officer who answered would be one of Eddie's friends too!

With her car blocked by the Caddy, there was no way she could sneak out to the VW and make a break for it. The only option was to escape through the back door, jump the fence and keep on running. But that would mean leaving Tina and Ricky vulnerable when they got home. Dang it!

Should she open the door? If Vic was with him, she was a dead duck. Who was she kidding? Even if Vic wasn't with him, she was a dead duck if Eddie wanted her to be a dead duck.

Hurrying to the utensil drawer, she grabbed the butcher knife. It was the only weapon she had. Of course, actually using it was beyond her imagination. But she needed something in her hand. Hiding it behind her, she marched to the door, unlocked the deadbolt and swung it open.

Eddie was alone. He smiled like he was a door-to-door salesman.

"I want to make you an offer, Miss Donovan. May I come in?"

He sounded as though he had a special deal on a set of Childcraft Encyclopedia.

He looked through the screen door as she struggled with how to answer. He seemed surprised by the nearly empty living room.

"We used to have furniture until *somebody* threw a tire iron through the picture window the other night."

Oh, the irony! He actually seemed to be concerned.

"The tire iron damaged the furniture?"

"It shattered the big window pane and pieces of glass stuck in the couch, the chair, the carpet and the drapes. They're out there on the lawn waiting to be hauled to the dump."

He glanced to where she pointed, then pulled his wallet from his back pocket and withdrew several one hundred dollar bills.

"Here," he said, holding them up to the screen. "This should help."

An interesting dilemma. He definitely owed her for the damage, the inconvenience and the stress. She could use the money. But if she accepted it, there would be repercussions. She'd made a lengthy statement to police about Eddie's drug business and about terrorizing her. If she took his money now, it would be construed as being on his payroll.

"I can't accept your money."

"Take it!"

He reached for the screen door handle. She held it shut from inside.

"Why are you here?" she said.

He slid the money in his pocket. "I need a savvy accountant. And you've proven you have guts. I appreciate a woman who has guts *and* good looks. I'll pay you four times what Harry pays you. The salary goes up from there."

With great effort, she managed not to roll her eyes. Did he honestly believe she might say yes? She wanted to ask if the tire iron through the window was his way of buttering her up. Funny that he was offering her a job after criticizing his brother for doing the same thing with the sales position.

"Not interested."

His genial façade vanished, a smokescreen swept away by a gust of wind.

"You shouldn't look a gift horse in the mouth, Miss Donovan."

"You're not a gift horse."

"Trust me, Miss Donovan. If you don't accept my gift, you'll discover that Eddie Carlisle is not a man you want to antagonize."

The friendly salesman eyes were gone, replaced by the dark beady eyes of a peregrine falcon closing in on a starling. Certain he was about to sink his talons into her, she prepared herself to slam the door, slide the deadbolt into place and make a break for it through the back door.

Eddie's hand moved first, reaching for the door handle.

She grabbed the heavy door and was about to slam it, but hesitated when she heard the familiar sound of a truck slowing on the street. It was Allan's pickup. Thank God!

"Pardon me!" she cried, chucking the big knife on the floor behind her. She forced the screen door open with her body, shoving Eddie out of the way, taking him by surprise.

Before he recovered, she bolted past him, down the steps and across the lawn, fearing he would grab her from behind.

"Good timing, old friend!" She called out, loud enough for both Allan and Eddie to hear. "I've got a roomful of ruined furniture that needs hauling to the dump."

She glanced over her shoulder to see Eddie staring after her from the porch.

Under the circumstances, it didn't occur to her that Allan would misconstrue her eagerness as romantic interest. Not until she noticed the fervor in his eyes.

"I arrived home about an hour ago," he said, a confused expression on his face.

"You just saved my life," she said, gesturing with her chin at Eddie.

"What happened? Who is he?"

"That's my boss's gangster brother."

"The one you thought was laundering drug money?"

"None other."

"Why's he here?"

"It's a long story." She really wanted to give him a big hug, she was so happy to see him. It was all she could do to keep her distance, knowing it would be misinterpreted. "I know you just got here but I really could use your help with this stuff." She pointed at the pile of furniture on the lawn. "And I need to get away from Eddie."

"Did he threaten you?" He watched intently as Eddie cranked his car and backed out of the driveway.

"How about I fill you in as we drive?"

Undoubtedly, he had expected something very different from this strange greeting. He'd probably fantasized about a passionate kiss, her arms around his neck. Poor Allan.

"I'll pull my truck into the yard," he said.

She ran inside to get work gloves, locking the house as she left. He backed his truck across the yard to the furniture.

She told him about the glass as she handed him a pair of gloves.

"And you think Eddie Carlisle was behind the attack?" he asked.

"He was behind several attacks."

"Why didn't you tell me?"

"I didn't want you to get hurt trying to protect me."

A look of annoyed disbelief was his reply.

They loaded the couch, chair, rug and drapes into the bed of his pickup, then got going.

"Okay, come clean," he said.

First, she commanded him not to tell a soul.

"This is a lot more serious than I thought when I first mentioned it to you," she said. "If you tell even a little of this to a friend who tells a little to one of *his* friends, it could end up reaching a police officer who's buddy-buddy with Eddie. If that happens, well, I won't need a job anymore. I'll be pushing up mushrooms in a remote wooded area."

"Maybe you shouldn't tell me. Sometimes I talk in my sleep."

It was good to have Allan back.

As they drove, she told her story. He hung on her every word. Especially when she got to the part about hiding in the closet to record the Carlisle brothers.

"I can't believe you did that. Didn't you understand how risky it was?"

"I thought I did. To be honest, when Mr. Carlisle opened the door and saw me on the floor with the tape recorder, the reality hit me – that I could get myself killed."

"I don't know whether to praise you for your bravery or whip your butt for putting yourself in such extreme danger."

"Better be the first option because nobody's going to whip my butt. Least of all, you!"

He let loose with his big Allan laugh, which made her feel safe and loved. Funny how that worked.

She went on with her tale of derring-do, telling him how terrified she was walking into the police chief's office, then listening to the tape with the lieutenant.

"I was about to hyperventilate. I wasn't sure I was dealing with the right people, you know? I thought to myself, what if Mr. C. tricked me? Then again, if he was on Eddie's side, things would've played out differently when he saw me in the closet. He would've told Eddie I was in there. Eddie would've pulled his gun on me while Mr. Carlisle tied my hands behind my back. And I would never have walked into police headquarters."

"I can't believe those words just came out of your mouth."

"I was shaking the whole time. Afterwards, I came home feeling a wave of relief. But then what happens? Eddie Carlisle shows up!"

"What did he want?"

"You won't believe this but he offered me a job as his accountant. He said he'd pay me four times what I'm making right now."

"It goes without saying that you turned him down."

"Are you kidding? I said to him, 'when's my first day? I could use the money.'"

His head jerked toward her. But he saw it in her eyes that she was pulling his leg.

It only took a few minutes to unload the furniture at the dump. Allan told her about his experience reporting for Reserve duty as they retraced their route home.

"I was nervous as hell even though I knew I'd be doing grunt work while the regulars took care of the dangerous stuff. But it made me tense being so close to Cuba. I kept wishing Kennedy and Khrushchev would come to their senses. Nobody wins a nuclear war."

"Remember that Gregory Peck movie, *On the Beach*? Even while fallout was killing everybody, they still didn't know who fired the first missile."

"Thankfully, things have turned out better in real life. At least for now."

"I guess your mom is glad you're home."

"She doesn't know yet."

"Allan! She's probably worried sick."

But he came to visit Cheryl first. His objective was plain. She pushed that thought away, wondering instead when Paul would return. She didn't know why she was so drawn to him. She was like a butterfly that couldn't resist a daylily. Which troubled her.

Allan was good-looking too. Smart. Funny. Kind. And it was as clear as the pristine new pane of glass in the picture window that he was in love with her. But she'd come to rely on his friendship.

"I have to admit, I'm awfully glad you came to my house first," she said. "I shudder to think where I might be right now if you hadn't interrupted Eddie's recruiting trip to my front door."

"Jesus, Cheryl, you need to hang out with a better class of people."

She socked him in the arm.

When they reached the house, Tina and Ricky were getting out of her car.

"Welcome home!" Tina cried.

Allan climbed out of the pickup. "Thanks! It's great to be *here* rather than *there*, if you know what I mean."

"I agree. I see you got rid of that awful junk pile for us. We owe you! Stay for supper."

Cheryl wished she hadn't done that. But Tina was being her usual friendly self.

Allan glanced at Cheryl.

"I'm not fixing anything fancy tonight," Tina said. "Hot dogs with chili and some other stuff. But I did make a dessert."

"Banana pudding!" Ricky rocked his head back and forth imitating a bobblehead dog in the back of an old Chevy.

Feeling cornered, Cheryl chimed in.

"We'd love for you to join us."

Allan agreed.

"Oh boy," Ricky said, taking Allan by the hand, leading him around the side of the house so they could play kickball in the back yard. Max joined in, chasing the ball.

Sitting down for supper, Cheryl sat next to Ricky, allowing Allan to sit across from them in the chair that was normally hers. Ricky immediately filled their guest in on a new dish they were having.

"Mommy learned how to make cold slop!" He pointed at the big bowl of coleslaw in the center of the table.

Allan chuckled as Cheryl and Tina tried to hide their amusement. "I like *cold slop*," Allan quipped, spooning a big serving onto his plate.

Noticing Ricky was watching Allan, Tina offered him a bite. He took a tiny taste, saying it "tasted good, kind of like smushed-up, crunchy pickles."

Conversation was light with Ricky adding his own comments whenever the notion struck. After serving dessert, Tina asked Allan about his experience. He told them about being nervous and then relieved when the trip to Florida was canceled.

"Are you a soldier?" Ricky asked.

"I'm in the Air Force. So I'm an airman, not a soldier."

"Air man?"

"The Air Force flies a lot of airplanes and helicopters."

Cheryl was nervous about the direction the conversation was taking.

"We have a friend who flies helicopters," Tina said. "But he's in the Army."

"Paul let me get inside his helicopter." Ricky's eyes gleamed at the memory.

"That was awfully nice of him, wasn't it?" Tina said.

Ricky nodded, spooning more pudding into his mouth.

"A US Army helicopter?" Allan asked.

Ricky nodded.

Allan glanced at Cheryl, apparently assuming Ricky was mixed up.

She was about to change the subject but didn't act fast enough.

"Paul is Cheryl's boyfriend," Ricky blurted, his mouth so full, a blob of banana pudding tumbled out, landing with a splat on the floor.

Tina closed her eyes in frustration as their fun supper hit the skids.

Cheryl had no idea what to say that wouldn't make things worse, so she said nothing.

Allan pushed his chair back, getting to his feet. "Great meal, Tina. I need to drive over and see my mom now. Thanks for the invite."

"It's the least I can do for a man who helped scare Nikita Khruschev into backing down."

She followed him as he made his way to the front door. Cheryl trailed behind, downcast. They stood on the porch as he took the steps two at a time.

"Thanks for hauling that stuff to the dump!" Cheryl cried, feeling like she had not only poured salt in Allan's wound, she had ripped the would open and dumped a whole box of salt in it.

He gave a quick wave without turning around, then drove away.

"He would've found out anyway," Cheryl said, knowing Tina wished Ricky had kept his mouth focused on chewing rather than announcing that Paul was her boyfriend.

"Still, I'm sorry. Allan's a good guy. But I guess he doesn't stand a chance against Paul McIntyre."

"Paul McIntyre may not stand a chance either," Cheryl said.

Tina's face showed surprise but before she could ask a question, Cheryl skedaddled inside to wash dishes.

Allan's look of rejection haunted her. He'd been willing to put his heart on the line where it was trampled like a set of dog tags left on the battlefield. He had to realize it would be a stinking rotten relationship if she didn't love him. Of course, this would likely accomplish what she hadn't been able to – make it plain she preferred him as a dear friend, not her beloved.

*

While Tina read Ricky a bedtime story, Cheryl worked on making the living room usable. It was better to stay busy rather than brood about whether she'd broken Allan's heart. Or, perhaps a more pressing issue, whether Eddie Carlisle was likely to return.

First she cleaned up the porch rocking chair. Then she put an old blanket under it and dragged it into the living room. Next, she carried the wooden rocking chair from Tina's bedroom into the living room, added a dining room chair, then Ricky's child-sized rocking chair. All four of them would have a place to sit while watching TV. The finishing touch – two lamp tables between the chairs. If she were lucky, she could replace some of the furniture soon. Until then, at least nobody would have to sit on the floor.

When it was her turn, she made her way into Ricky's room to kiss him goodnight. The ritual was the highlight of her day. Ricky hugged her neck as she gave him a smackaroo on the cheek.

"Goodnight, Cheryl."

"Goodnight, sweetie. Love you a bushel and a peck!"

"Well, I love you a wagon of rain!"

She grinned as she backed away, blowing a kiss from the door. He tried to do the same, but looked as if he was throwing a rock at her.

She was ensconced in the porch rocking chair when Tina strolled into the living room a short time later.

"I was hoping you and I could talk before Peggy gets home."

"Sure." Cheryl jumped up, crossing to the TV to turn it off. "I need to tell you something too. But you go first."

Tina took a moment to get seated in the smaller rocker, adding a throw pillow behind her back, turning her chair in her friend's direction. She was stalling.

"Can't wait till we get some real furniture in here," Cheryl said in apology.

"I have some news," Tina said, then raised her glass of iced tea for a sip. "God, I didn't know this would be so hard."

"What is it?"

"Well, you'll have to look for a new roommate." She hesitated, but as Cheryl opened her mouth to speak, Tina raised her hand. "I'm moving out. Moving away."

Cheryl felt like she'd been sucker punched.

"Me and Ricky are moving to Oregon. Peggy is coming with us."

Cheryl's mouth opened but she had no words. She was knocked sideways.

Tina was too nervous to be joking. But it was unthinkable that she would really pull up stakes and leave. Granted, she'd always wanted to put some distance between herself and her parents. And no one could blame her. It was also understandable that she wanted to get away from Wyatt, who was so much worse than merely a bad father. He was careless and negligent and drunk half the time. But what about their friendship? She and Tina were close. Very close.

"If it's about the vandalism and the threats," Cheryl said, "I'm sorry about not going to the police sooner."

"That has nothing to do with it. This is about reinventing my life in a place where I'll be accepted. Where Ricky will be safe. Peggy wants that too."

"But..."

"I know, you're thinking, 'she can't leave me, she's my best friend.' But If I stayed, one day *you* would leave *me*. You'll find a man to marry. It's inevitable. You may have already found him! We won't always share our lives as we have in the past."

Cheryl looked lost. "Why now?"

"Ever since the president said we were on the verge of nuclear war, I've dreaded the moment a warhead would be launched. Living with that kind of fear did something to my brain. And my heart. For a long time now, I've been waiting for things to get better, thinking there's plenty of time. But believing there was plenty of time made me lower my standards for all kinds of things. Like happiness – my happiness as well as Ricky's. That's one good lesson that came out of this past week and a half. I was terrified Ricky wouldn't live to grow up, that I wouldn't live to grow old, that our whole civilization would go the way of the dinosaur. When we heard that Kennedy and Khruschev had come to an agreement, it lifted a terrible weight. I realized how short our lives are. You don't even know if you'll arrive home safely from work every evening. Time isn't guaranteed. Life could be over in an instant. One trigger-happy soldier and the whole world could be a burnt roast beef circling the sun. So I'm not going to wait any longer for my life to get better. I've got to break free and find joy each and every day. To do that, I'm moving to Oregon."

"Can't you reinvent your life here?"

Tina sighed, looking at Cheryl like a mother trying to calm a clingy child. She closed her eyes for a moment. "There's something else I need to tell you so you'll understand. I've been keeping a secret from you for years." She dropped her hands into her lap. "At first I was afraid you'd turn away from me. Later, I thought it would complicate our friendship. But the time has come to tell you."

"Tell me what?"

"Remember when we first met in ninth grade English class?"

"How could I forget?"

"You were the new student. Everybody already had their friends and gave you the cold shoulder."

"You came over and introduced yourself," Cheryl said. "You sat with me at lunch. You showed me how to work a combination lock so I could get into my locker. You basically saved my life."

"What you don't know is that you saved my life too."

That surprised Cheryl.

"You see," Tina went on, "I was an oddball. A queer bird. Literally." She let that sink in before continuing. "My classmates didn't hate me exactly but they didn't want to be friends either. They sensed I was different."

"What do you mean? You were as witty back then as you are now!"

"Only you saw me that way. You didn't have any preconceived notions. Being with you was truly the warmth and beauty of springtime after a decade of winter. I felt it immediately. When we met that day, it was love at first sight."

20

Cheryl needed to sit down. Except she was already sitting. She stared at Tina, toying with the idea of asking her if she was joking. But it was all too obvious she was sincere.

Her eyes became unfocused as she mentally searched for clues that she'd missed all these years. But Tina looked the same as she always had – like Tina. Tall and striking, with piercing, intelligent eyes, smart aleck crinkles at the corners of her mouth, ready to transform her face in an instant.

"Are you saying..." she began.

"...that I'm a lesbian? Yes," Tina said.

If Tina was telling the truth – and she always told the truth – she'd hidden her feelings for twelve years, the entire time they'd known each other. Which meant Cheryl hadn't taken the time to really get to know the person she was closest to in the world. She'd been oblivious to Tina's pain and frustration.

"I must be blind," Cheryl said. "I always believed you liked me as your friend."

"Oh, I did! From the moment we met, you were my best friend. My only true friend. But you see, in ninth grade, I was still trying to figure out my feelings. I was unsure about a lot of things, including my sexuality. I just knew you were the one I loved. But it quickly became obvious you didn't return my feelings. You were definitely a girl who went for boys. While I wished it were otherwise, I still loved you as my best friend."

"I didn't mean to be so stupid."

"You weren't stupid. You are who you are. I am who I am. I wouldn't have missed our friendship for the sun and the moon and all the stars in the Milky Way. You gave me affection when no one else did. Eventually, I found other girls who were like me. I had to keep it secret, though. Even from you."

"You couldn't trust me."

"I almost told you – jeez, I can't remember how many times. But I didn't want to lose you as my best compadre."

Cheryl's shock turned to remorse. She always thought of herself as a sensitive person. But there was no defense for being so self-centered that she failed to notice her most wonderful friend and companion was suffering.

When her eyes began to sting, she looked down so Tina wouldn't see. Too late.

"Don't do that," Tina said, grabbing Cheryl's shoulders.

"I'm so sorry I let you down." When two tears escaped, Cheryl wiped them with the back of her hand. "I was too wrapped up in myself."

"No you weren't. You've always been a caring person. I was too timid to tell you the truth. We were ignorant teenagers. Thank God, we were ignorant teenagers *together*!

They hugged each other.

"Who else would've danced "Rock This Joint Tonight" with me at the prom when our dates chickened out!" Tina said.

Their girlish giggles eased Cheryl's guilt. Now it made more sense why Peggy moved in with them.

"So Peggy...?"

"We've been together for two years. We have to be cautious. I've been uneasy about my parents finding out and using it to get custody of my precious child. After the Cuba thing began, Peggy called our former math teacher Miss Darnell. You remember her?"

Cheryl nodded.

"Miss Darnell is a lesbian. Peggy became friends with her after graduation. When Miss Darnell moved to Oregon, Peggy exchanged letters with her. Last week they talked and she's helping us move out there where she lives."

"But there's one thing that doesn't add up. Why on earth did you marry a guy who cleans his ears with his car key?"

"I know it's hard for someone who's always had loving parents to imagine the family I grew up with. Life at home was hell. By the time I reached my junior year, Mom was after me about why I wasn't dating. Embarrassed is what she was, especially at church with the other ladies. She always said I wasn't feminine. She'd get furious if I refused to wear a dress with a full skirt like other girls did.

"During senior year, I couldn't take it anymore. So I flirted with several guys. Wyatt was the first one who asked me out and I said yes. I had to get Mom off my back. She was wearing me out. It worked. She told all her Sunday school ladies I was dating a boy named Wyatt Armstrong who played center on the football team. I figured we'd date senior year, Mom would leave me alone, then he and I would go our separate ways."

"Except you married him."

"That was not supposed to be part of the plan. After graduation he surprised me with an engagement ring. I made the mistake of telling you on the phone one night that I was going to return it and tell him I couldn't marry him. My mother overheard every word. She had a flair for eavesdropping."

"Yeah, I remember that conversation. That's why I was so surprised when you went through with it."

"When I hung up, Mom went on a tirade worse than all the other times she'd jumped down my throat. She turned red in the face, she was in such a rage. She yelled 'what are you – a homosexual?' She said the meanest things she could think of. She didn't know she hit the bullseye. I figured if I didn't do something, she'd find out. I wanted to escape so bad, I agreed to marry him, even though he was a numskull. I figured I'd get some kind of training so I could earn a living. And as soon as I did, I'd file for divorce. But..."

"But then you got pregnant."

"I thought I was being careful. Not careful enough as it turned out. All I can say is thank goodness. If I'd succeeded in being careful, I wouldn't have my darling little boy. I believe he was a gift from God. My soul needed the love and joy Ricky brought into my life." She was teary eyed. "You've always been there for me, Cheryl. You loved him from the moment you held him in your arms. He loves you too. Even more than he loves tuna roll-ups!"

Cheryl chuckled softly as Tina smiled.

"Boy, is he gonna miss you," Tina continued. "You're family to him. And to me."

It had been a struggle for Tina. Now Cheryl knew it had been much more challenging than she ever dreamed.

"I'm sorry I was blind for so long," Cheryl said.

"You always saw me as a person you cared about. For that, I will be eternally grateful."

"I've been such a pest, trying to fix you up with men."

"You meant well."

"Jeez, you would forgive a cockroach in the kitchen because he's just doing his job cleaning up after you."

Tina snorted.

"I want to know and I don't want to know," Cheryl said. "When are you leaving?"

"We got word today that an apartment is available. Miss Darnell gave them the deposit money we sent her, then called Peggy with the news. We leave this Friday."

"This Friday?"

Friday was much too soon. Their departure would create a huge hole in Cheryl's life.

"Ricky doesn't know yet," Tina cautioned. "I didn't want to put pressure on him to keep a secret. I don't want to tip my hand to Mom and Dad. I'm waiting till the last minute to tell Wyatt. As for Ricky, I'll tell him Thursday morning."

They were quiet for a moment, Cheryl trying to accept the new reality and Tina giving her time to do so. It was going to be a colossal adjustment.

Cheryl forced back tears, certain that it would be a sign she was still thinking of herself, not Tina. She had to be strong for them.

"It's not the end of the world you know," Tina said.

"I was just mulling over how soon I can come out west to visit you guys."

Tina pulled her into a hug. "You're the only reason I'll ever be nostalgic for my youth."

"My dearest friend," Cheryl said.

"I need to pack up a few things," Tina said, turning to go. "Oh, I forgot. You wanted to tell me something too."

Cheryl had to stop and think before remembering she was going to tell Tina about Eddie's scary visit.

"Oh, I was just going to remind you to make sure your bedroom windows are locked. And Ricky's windows. I'm making the rounds in a few minutes to check the rest of the house. We've opened windows recently with the nice weather. And sometimes we forget to lock them again."

"Sure thing."

Tina headed to her room.

Cheryl spent the next few minutes making sure all the windows were locked securely. She also checked the back door. Then she dashed out front and checked that her VW and Tina's Ford were locked.

Then she fixed herself a little bowl of canned peaches and sat on the front porch wrapped in a blanket. Her mind was consumed with thoughts of Tina. She should've had some inkling. She remembered all the times Tina had said "he's not my type." To which Cheryl had some smartass comeback, making fun of her. God, she'd been living with blinders on. She wondered how many times she'd been dismissive or mean.

Tina was turning the corner to follow a road she hadn't had the chance to travel on. A road leading to acceptance and openness. What was it she said? Life is too short to accept unhappiness and frustration. It was the threat of an apocalypse that gave her the push she needed.

The phone rang. She ran inside. It was long distance from Paul. She waited till he dropped his coins in the box.

"I'll be home tomorrow!"

She hadn't expected to feel this way but realized her skin was prickling. All she could think about at that moment was his arms around her, his lips on hers.

"Oh, Paul, that's fantastic!"

"Yeah, they need me back at Fort Bragg. As soon as I get there I'm driving over to your house. Well, first I'll take a..."

There was a click, a buzz and then the line went dead. She waited for him to call back but he didn't. What if he'd been caught off base without permission? What if he'd been hauled back to his unit for punishment? Her stomach was in knots. Now she didn't know if he would arrive the next day or not.

She heard the front door open. Peggy slipped in quietly as she always did. Finding no one in the living room, she made her way to Tina's bedroom. The door closed with a soft click.

Cheryl had felt twinges of jealousy ever since Peggy moved in. Those twinges now turned into spasms. She used to believe Tina confided in *her*, rather than Peggy. Turned out there was a lot Tina hadn't felt comfortable sharing with her oldest friend. Now Peggy would be her best friend and much more. But Cheryl wanted happiness for Tina, so she pushed the jealousy aside. She genuinely hoped they would make a good life together out west. She also hoped Peggy would love Ricky at least half as much as she did.

The last thing she did before heading for bed was to check that the front door was locked. But it didn't prevent bad dreams from interrupting her sleep. She couldn't remember much, except for the mushroom cloud in the sky like a giant monster.

*

Drizzle made the roads wet Wednesday for her drive to work. She hoped the weather would improve. Tonight was Halloween. Definitely not fun to trick-or-treat in the rain. Thankfully, the cold snap had eased.

The mood seemed off kilter at work. She couldn't quite put her finger on why.

Mr. Carlisle worked in his office. A couple of salesmen were in the building. The others were showing houses again now that people believed there would be a tomorrow. On the surface, it was the same as a regular day before the nuclear crisis tapped the brakes on the local real estate market. Still, the uneasy feeling stayed with her.

Of course, she was nervous about Eddie. She had listened all night, fearful that he would break into the house and kidnap her. She glanced with alarm around the lobby half expecting guerilla fighters to charge into the room at any moment, armed with fixed bayonets.

Morbid, she thought. She needed to find another task to do. She should check with Mr. Carlisle but she dreaded facing him. The last time they crossed paths was when he opened the closet door in his office Monday night. She didn't know what to expect.

She waited until line three went dark before grabbing her steno pad and pencil and making her way to his office. Through the open door she saw him sitting stock still at his desk, staring straight ahead at the opposite wall.

"Mr. Carlisle, anything I can do for you?"

He didn't move.

She walked a few steps closer.

"Mr. Carlisle?"

Silence. She moved forward, this time angling to the right so she could stand in front of him and see his face. He was silently weeping. He made no move to wipe the tears, not seeming aware of her presence.

She took two tissues from the box on his desk and set them in front of him.

"Mr. Carlisle?"

His eyes regained focus, meeting hers. There was pain in his gaze.

"My son woke up last night."

"That's good news."

"That's what I thought too, at first. He hasn't said a word yet. He seems to know who we are, I think."

The faraway look returned.

"The doctors will help him," she said.

"We don't know if he'll ever regain full use of his mind."

She struggled with something to say.

"Goddam drugs!" He sounded so tired, so bitter.

She turned to leave but he stopped her.

"Cheryl, please don't mention anything about Dean to anyone else."

"Of course."

"I shouldn't have said anything."

She nodded, then eased out the door.

For Mr. Carlisle, even Monday night's faceoff with Eddie didn't qualify as a major concern compared with his son's life. Even the nuclear stalemate had seemed irrelevant to him and his wife. They'd been far too preoccupied worrying about their son. Cheryl hadn't met Dean but couldn't help feeling tremendously sad for him and his parents.

Later, the telephone rang as she was about to take her sandwich to Jerry Inman's empty office to eat lunch.

"Miss Donovan?"

"This is she."

"This is Vernon Swaney at Sandhills High. The secretary job is yours if you're still interested."

"Yes, I am!"

"Glad to hear it. I'm pleased you'll be joining our staff. Your first day here will be two weeks from tomorrow. Which leaves you time to give notice at your current job today."

"Consider it done."

"It'll help if you drop by Monday morning about eight forty-five. I have a couple of forms for you to sign before we add you to the payroll."

"I'll be there."

After they hung up she rubbed her hands together, flooded with relief. She would soon be out the door here at Sleazy Realty and Money Laundering Incorporated, as Tina put it. She couldn't wait to tell her.

Coming on this unsettled day, knowing Tina was leaving added to her distraction. Tina would drive away in two days' time, taking Ricky with her. If only she would stay.

She was also worried about Eddie and Vic, wishing she had the nerve to call the police chief to ask if they'd been arrested yet. Perhaps Lieutenant Malone would be easier to talk with. She worried about how much she had hurt Allan.

Then there was Paul. He told her he would arrive today, that he would come to see her first thing. Then the line went dead. She was afraid he'd been thrown in the stockade for sneaking off to call her.

She craned her neck, searching the parking lot for his Sapphire Blue Stingray. It was nowhere to be seen.

Why did she suddenly feel such urgency to see him? Perhaps it was true that absence makes the heart grow fonder. Those troubling reservations she'd had ten days ago had collapsed in the wind. She only knew she needed to see him. The threat of an apocalypse may have made her cling to Paul because when she was with him, the urge to live in the moment was strong. Especially when there were doubts that there would be a tomorrow.

She sat gazing through the wall of windows, daydreaming about him, daydreaming that they were driving on a beautiful fall day, the slanting sunlight transforming the trees with vivid colors. He made the natural world more beautiful, life more joyful.

Enough daydreaming! Time to get back to work. She ordered a box of pink phone message pads. Someone had snitched what was left of them in the storage room. She'd been cutting sheets of paper into fourths to tide her over, the scissors still lying on her desk. She double-checked the design and lettering for new magnetic car signs the sales staff required. She sorted through the stack of mail, then distributed it to the staff mail boxes. Returning to the lobby, she noticed a man in fatigues waiting by her desk. Dan O'Keefe was number one on the floor today. He'd be pleased to get a walk-in, even if the guy was breaking regulation by wearing fatigues off duty.

Hearing the click of her high heels on the floor, the man turned around. It was Paul!

He rushed to her, lifted her off her feet and swung her around. The way he kissed her, you'd have thought he hadn't seen her in a year. It wouldn't help her reputation being caught kissing a man in the lobby. But she wasn't about to push him away. So she took him by the hand and led him outside to her Volkswagen. Unlocking the door, she folded the driver seat forward and climbed into the cramped back seat. He didn't have to be told to follow.

Pulling down the shades on both windows, they picked up where they left off, their kisses becoming more passionate.

"Damn, I've missed you so bad," he murmured in her ear. "Another day and I would've gone AWOL and hitchhiked up here to see you."

"Then, I'm doubly thankful the crisis is over. Not only do we avoid nuclear war, we also avoid having you locked up. I thought that's what happened last night."

"My ride was leaving. I had to hustle."

She was as giddy as a child at the county fair.

He kissed her again. "I didn't have any idea the back seat of a VW could make me this happy."

"You don't have to go back, do you?" she asked.

"Nope. I'm yours to wrap around your pinky finger."

She touched his cheek. He shivered, then pulled her closer and they lost themselves in each other's arms. Luckily, it was daytime and not a moonlit night.

"I need to get back to my desk," she said.

"But I need five more minutes to soak in your beauty. There's a glow in your cheeks."

"Well, today is a good news day. You returned from the front and the principal of Sandhills High School offered me the school secretary job. My first day is in two weeks."

He kissed her nose. "Better call him back and tell him you don't need the job after all. Tell him your man came home and will soon be carrying you across the threshold of your new home as Mrs. Paul McIntyre."

There it was. She stiffened, then removed her arms from around his neck and straightened her clothes.

"I need to get back inside and get my ducks in a row," she said.

With that, she opened the door and squeezed out of the tight back seat. He was right behind her.

She locked the car before turning to face him. "So glad you're back safely."

"Not even a good-bye kiss?"

She glanced toward the building. "I think we stocked up pretty well. Plus, they'll be looking for me." She smoothed her hair and walked away.

It wasn't fair that so many things about Paul were perfect: the easy conversation, the way he joked with her and the sizzle in her blood when they were together. There was something about him that said they belonged together, that they were two halves of a whole.

But – and it was a massive 'but' – he was a gentlemanly throwback to an earlier era when a man was expected to protect a woman, provide for her and, worst of all, to govern her. Over the last ten days, as a nuclear cataclysm loomed, she'd glossed over these things. Now that he was back, already telling her to take a pass on the new job, the issue was front and center once again.

She didn't want falling in love to mark the end of living her own life. She didn't want to suffer as her mother did, having a dream but giving up the chance to pursue it.

Forcing herself to get back to work, she was about to type a letter when the boss summoned her on the intercom.

Reporting to his office, he said he needed for her to drive to Odom Realty and get a document from Perry Odom related to their proposed partnership. Then she was supposed to drop by the printing office to pick up the first draft of a brochure they were producing for their joint venture.

First stop, Roger's office to let him know someone would need to cover the phones. But Roger wasn't there. None of the salesmen were in the building at the moment, which happened from time to time. She would get ready to go and wait for someone to show up. Taking her purse with her to the ladies room, she brushed her hair and touched up her lipstick. When she walked down the sales hallway again, the offices were still empty.

Sitting down at her desk, she wished she could leave early. Tonight she wanted to accompany Ricky and Tina trick-or-treating, especially now that they were leaving town on Friday. As she waited, a man in a sport coat and tie entered the lobby, approaching her desk.

"I'm here to meet with a new sales agent named Phil Boyer."

She didn't want to let on that she hadn't heard of Phil Boyer. She simply told him she'd be back in a moment and headed for the sales offices. She ran into a stranger in the hallway wearing a blue suit.

"You wouldn't happen to be Phil Boyer, would you?"

"That's me."

"A customer is asking for you."

He thanked her and hurried to greet him.

Cheryl returned to her desk wondering if she could leave now that this new guy was here. Mr. Carlisle must've hired him after she said no to the job. He should've told her.

Before she could make up her mind, a streak of red drew her attention to the front. Pulling into a parking space was the dreaded Cadillac. Eddie and Vic emerged, then walked toward the building. Why hadn't they been arrested yet? Lieutenant Malone assured her that would happen. Her heart raced as the two of them approached.

She pretended to study a file on her desk as they walked through the front door, watching them out of the corner of her eye.

Vic stayed near the door as Eddie swept across the lobby, bringing to mind a galloping centaur. He stopped at her desk, leaning across it so his face was inches from hers.

"When I'm done with Harry, you're coming with me for a tour of your new office."

He regarded her as though she was a steak. There was a hint of whiskey on his breath. He chortled as he walked away, signaling Vic to keep an eye on her.

Without so much as a knock he disappeared into his brother's office, slamming the door behind him.

Loading paper into her typewriter, Cheryl typed as if her life depended on it, secretly keeping watch. Vic sat down on one of the Danish modern sofas that looked much too small for his large frame. He faked reading a magazine, watching her above the page. His job was to make sure she didn't leave. Eddie had plans for her. She had made it clear to Lieutenant Malone that her life was in danger until they were behind bars. Why were they still free?

An escape plan took shape in her mind. She would make a break for it through the back door. Hopefully she could take Vic by surprise. She'd hide somewhere in the mess behind that auto repair shop next door. She was about to grab her purse and head for the rear exit when the boss's door opened.

"Can I get you a cup too?" Mr. Carlisle said, louder than usual.

"No! Will you hurry up? I haven't got all day." Eddie was his usual congenial self.

Mr. C. crossed to the sales hallway, ducking into the break room. The electric percolator was always ready with a pot of coffee. Odd, though. He didn't normally drink coffee in the afternoon.

As she waited for her chance to run, she noticed something curious. The new sales guy and his customer were sneaking glances at Vic.

That's when a noise came from the back hallway, followed immediately by the front door opening with a thud. She couldn't believe her eyes! A column of armed police officers stormed into the lobby. Mr. Boyer and his client both ran toward Vic, pulling guns from inside their jackets. Vic evaded them, lurching toward Cheryl. She screamed and dropped to the floor to hide under her desk. Vic was beefy but he was fast. He grabbed her arm and yanked her to her feet before the other men reached him. Then he pulled her firmly against his body from behind. His grip around her middle was so constricting, she thought her ribs would snap.

The officers came to a halt, weapons drawn. But when they saw the muzzle of Vic's gun pressed against her right temple, they held their fire.

21

There were ten armed policemen and two plainclothes officers – the fake salesman and phony client. But as long as Vic held a gun to Cheryl's head, there was nothing they could do. She had relaxed about surviving to live another day when the threat of nuclear war eased. Now she was one bullet away from becoming a casualty in a war between drug dealers and police.

"Where's Eddie?" Vic demanded.

"On his way to jail," a tall officer replied. It was Lieutenant Harvey Malone, the man Chief Girard trusted with his life.

"I don't believe you," Vic said. "Bring him here so I can see him."

"He's gone. He was escorted out the back door."

Vic tightened his grasp on Cheryl's waist with his massive left arm while his gun dug into her temple. She struggled to loosen his grip but she might as well have tried to detach herself from a giant grizzly.

Mr. C. must've sent her on that errand to get her out of the building. When he went to the break room, asking Eddie if he wanted a cup of coffee, he was actually clearing out so police could move in. She fouled things up staying at her desk, worried about the phones. Mr. Carlisle made the faulty assumption that she would walk out the door when he gave her the errand. But it was the undercover cops who deserved to be horsewhipped for not insisting she leave immediately, knowing what was about to happen.

"Let her go, Acosta," Lieutenant Malone said. "You don't want a first degree murder charge on top of drug charges."

"Eddie?" Vic bellowed.

Silence.

He twisted to the left, craning to look through the front windows. Cheryl did too. A dozen police cars were visible. Armed officers were hiding behind them, rifles aimed at the building.

All that firepower and they didn't dare shoot. The more she thought about the situation, the madder she got. If she was going to die anyway, she wanted to have her say.

"I have a question," she said, causing Vic to stiffen. She ignored him, looking at Malone. "Why didn't you evacuate the building? You wouldn't have a hostage situation now if you'd done your job."

Silence.

"Because you're in charge, Lieutenant Malone, I hereby give you an 'F' on your report card. 'F' means failure. It also means fired. As in, you're fired."

Vic's body vibrated. Amazingly, he was chuckling. Which only served to encourage her.

She addressed her next comment to the men who played the new salesman and the customer before the phalanx of armed officers charged in. "Are you undercover guys really so stupid you didn't realize I was in danger?"

She flapped her arm in frustration. Vic didn't tighten his grip this time.

They didn't answer. Lieutenant Malone did.

"I'm sorry, Miss Donovan. We were told you left."

"That makes me feel so much better."

There were some uneasy glances among the officers.

"Mr. Acosta, you need to drop your weapon and ..." Malone said.

"I'm not finished!" Cheryl blurted. "I'm entitled to make a final statement before I die."

Vic's body shook. He was enjoying himself even with a dozen guns trained on him. Of course the bullets had to go through *her* first.

"I wish I could give you guys another chance at doing this properly, Lieutenant," she continued. "You could send a plainclothes officer into the building first. He would flash his badge and tell me I need to clear out." She raised her hand in the air for emphasis. "I, for one, want to do this whole thing over. You ready?"

She gritted her teeth and doubled over fast and hard, sticking her butt out as far as she could, slamming it into Vic's groin. He struggled to keep his balance and hold onto her at the same time. That little bit of movement was enough for Cheryl to reach the scissors still lying on her desk. She clutched them in one hand, letting the blades fall open, then swung them with all her might toward Vic's right arm. He gasped when a blade sliced his wrist, almost dropping his revolver. He pawed at her, trying to pull her back as he struggled to hold onto his gun.

A throng of policemen converged on him. Some strained to pry the weapon from his hand, others tried to pin him to the floor while two others labored to wrench Cheryl away from him. They all ended up on the hard floor, Vic's powerful legs wrapped around Cheryl's waist.

Through all of that, she managed to hold onto the scissors. She flailed her arm, stabbing Vic in the thigh.

He growled in pain as she thrashed one way and the other, further loosening his grip. Then two officers – one of them was Lieutenant Malone – pried his legs apart just long enough so she could pull away. Clambering to her feet, she pushed past them as the life or death struggle continued behind her. She grabbed her pocketbook and ran for the door. No one was going to stop her. As she jumped into her car, there was a gunshot, followed quickly by more gunfire. She tore out of the parking lot as fast as her old Volkswagen would go.

Even after she was safe at home, her hands continued to shake. She paced from the living room to the hallway, from the hallway to the kitchen, then through the dining room and back to the living room. Each time she circled through the living room, she scanned the street for red cars. Instead, a black and white police cruiser glided to a stop out front. It was Lieutenant Malone, another officer and a woman.

Cheryl moved to the front porch.

"Miss Donovan!" Malone said, stepping from the vehicle. "You're not hurt, are you?"

"Whyever would I be hurt? You and your officers did such a fine job of protecting me this afternoon."

The lieutenant stopped at the foot of the steps.

"I apologize for that. Your boss told us his brother said he would be alone."

Cheryl shook her head like that was the most pathetic thing she'd ever heard.

Lieutenant Malone looked chagrined.

"Please tell me Eddie and Vic are behind bars," she said.

"Edward Carlisle is in a jail cell. Vic Acosta was shot dead after seriously wounding one of our officers. Harold Carlisle was arrested on lesser charges."

She took a slow, deep breath, closing her eyes as she struggled to get her emotions under control. The news that someone had been killed rattled her.

He gave her a moment before he went on.

"I know you're running on empty, Miss Donovan. But we need you to give us a statement about today's events."

A disbelieving glare was all she could manage.

"This is extremely important to our case," he went on. "You witnessed our attempt to take Mr. Acosta into custody."

"What I have to say won't make your department look good."

"Don't worry about that. The judge and jury will need to know Mr. Acosta put your life in danger trying to avoid arrest."

"There were a dozen police officers who saw the whole thing!"

"But you were the one whose life he threatened. It won't take long. You don't have to go to headquarters. Officer Nash can record your statement here at your house." He gestured at the policeman in the car. "Gail Douglas will take notes." He pointed at the woman in the back seat, the same stenographer who took notes when Cheryl gave her first statement at police headquarters.

Thirty minutes later they were gone, her statement done.

She sat on the porch swing to wait for Tina and Ricky. She was spent. But it was Halloween. Ricky would be talking loud and fast, his engine revving as he waited to get his costume on. She didn't want to ruin his fun so she wouldn't say a word about what kind of day she had. She would store today's harrowing experience in a corner of her brain where she could save it for another time.

There they were. Ricky jumped out of the car almost before it stopped. He ran to the house, his untucked shirttail flapping behind him.

"Cheryl! Cheryl! It's Halloween! Me and Tommy are going trick-or-treating!"

"Can I tag along?"

"What're you gonna be?"

"How about a witch?"

"Yeah!"

Peggy arrived then, after her last day on the job. She had picked up her transcript that morning so she could transfer to another dental hygienist program in Oregon. She would hand out candy and homemade cookies while Cheryl and Tina chaperoned the boys.

They ate a quick supper of sandwiches and chips and were ready for action when Tommy showed up.

He was dressed as a hobo in torn pants and shirt with a real cigarette to put in his mouth. He was impressed by Ricky's olive drab jacket and helmet. But he insisted Ricky had to have a rifle if he was going to be a soldier.

"No I don't. I'm a soldier that marches for peace." Ricky proudly held his homemade sign above his head. It said, "Peace," hand lettered by Ricky himself, the word slanting from the bottom left corner to the upper right corner.

Tommy looked unconvinced.

Cheryl let the boys watch her get ready. She put on a tangled, misshapen dime store wig over her own hair with a few bobby pins. Then she slipped on an old, black raincoat.

"What are you s'posed to be?" Tommy asked.

That's when she opened her mouth, showing off her teeth, which were mostly blacked out with liquid eyeliner. Then she cackled loudly using what Ricky said was her piggy voice.

The boys fell into a fit of giggling. They weren't merely walking on air, they were skipping and bouncing on air.

With flour on her cheeks and an old floral apron tied around her waist, Tina looked like a cook. She even carried a long handled cooking spoon.

Before they left the house, Peggy took pictures with Tina's Brownie as everyone mugged for the camera.

"Now, let's hit the road, Jack!" Tina said.

"My name's not Jack!" Ricky said, laughing.

"Mine neither!" Tommy said, grinning with excitement.

The women hung back, keeping watch without hovering.

"I called Wyatt a while ago and told him we're moving away," Tina said.

"You really think giving him notice is a good idea?"

"Well, he is the boy's father."

"Wyatt is a cross between a fox, a snake and a slug. No offense to foxes, snakes and slugs."

Tina snorted. "With the restraining order in effect, I contacted police too and told them I was letting him come over to say good-bye tomorrow afternoon. I assured them I'll be with him and a male friend is coming over as a precaution."

"I don't know, Tina."

"Don't worry. Allan will be here to help us pack up anyway."

"Allan?"

"He's my friend too, you know."

Cheryl dreaded the awkwardness.

"Plus, the things you said about him when you tried to set us up are true. In fact, he's the most modern man I know. Treats women how they should be treated. As equals."

Cheryl knew Tina was right.

"Besides," Tina continued, "He and I have something in common. We both fell in love with a girl who couldn't love us back."

Cheryl wrapped her arm around Tina's shoulder, giving her a little hug.

She waved at a couple walking toward them on the other side of the street. They looked away. As they passed by, Cheryl heard the woman tell the man, "See? They're lesbians." He shushed her. Cheryl didn't comment, hoping Tina hadn't heard. No wonder Tina kept her secret to herself. Now that she thought about it, maybe that was why Tina's boss always gave her a hard time.

"You know, I caught the tail end of a newscast on my way home this afternoon," Tina said. "The news guy said there was a shooting at a Fayetteville realty office. You wouldn't happen to know anything about it, would you?"

"As a matter of fact, I would."

"I was afraid of that."

"Yeah. It was sort of the *Gunfight at the OK Realty Office.*" Cheryl's attempt at a chuckle came out more like a groan.

Tina slipped an arm through Cheryl's like they used to do in school. They walked arm in arm, keeping an eye on the boys as Cheryl told her story.

It was a frightening tale that underlined how close she'd come to having a date with the Grim Reaper. Relating how Vic held a gun at her temple gave her the shakes all over again. Oddly, knowing police shot him dead as she fled the building upset her all the more, in spite of how she had hated him.

"When we got home this afternoon, I thought you were troubled. Why didn't you tell me?"

"I didn't want to ruin Halloween."

"I figured it was over after you met with the police chief."

"Me too."

"Are you okay?"

"I will be.

That's when a child's cry drew their attention to a side street.

"That car looks like Wyatt's," Tina said, pointing to a big car parked under a tree.

"Is it light blue? I can't tell."

"Where are the boys?"

They trotted along the street looking for a soldier with a peace sign and a hobo with a cigarette in his mouth.

Picking up their pace, they scanned bands of children singing out "trick-or-treat!" as they held out their bags under porch lights. There were princesses and ghosts and all manner of Halloween ghouls, but no soldier and no hobo.

Tina grabbed Cheryl's arm, forcing her to stop.

"That car," she said. "Let's go back to that car!"

It was a foot race to get there first. As they approached, the car's headlights came on. A child was bawling. Nearing the intersection where the car sat idling, they could tell the sound was coming from inside it.

"Ricky?" Tina sounded panicked.

The car moved toward them, headlights blinding them. Cheryl stood in the street to block the driver. Suddenly the front window rolled down.

"Can I help you ladies find your children?"

It wasn't Wyatt. The driver was a man she'd seen on their street in his white Plymouth Fury. Which is what they were looking at. Not a light blue Chrysler New Yorker.

"I hear him!" Tina took off the way they'd come, leaving Cheryl to apologize to the man.

"I'm so sorry. We mistook you for someone else." She looked behind her a couple of houses away and saw Tina lift a little soldier in her arms while a hobo watched.

"No problem."

There was that noise of a child squalling inside his car. No, it was a baby.

"That's my dumb cat. Her name is Puddy Tat."

"Thank goodness," Cheryl said, then jogged to catch up with Tina and the boys. She was relieved and embarrassed.

When Tina announced it was time to eat some candy, the boys happily returned to the house, skipping along the street ahead of their chaperones. Tina told Cheryl on the way home that she overreacted, thinking Wyatt had kidnapped Ricky again.

"It's understandable."

"Yeah, that's another reason I need to leave. If we stayed here, I'd be a paranoid neurotic in no time. But I wouldn't just be worried about Wyatt abducting Ricky, I'd also wear myself out worrying about the impact my hateful parents would have on him. It's exhausting."

The guys were still in their costumes at the kitchen table, digging through their sacks when the doorbell rang.

Expecting trick-or-treaters, Cheryl had the candy bowl in her arm when she opened the door. A big guffaw greeted her. It was Paul.

Remembering she was still in costume with blacked-out teeth and that crappy hair piece poking out in all directions, she decided to make the most of it. One thing she didn't want was another serious heart-to-heart. Using her nasal voice, she fired off a maniacal cackle. Which made Paul laugh harder and brought the boys to see what they were missing.

"She's a witch!" Ricky said, bouncing up and down.

"Do it again!" said Tommy, copying Ricky.

The boys became crazed squirrels when she cackled, chasing each other around in a circle.

"That's one reason I'm in love with you," Paul said, stepping inside. "Your hidden talents are awe-inspiring!"

She chuckled as she led him to the kitchen. He helped pull the table away from the wall so all six of them could sit around it. Cheryl fixed glasses of Ginger Ale and they nibbled on Tina's homemade cookies and an occasional piece of candy. The boys regaled them with descriptions of the costumes they'd seen and which houses gave out the best candy. When it was bath time, Peggy walked Tommy home while Tina got Ricky in the tub.

Cheryl pulled the shower curtain across so Ricky could have his privacy while she removed the eyeliner from her teeth. She threw the ugly wig into a box of junk before returning to the kitchen.

Tina was telling Paul how she panicked, thinking Wyatt was trying to snatch Ricky. She told him about letting Wyatt come over the next day to say goodbye. She explained she needed a couple of men on hand to discourage her ex from trying to pull off another abduction, in addition to helping them load their belongings for the trip.

"Saying goodbye? Trip?"

"We're moving away. Friday morning."

He looked from Tina to Cheryl.

"Me and Ricky and Peggy," Tina added, seeing his confusion. "We're moving to Oregon. Although I haven't told Ricky yet."

He relaxed. "That's a long way."

"So if you're not busy tomorrow, could you help?"

"I'd be happy to."

Eventually Cheryl and Paul were left alone, Tina reading bedtime stories to Ricky while Peggy watched *Wagon Train*.

"How about an evening stroll?" Paul said softly.

"My feet are screaming at me already."

"Another hidden talent – feet that scream." Said with a mischievous wink. "How about we sit on the porch swing with our coats on."

She knew how that would play out.

"I'd rather stay here," she said.

His disappointment was palpable.

"We don't need a romantic tête-à-tête," she said.

"We don't?"

"That won't solve anything."

"There's nothing to solve."

"That you don't understand there's a problem, is a big problem."

"You're speaking in riddles."

"Listen, Paul, I refuse to get serious about a man who thinks a wife has to quit her job."

"Any other woman would be thrilled if a man said he wanted her to stay home after they were married."

"I think you're seriously out of touch."

"Come on, you know I'm crazy about you. And I know you love me. I can feel it. You've got this idea about being an independent woman stuck in your head. Next thing you know, you'll say you don't want to cook your husband's meals or take care of the children!"

She popped up out of her chair, giving him a hard look.

"What I don't want, for your information, is a man telling me what to do. I gave you a second chance when you took off for Florida. Now I hereby award you an "F" on your report card!"

"Marriage is about compromise."

"If there's one thing I know, it's that you need to love a person for who they *are*, not who you hope you can mold them into. Why would you fall in love with someone because of who she is, then tell her to change?"

Silence.

She marched back to her bedroom, ignoring secret glances from Peggy and Tina who pretended to watch TV. As she shut her door, she realized she'd also closed the door on a future with the man who made her heart sing. She could imagine her mother telling her she was being hardheaded. Mom would say, "a marriage is made of a thousand compromises." But the intense attraction between them would wane like a full moon that becomes smaller until you can hardly detect it in the night sky. If their relationship wasn't built on a lot more than romance and lust, there could be decades of dark skies.

22

Thursday dawned grey and misty. Tina and Peggy had already worked their last day. Cheryl was out of a job with Carlisle Realty closed till further notice. Mr. Carlisle would be in jail for a while. Auditors had to check the books before the business could reopen.

The four of them had breakfast together, as usual. Afterwards Tina took Ricky into his room to explain what was about to happen. Cheryl worried about how he would take the news.

Peggy washed dishes, leaving Cheryl free to eavesdrop. She stood silently in the doorway to her bedroom.

Sounding artificially perky, Tina described how they were going to drive all the way across the country to their new home in Oregon. There would be new friends and a nice new school. And, yes, they were taking Max and Pinky.

"Is Cheryl coming too?"

"No, but Peggy's coming with us."

"Why can't Cheryl come?"

"Well, she'll come and visit us from time to time."

"But isn't Cheryl your bestest friend, Mommy?"

"Yes, sweetie. But Peggy is my other best friend."

"But…"

Cheryl felt wretched. She gently closed her door, then sat on the side of the bed blotting her eyes with a tissue. She wondered if Tina was wrong to move so far away. She also wondered if she, herself, had been negligent not preparing Peggy for her new role.

The drizzle ended by the time Tina took Ricky with her to pick up his school record. This would make the transfer to his new school smoother. While they were gone, Cheryl used the opportunity to rub elbows with Peggy, grabbing a kitchen towel to dry the dishes.

"Peggy, I want to apologize for not treating you as a friend."

"You don't have to say…"

"I *do* have to say I'm sorry. I've been so caught up in my own life, I haven't been very nice to you. Plus, I was feeling this weird kind of jealousy, thinking I was Tina's closest friend."

"Don't feel bad. Before I got to know you a little bit, I felt the same thing. But I think Tina's heart is big enough for both of us. After you-know-who of course."

Cheryl smiled at that. "Still, there's something important I should've already discussed with you."

Peggy gave her a wary glance as she rinsed the frying pan.

"This move will be hard on Ricky," Cheryl said. "In time, I know you'll grow to love him as I do. But being uprooted, he's going to need you to be his buddy pretty quickly."

"I've been concerned about the same thing. Tina thinks as long as he's got his mommy, he'll be all right."

"God, I'm so relieved you understand. There's not much time but I've got an idea. If you and I let him see that we like each other, I think that would help. It would be great if you could join us to play with the tape recorder later. I'm giving it to him as a surprise going-away present tomorrow morning. If you operate the recorder for him, I think that'll help pave the way. Another idea – you've noticed he loves to joke around – if you could find ways to do that with him, it could make a big difference. And if you have any weird childhood skills that would amuse a first grade boy, this is a super time to unpack them from moth balls."

"I can wiggle my ears and flare my nostrils at the same time."

Cheryl laughed, elated that Peggy was on board.

Tina and Ricky weren't gone long. When they got home, they were pulling a U-Haul trailer behind them. Ricky was excited now, anxious to show Cheryl the trailer.

Next on the agenda was disassembling the beds and packing the boxes. It was a busy morning. Allan and Paul both showed up. They were friendly but there was a competitive undercurrent. They loaded furniture into the U-Haul, working together as a well-oiled team.

When they stopped for a break midmorning, Cheryl was surprised that Allan mentioned a proposition he'd made to her a couple of weeks ago in private.

"So, Cheryl, have you given any more thought to forming an accounting partnership?

There was an aura of resentment hovering around Paul, who reacted as though Allan had asked her to go to bed with him. Allan seemed on pins and needles anticipating her reply, which he might take as a signal that there was hope for romance yet.

"To be honest, I'm still mulling it over," she said. "If I were to eventually sign on – and that's an 'if' the size of a Mack truck – I have some concerns. First, if we set up our own accounting firm, we would both be newcomers with no accounting job history. Which would make it hard to win big accounts. We'd be able to do taxes for individual customers and other small jobs, but that wouldn't be sustainable unless we worked day jobs, so to speak, to pay the bills and did accounting in the evenings. A more realistic plan would be to hire on at an established firm to build a track record before establishing our own company."

"You *have* given it some thought," Allan said, looking more like her old friend than the melancholy suitor he'd turned into.

"But, as I said, I'm not ready to make a commitment."

Paul seemed taken aback by the exchange. It occurred to Cheryl that Allan brought it up now for that very purpose. To let Paul know he had a rival.

They were a colony of busy bees again by the time the light blue New Yorker pulled up.

Wyatt hurried up the driveway to where Allan and Paul were loading a mattress and box springs into the orange and white trailer.

"Jesus Christ!" Wyatt shouted. "Haven't you heard the news?"

"What're you talking about?" said Tina, adding another cardboard box to the growing stack on the grass.

"A nuclear warhead has been fired! It's on its way to Washington! Our guys have probably already fired back."

"I thought it was over!"

"Yeah, so did the president."

This is exactly what Cheryl had feared. That both sides would let their guard down and some fool would push a button he wasn't supposed to.

"Where'd you hear that?" she said.

"On the radio as I turned onto your street. Instead of packing that damn U-Haul, you need to get your asses down to the basement!"

Tina dashed into the house, nearly colliding with Ricky on his way out. She scooped him up, fear in her eyes, then made her way inside. Cheryl gave Paul and Allan a skeptical look. Peggy came through the front door carrying another box. She stopped in her tracks, looking around at the stunned faces.

"What's wrong?" she said.

Before anyone could answer, the sound of a radio blasted through the open front door. Tina had turned the volume all the way up trying to find a news bulletin. A short segment of a song would play, then she would turn the dial to another station where a song would play for a few seconds, then another station and another, searching for news.

A moment later Tina returned to the front porch with Ricky in tow.

"I can't find a newscast, but we're going down to the basement just in case. Is anyone else coming?"

"I think Mr. Armstrong got his months confused," Allan said. "Instead of playing an April Fool's joke on the first of April, he's playing an April Fool's joke on the first of November."

"You calling me a liar?" Wyatt's eyes blazed.

Allan shook his head. "I'm calling you a joker."

"I heard it on the radio! A Marty Robbins song was playing, then some guy broke in and said a missile was headed for the White House."

"If that were true," Cheryl said, "it would be on every radio station."

"Yeah," said Paul, "and we'd hear the sound of jets flying overhead from Pope Air Force Base."

Tina's eyes drilled into her ex.

"That's a sick joke, Wyatt."

"It's not real, Mommy?" Ricky asked.

"No, honey, your daddy was joking, trying to scare us."

Ricky squatted down to pet Pinky who had begun rubbing against his leg.

Wyatt crowed as if he'd told a good one to some buddies at his favorite Hay Street bar. He jutted his jaw in victory, then called his son's name, waiting for him to run into the yard.

But Ricky didn't react as he usually did. There was a new cautiousness that didn't used to be there.

"Your mother says y'all are moving away," Wyatt said.

Ricky nodded solemnly, scratching the cat's ears.

"Far away," Wyatt said.

Ricky didn't look up, focusing on petting Pinky.

"So far away," Wyatt continued, "that I won't be able to come see you."

Ricky looked up at his mother.

"I'll go halfsies with you on airfare so you can visit now and then," she said. "Under my supervision, of course."

Wyatt gave her a hostile look. "Come on, boy. Let's go get a milkshake."

Ricky looked at his mother again.

"You have permission to visit *here* under my supervision for a few minutes," she said. "You can come up on the porch with us. Sorry it won't be a private goodbye but that can't be helped."

He rolled his head back in frustration.

As he walked toward the house Tina took a seat on the porch swing. Ricky climbed up beside her, suddenly shy. Cheryl brought a kitchen chair for Wyatt to sit on since the rocker was in the living room. She and Peggy sat at the edge of the porch, their legs dangling down. Paul and Allan joined them, standing on the ground. The four of them gabbed quietly about their experiences on the road, giving the father and son a modicum of privacy.

Ricky sat quietly and listened while his dad told him about getting a job at a car dealership, announcing that he was now a mechanic.

"No more pumping gas and cleaning bug guts off windshields for me."

He talked about engine parts and how he diagnosed problems. When he couldn't think of anything else to say, he stood and announced he had to get back to work.

"Tell your daddy goodbye," Tina said.

"Bye, Daddy," Ricky said, sounding like a timid little boy.

"Bye, little pardner." Then Wyatt turned to go.

"Why don't you give him a hug?" Tina said to her ex-husband.

"Hugging is for sissies."

"No it's not. Hugging is for everybody."

Wyatt gave her a cold stare. "You're such a fucking goody-two-shoes. You're turning my son into a sissy. A mama's boy!"

"Hey, that's enough of that," Allan said as all eyes settled on Wyatt.

Tina's face flushed as she jumped to her feet. It was plain she was about to clobber him with a few choice comments. But she glanced at Ricky who was about to cry. So instead of giving her ex a piece of her mind, she turned to Cheryl.

"I'm taking Ricky in the house."

She hoisted him onto her hip and carried him inside, closing the door behind her.

Wyatt turned to leave but Cheryl had gotten to her feet and moved to block his path.

"You have now confirmed my opinion, you ugly nosepicker! You're a slug, a fox and a snake all rolled into one. You don't deserve that precious child. You don't know the meaning of the word father! The sad thing is – you don't even care!"

Like a big bully on the playground, Wyatt shoved her out of his way with both hands. She fell backwards, tumbling off the porch where Allan and Paul stood ready to intervene. The two men managed to break her fall as Wyatt hustled down the steps.

Seeing that Cheryl was unhurt, Paul and Allan took off after him.

"Let him go!" Cheryl cried. When they turned to look at her, she waved them off.

Wyatt jumped behind the wheel of his New Yorker and backed out so fast, he nearly hit the mailbox.

"He's not worth it," Cheryl said. "I'm pretty sure he'll get what he deserves in life."

"Wise call," Allan said.

Paul nodded.

While the men got back to work, Cheryl asked Peggy to go inside with her. She found Tina reading a book to Ricky.

"Do you suppose he wants to play with the tape recorder for a little while," Cheryl said. "Peggy wants to see how it works."

"That's a great idea," Tina said.

By the time they had the recorder set up on the kitchen table, Ricky seemed to have recovered from the ugly scene on the porch. Cheryl guessed he'd gotten used to his daddy's bad behavior, which was one of Tina's concerns – that he could think such behavior was normal.

He climbed into his usual chair, raising himself higher on his knees. He talked into the mike about how he would have to help take care of Max and Pinky on the long drive to Oregon. Peggy watched as Cheryl pushed the buttons for the first few minutes, then she took over, getting in the spirit of things by quacking like Donald Duck. Ricky was impressed, asking her to do it over and over. When it was time to put the recorder away, he looked sad, believing it was the last time he'd get to play with it.

When the trailer was full, Tina locked it. They left space for her full-size mattress which she and Peggy would use for a bed that night on the floor of her room. Ricky was excited when Cheryl told him he could share her bed. His bed had already been loaded.

Peggy volunteered for a pizza run, prompting everyone to hand her some cash. She was back a short time later with pizzas and beer. They ate together in the back yard at the picnic table. There was lots of small talk and joking around. There were some serious moments too, including when Paul and Allan gave Ricky their parting gifts.

Allan gave him a Brownie camera, saying he could learn to take his own pictures as he got older. Ricky said thank you but didn't really grasp what a special gift it was. Before he stepped aside, Allan leaned down to give him a quick hug.

When he opened the gift from Paul, he could hardly wait to get the toy helicopter out of the box so he could make his rotor noise and fly it all around the yard. His thank you to Paul was effusive. Paul followed Allan's lead, giving the little boy a hug.

Tina grew misty-eyed that the guys had validated what she told Wyatt, that hugging is for everybody. She gave the guys her own hug in appreciation.

Their peaceful lunch was interrupted when Max ran to the gate barking. Tina cringed, grumbling to Cheryl that she hoped it wasn't her parents. Cheryl headed to the gate, intending to force Mr. and Mrs. Rossi to leave rather than let them add yet another layer of anxiety to an already anxious day. But it wasn't the Rossis. It was Audrey Quinn, their old friend from high school who'd been traveling the world as a teacher, most recently to Okinawa.

"Cheryl, you look wonderful!"

Audrey was the one who looked wonderful. Her dark glossy hair was cut into a pretty page boy. She was dressed in grey slacks with a stylish blue sweater. What a change from their teenage years.

"Good to see you," Cheryl said, wishing she could tell her that now was a bad time to stop in unannounced.

"Tina told me you need a new roommate. Thought I'd drop by and ask about it."

Cheryl turned to look at Tina who walked over to join them.

"I forgot to tell you she phoned," Tina said. "There's been so much going on, I let it slip my mind."

They ushered her into the back yard and introduced her to Ricky and Paul. She already knew Peggy and Allan from high school. Audrey quickly understood that they were loading Tina's things for her move.

"Gosh, I'm sorry for the intrusion. I can come back another time."

But Cheryl insisted on walking her through the house and filling her in on rent and utilities. Their brief visit left her with a good feeling. She hoped it worked out that they could share the house until the Donovans came home next summer.

After Audrey drove away, Cheryl returned to the picnic table in time to say goodbye to Allan. He wished Tina, Peggy and Ricky the best of luck.

Paul, on the other hand, waited around until the others went inside, leaving the two of them in the yard.

"I don't mean to pry, but are you involved with Allan?"

"Allan and I have been friends a long time. He's a great guy. But no, I'm not involved with him." No point telling him that Allan wished they were involved.

"Yet you're considering becoming partners?"

She was torn between expounding on how a man and a woman could be business partners and not lovers, or walking away and letting him stew over it a while and possibly work it out for himself. If he could get past the green-eyed monster, that is.

"It's one of the options I'm looking at. He's smart, trustworthy and kind. Plus he's got a fun sense of humor that keeps things from getting boring. Romance isn't part of the equation."

"But Cheryl, what about getting married and having children?"

"What about it?"

That threw him. He sat silently for a moment, his forehead pinched.

"You can't promise to be his business partner and then get married. You'd have to..."

"No, Paul, I would not have to quit my job."

"But..."

"And if I eventually choose to have children, I still wouldn't have to quit my job. Allan understands this. As I said, he's a smart guy."

He stood up, leaving his plate on the picnic table. "I think Allan is in love with you."

"And I suppose you think I'm in love with him."

The intensity of his stare made her itchy. She refused to scratch.

"Thank you for giving Ricky a hug," she said. "That was thoughtful of you and Allan. And the toy helicopter – a fantastic gift. Now, I've got to get busy."

"Wait!"

She took her paper plate with her as she headed for the house.

"You know why I'm saying these things," he said.

"I have to go inside now."

"I love you, Cheryl."

She loved him too but those words would not pass her lips. Resisting him was the hardest thing she'd ever had to do. Even now her desire to be with him was powerful. But she wasn't a teenager anymore. The yearning that made her blood thrum in her ears would have to be put on ice. Giving in to longing wouldn't bring happiness.

"You need a man to love you and protect you. I'm that man."

She spun around. "This is not the Middle Ages! I don't need a knight in shining armor!" She continued toward the back door at a brisk pace.

He blinked as though a bright light had blinded him. "I'm not giving up, Cheryl. Not when I know you're the only woman for me."

She faced him.

"What you apparently don't comprehend is that I'm *not* the woman for you if what you want is a woman who treats you as lord and master. I will always be my own boss."

"Most other women would be happy to have me!"

"Go get 'em!"

"Cheryl!"

There would be no turning around and looking into his eyes. She bounded up the back steps and escaped into the house.

23

"Why do you enjoy this book so much?"

Leaning on pillows at the head of her bed, Cheryl and Ricky had settled in for a bedtime story on his last night on Loblolly Lane. He had asked her to read from *Half Magic*, the book his mother had read him.

"I like it cuz of the magic. They get half a wish, so they wish twice as big so they get their whole wish."

She gazed down at the earnest little boy sitting beside her.

"Wanna know the bestest wish of all?" he said.

She nodded.

"At the end, they wish their mommy would marry Mr. Smith. They like Mr. Smith a lot and their mommy is lonesome. And guess what? Their wish comes true!"

He seemed the very embodiment of generosity and love.

"If I had a magic coin," he said, "I'd wish Mommy was happy the same as their mommy is happy at the end of the book."

"Well, you know what? I think your mommy *will* be that happy once you get settled in your new home in Oregon."

"You do?"

"Yes, I do."

His contented expression made her smile.

After reading only a few pages, his eyelids grew heavy. She tucked him in and kissed him goodnight, then summoned Tina so she could give him his nightly dose of mommy love.

*

Friday morning's blue sky was a good omen for a cross-country trip to Oregon in an old car pulling a U-Haul trailer. For that, Cheryl was grateful. But it was dark and rainy in her soul as she braced herself to say goodbye.

After a big cheerful breakfast around the kitchen table, the brushing of teeth and loading of final items for the trip, Cheryl grabbed her camera.

"Time for a few snapshots. Tina, you and Peggy and Ricky stand by the U-Haul."

Wearing warm coats in the cold morning air, they followed orders, saying cheese four times.

"Peggy, can you take a few of the three of us?" Cheryl said, handing her the camera.

Cheryl forced a smile as she posed with Tina and Ricky, knowing these photos would mean a lot in the years to come.

"Send us reprints," Tina said.

With that, the dreaded time for farewells arrived.

It was easy giving Peggy a brief hug and exchanging words of support and thanks. But when she carried the box to Ricky with her parting gift inside, she had to blink repeatedly to make her tear ducts behave.

"Guess what I'm giving you as a going-away present!" she said.

His eyes brightened as he studied the cardboard box in her hands. "A stuffed Yogi Bear?"

"Nope."

She leaned over so he could open the lid and see for himself.

"It's your tape recorder!" he said, bewildered.

"Now it's *your* tape recorder. I want you to have it. Peggy knows how to push the buttons. I thought you two could play with it on the trip to your new home!"

The wonder in his eyes was replaced by sadness. He sniffed, rubbing his eyes with the backs of his hands.

Cheryl set the box on the grass and wrapped him in her arms, struggling with what to say that wouldn't make him sadder. She decided to say what was in her heart.

"Good golly, I love you. And I'll be coming out to see you very soon."

"You will?" he snuffled into her neck.

"Yes siree Bob! You can count on it! You're my best buddy!" She kissed him on the cheek, then loosened her hold so she could see his face.

"Well, you're my bestest buddy too!" he replied. "Even if you are a girl."

Which was a nice touch.

"Do me a favor and remind your mommy to write me a letter when you're ready for me to visit. Do you think I could sleep on a pallet on the floor of your new bedroom?"

"Yeah! And we could play with the tape recorder before we go to sleep!"

"Man oh man, that'll be loads of fun!"

She blotted his face with a tissue she'd stashed in her pocket and wiped his nose, relieved his smile had returned.

Then she retrieved a cardboard tube from where she'd dropped it on the grass and faced Tina.

"First, here's some money so you can buy a pallet for me to sleep on," she said, handing over a hundred bucks in tens and fives.

"Are you crazy? That'll buy six or seven pallets!"

"Keep the change. You'll need it. Hide it in your money belt."

Then she withdrew a large sheet of art paper from the tube, holding it up for Tina to see. "This is your moving-away present."

Peggy and Ricky moved over to get a better view.

Tina's eyes welled up. "Oh, Cheryl, it's magnificent. Truly magnificent."

"That's me and you, Mommy!" Ricky said.

It was a pen and ink drawing of Tina and Ricky seated side by side on the porch, the two of them gazing into each other's eyes. Looking at it, you could feel the love between them.

"I worked on it in the spring and finished it after you gave me a talking-to."

"Well, abracadabra! You found your creativity!"

Cheryl pulled her dearest friend into an embrace. "You're the bravest woman I know."

"I think bringing down a drug lord was pretty damn courageous," Tina whispered.

"You mean the world to me," Cheryl said.

"Ditto, my friend."

That's when the dam burst for both of them. They were still for a moment, tears spilling over. Then Tina grabbed her friend's shoulders and locked eyes with her.

"You should move out there too. You can be a CPA in Oregon as easily as you can be a CPA in North Carolina."

"Yeah, Cheryl!" Ricky cried.

"Yeah, Cheryl!" Peggy said.

Everyone smiled and laughed.

On that note, it was time to pile into the car. Pinky was already settled in a shoe box on the front passenger seat while Max sat with his tongue hanging out in the center of the back seat. Tina slid behind the wheel. Peggy joined Ricky and Max in the back, which made Cheryl happy. Still, it was going to be a challenging trip, no two ways about it.

Cheryl mustered a smile as the Fairlane pulled out of the driveway, the orange and white trailer bobbing along behind. She waved until she could no longer see them, then let her arm hang limp at her side.

Turning toward the house, she couldn't stand the thought of going inside. She didn't want to see their empty bedrooms. She didn't want to walk through the ruined living room with only the porch rocker, a dining room chair and two lamp tables for furniture. She didn't want to hear the echo of her footsteps on the hardwood floors. She felt like a warship listing on the ocean after being torpedoed by the enemy.

She took a seat on the porch swing, letting her mind wander as she hugged herself to keep warm. Without a doubt, Tina was a perfect example of a courageous woman. She and Peggy pulled up roots to spend a week on a cross-country drive to start anew. She was so proud of her friend. A leap of faith – that's what Tina was willing to take. She said facing a nuclear holocaust made it clear the future wasn't guaranteed, so she had to make every day count. She was onto something.

But Cheryl would mourn her friend's absence. And Ricky's. They had become family.

The phone rang, jangling even louder than usual with the echo. She didn't budge, a great fatigue weighing her down.

She was tired of answering the telephone. But what if it was her mother? Or Tina.

She plodded inside, through the dining room to the kitchen. It was Allan.

"Hey! Thought you might be feeling lonesome about now."

He had good instincts, she had to give him credit.

"You could say that."

"When I get off work this afternoon we could go to the movies."

"Tina said I should move to Oregon too and work as an accountant out there."

"Are you...?"

"I don't know."

"I'll take another day off. I can be at your house in half an hour."

"No, I need to think."

"Cheryl, I care about you deeply." He lowered his volume so no one could hear.

"That's part of the problem, Allan. I want us to go on being friends. You know, good buddies. I don't have romantic feelings for you. I hate to disappoint you. And the last thing I want to do is hurt you."

There was a brief silence.

"I wish I was there so we could talk face to face. Please let me come over."

"Allan..."

"Come on, give me a chance."

He was the perfect man except he didn't make her tingle. Paul made her tingle but his attitude would send her to a divorce lawyer within a year. She needed a cross between them. Was such a man out there somewhere? Maybe in Oregon?

"Please say you'll always be my friend and that you won't hate me for not drooling over your body and pining for your soul."

"See? That's why I..."

"Friend, Allan. I need a friend."

He sighed.

"Maybe I *should* move to Oregon."

"Gotta go," he said. "Someone needs the phone."

She hung up.

The house felt deserted. She didn't want to be in this lonely place. She had to force herself to wash dishes, already wondering how far the Fairlane had gone. She'd marked a map with the route to Oregon and written up a highway-by-highway set of directions for them. Too bad they couldn't have flown out there and hired movers to bring their things. That would've been too expensive, of course.

The possibility that Audrey Quinn might move in with her had been left up in the air. Audrey said she'd call. But what if she didn't? An ad needed to appear in the paper soon seeking a roommate. Paying full rent meant she couldn't afford her classes in the spring, which would delay finishing her degree. That would hurt. She needed a housemate.

Sitting down at the kitchen table, she put pen to paper. "House to share," she began. After briefly describing the house and mentioning the rent, she spelled out what kind of renter she was looking for. "Must be neat, honest and considerate. Must have your own car and be a non-smoker. Cooking skills a plus. Looking for someone who prefers a quiet homelife." God, she was describing Tina. How many potential roommates could come close to filling Tina's size eights? Her vision blurred.

A knock at the door roused her from her stupor. She blotted her eyes with a napkin and made for the door, hoping it wasn't Allan. It wasn't.

"Looks like I've got better timing today," Audrey said.

"Speak of the devil."

"The devil, huh?"

Cheryl opened the screen door.

"I was thinking about submitting an ad to the paper for a roommate."

"That's exactly why I'm here. If the offer is still open, I'd like to be your roommate until next summer, as you mentioned. This is a nice house in a good neighborhood and you're someone I know and trust."

"Now I can throw the ad I was writing in the trash."

Cheryl fixed cinnamon toast and a fresh pot of coffee. Figuring Audrey should know why the living room was such a shambles, they sat at the kitchen table so she could give her the short version. She told her about Eddie Carlisle and his hired thug, about the drugs and money laundering, and the tire iron through the picture window. She told her about the stand-off at the realty office and how Vic ended up dead.

"I'll have to testify when the case comes to court."

"Here I was thinking my life was pretty exciting," Audrey said.

After her new roommate was gone, Cheryl felt a wave of relief. She would miss Tina and Ricky intensely, but she was relieved and looking forward to getting to know Audrey. She definitely wanted to hear about her travels.

There was another knock at the door.

"Please don't let it be Allan or Paul," she said to herself.

Pulling the door open, she found Paul standing there, an apologetic expression on his face.

"I had to come by and see how you're doing today."

The handsome, tingle-inducing lieutenant somehow managed to take off from work whenever he pleased. Was he flying a helicopter to her neighborhood or something? She hadn't heard that whoop-whoop-whoop.

Despite her head telling her he was all wrong for her, her heart continued to pump faster when he was near. But the last thing she wanted was to go another round with him. Too painful.

"I've got errands to run," she said, wanting badly to avoid more torment.

"I have to talk with you. Can I come in? Or we could sit on the porch?"

"Don't have time, Paul. Sorry."

She pushed the door to close it but he opened the screen door and placed his foot in the doorway.

"Five minutes," he said.

"Why does everybody want five minutes?"

"Two minutes!"

"Okay, two minutes. Move your foot."

He removed his foot and stepped back.

"Please don't slam the door in my face."

"Your two minutes began five seconds ago." She checked her watch.

He took a deep breath. "First off, blunders were made and I'm the one who made them."

She looked at her watch again.

"I talked with Allan last night," he said.

She couldn't help rolling her eyes.

"It's not what you think. I didn't do it because I'm jealous. I didn't ask him to back off or stay out of my way. Although it did cross my mind. You see, I needed to understand how he could ask you to be his business partner. I wanted him to explain why he thinks it's proper for you to work even if you get married."

"And?"

"He said you two have been friends a long time. He's always thought of you as an independent person, an adult capable of handling her own life. He didn't think of you as his girlfriend so he didn't have a vested interest in trying to tell you what to do as a husband or boyfriend. He told me he knows you pretty well and says you aren't the type to accept an old-fashioned guy who thinks he's above a woman."

She gave him a slow nod.

"Allan's a good guy," he said.

"He's the best."

A grimace appeared on his face but vanished as he continued speaking.

"Anyway, I thought long and hard about what he said and decided he knows what he's talking about. I also don't want to be a Yellow-bellied Sapsucker and let you slip away because I'm scared of a woman with ambition. So I won't say another word about you quitting your job when we get married. I mean *if* we get married."

"I don't know, Paul. I don't think a zebra can change his stripes."

"This one can." Said with a hint of a smile. "I thought a lot about the things you've been saying to convince me you don't love me. The thing is – I know for a fact you *do* love me. I can feel it. I can see it in your eyes. It finally dawned on me that you're willing to ditch me rather than abandon your principles. That's how strongly you're committed to them. So from here on out, I will respect your beliefs. I love you way too much to let you walk away. I won't be your knight in shining armor and I won't tell you to quit your job."

Oh how she wished she could believe him. But he was just changing tactics.

"All right," she said, "answer me this: what if your wife, whoever she might be, has to travel in her job? For instance, if she has to fly to New York. What would you say?"

"I'd say, 'be careful, honey. Come home quick as you can.'"

"What if you and your wife, whoever that might be, have two young children and your wife has to fly to San Francisco for several days?"

He hesitated, thinking hard.

"I'd ask my mother if she could stay with us to help take care of the children. If she couldn't, I'd ask your mother, I mean my wife's mother. If neither one was available, I'd hire a reliable babysitter for the time I'm at work."

"It's possible your wife, whoever she might be, would make more money than you. Would you be embarrassed?"

He had to think about that one for a minute.

"I have to confess that would take some getting used to. But I would get used to it. And I'd learn to appreciate it."

A fine answer, but she knew it would hurt his ego. She opened her mouth, ready to ask another question but he held up his hand.

"Now I have a question for *you*. What if I have to go overseas for a couple of months? Or worse, what if I'm sent off to war? What would my wife do, whoever she might be?"

"Your wife – and I assume she would be a smart cookie since you wouldn't marry a dumb bunny – would expand the childcare arrangements already in place, leaning on parents, friends and babysitters so she could continue working while making sure the kids were taken care of. And if your wife was an accountant, it's possible she could work at home sometimes."

He nodded like he hadn't thought of that.

"Now, I have a small request," he said.

She waited.

"I respectfully request that the woman of my dreams, whoever she is," he snickered before continuing, "that she enter into a marital partnership with me based on our mutual understanding that neither of us will ever attempt to usurp power by telling the other one what to do or how to do it, not including occasional advice."

"That's not exactly a *small* request."

"True. It's the most important life-altering request I've ever made or ever will make."

Could she trust this sudden change of heart? What if all those old-fashioned beliefs resurfaced after they tied the knot? It was a trap. Not that she believed he was intentionally setting a trap. It was the kind of trap people set all the time – misleading the person they want to impress by making themselves seem more sophisticated, pretending to be interested in what the other person is interested in, telling tall tales about themselves so they seem ever so much more interesting than they really are, that they're older than they are, or younger. He took her out to a romantic lake in his gorgeous Corvette, then as soon as they kissed a couple of times, he mentioned getting a family car instead. It was an instinctive trap, unconsciously set by both men and women who were filled with romantic aspirations.

Still, Paul had been open with his opinions about a woman's role from the beginning. He could've hidden his outdated views from her and ambushed her later. But he was always himself. And he was genuinely surprised when she objected.

"Would you agree that you and your wife would own property jointly – the house, the cars, the furniture, the land?"

"Gladly."

"You should know that I have a divorce lawyer's business card in my wallet. If one day I become someone's wife, I wouldn't hesitate to contact said lawyer to represent me if my husband failed to keep his end of the marital partnership. Whether there are children or not."

The glint in his eyes made her stomach do somersaults. But if she used her head and did the smart thing – the logical thing – she would tell him she couldn't put her faith in his newfound intentions. Having good intentions was like making a peanut butter sandwich for someone. Turning good intentions into reality was like preparing Thanksgiving dinner so that all the food was ready at the same time and everything was delicious. It required work and commitment.

If she listened to her brain, she would call Allan and tell him that, yes, she would go to the movies with him. In the darkness of the theater she would hold his hand on the armrest between them. He was the kind of man she preferred. Plus, he was fun to be with. He would be a good husband, a faithful husband. He *lived* his good intentions. He loved her. And if she threw herself into it, she would come to love him too.

If she listened to her heart, and maybe her hormones, she would say yes to Paul, pull him inside, close the door and lead him to her bedroom where they would make love for the first time like lovesick teenagers. God, it was tempting. But she could imagine the little digs he would make when he arrived home from work before she got there. When supper wasn't on the table, he would say, "They're having pot roast next door. I know because I smelled it when I pulled in the driveway." If he arrived home first, he would sit on the couch reading the paper while waiting for her to come home so *she* could get busy in the kitchen.

Allan, on the other hand, would learn to cook. Supper would be on the stove when she got home and they would finish it together. Or the food would already be on the table. He was the smart choice. The logical choice. They'd been friends for nearly a decade. He didn't need to alter his outlook about women. He was ahead of the curve, not behind it.

Regardless of what decision she made now, one day when she was old, she would understand how deeply she had loved Paul. The only question was whether it would be a treasured memory or whether it would be a painful memory about the love she rejected. A rejection that stemmed from her skepticism about human nature and how deep-seated beliefs couldn't be erased with a snap of the fingers. A rejection based on her unwillingness to take chances. Except for when she recorded the Carlisle brothers talking about hiding drug money. If she could risk her very life doing that, why couldn't she be brave when it came to a decision that would lay the groundwork for her happiness?

Tina was courageous. She threw timidity out with the garbage. She was willing to leave the safety of her closeted cocoon as she created a new life of her own choosing with the woman she loved.

Of course, Cheryl didn't have to choose at all. She didn't have to marry anyone.

"Cheryl?"

But she needed to seize the day. Seize the month, the year. Hell, she needed to seize the rest of her life.

"I'll love you until the twelfth of never," he said soft and low.

"When is the twelfth of never?"

"A day that never comes."

She let that sink in, yearning to caress his face.

"Well," she said.

There was a lot in that 'well.' That 'well' was deep. Her future was wrapped up in that 'well.' It was a word that meant she was weighing what to say next, debating what the next step should be. As the word hung in the air between them, her eyes remained unfocused while her mind and heart argued. At last, her attention returned to the man watching her patiently from the other side of the screen door.

The tenderness in his eyes undid her.

"Can you please restate your request?" she said.

He sucked in a lungful of air. "To put it succinctly, will you marry me?"

Opening the screen door, she moved aside, allowing him to step across the threshold. He stood in front of her, holding her hands in his.

"Possibly," she whispered.

"Possibly?"

"I need an unhurried engagement that'll give us plenty of time to decide whether we're well suited for each other."

"Cheryl, we were made for each other!"

"Do you agree to an engagement that lets us make sure of that?"

"I do." He smiled.

They gazed into each other's eyes.

"Your conditional fiancée has a burning desire to kiss you."

"The ultimate romantic. When I introduce you to my parents, do I have to tell them you're my 'conditional fiancée?'"

"Um…"

"Are you going to give me a report card and a grade?" He grinned, enjoying himself.

"As a matter of fact, I am."

With that, she placed her hand behind his neck and pulled his face down to hers. As he wrapped her in his arms, she kissed him like there was no tomorrow.

24

The passionate kiss in the doorway turned into two, then three, then she lost count. Instead of leading Paul to her bedroom, she cradled his face in her hands and asked if he was hungry.

"Yes," he said, breathless.

She took him to the kitchen where she whipped up deviled egg sandwiches and a quick fruit salad. Sitting side by side, his right arm touched her left arm as they ate.

Their conversation was about Tina and Peggy and Ricky. And about Audrey. About his time in Florida. She told him all about the Eddie Carlisle nightmare, including her evening in the boss's closet. He was aghast that she had put her life in such danger, begging her never to do it again. They could've talked all afternoon, but they were interrupted by the ringing of the blasted phone.

"Can't you ignore it?" he said.

"I wish I could. But not until Tina is safe in Oregon."

It wasn't Tina. It was Audrey.

"I meant to ask you something when we were having coffee. I wanted to clarify whether you're dating Allan."

"No. We're old friends. Good buddies."

"I thought so. I had a feeling you were involved with the other man. Paul, I think his name was?"

"Correct on both counts."

"Could you give me Allan's number?"

"Gladly."

As soon as she passed his number along, Audrey said thanks and goodbye. Cheryl was impressed by her directness. She also approved of her taste in men.

She filled Paul in.

"What a relief," he said.

She didn't let him know she wrestled with choosing Allan because he was the logical choice. Hopefully the two teachers would have a lot in common. It would be wonderful if Allan fell in love with a woman who could love him back.

No sooner had she hung up than someone was at the door. It was Tina's parents, undoubtedly stopping by to make more trouble. Tina said she would mail a letter to her parents on their trip out west. Until they received it, she'd coached Cheryl on what to say.

"We're here to visit Ricky. Tina phoned to say he wasn't going to school yesterday, that he had a cold. Then she called this morning saying he wasn't going to school today either."

Mrs. Rossi put her hand on the screen door handle but Cheryl held tight.

"He was much better this morning," she said. "In fact, they left a while ago on a trip to see friends."

Mrs. Rossi's eyes narrowed as she looked beyond Cheryl into the house. "Are you hiding them? I'll bet they're inside right now." She moved to open the screen door but Cheryl latched it. "How dare you treat me this way!"

"Mrs. Rossi, last time you were here, I pointed out that I'm the legal resident. I'll remind you of that today and warn you to stay off my property. Don't knock on my door again. Ever."

"You can't talk to me like that!"

Cheryl was about to close the door when Paul appeared by her side, giving the middle-aged couple a challenging glare.

"Mr. Rossi," Cheryl said, looking beyond Tina's mother, "please make sure she doesn't turn up at my house anymore."

She closed the door as Mrs. Rossi huffed and puffed.

"I can only assume she deserved that," Paul said, grinning.

"I've been trying to figure out whether Mrs. Rossi was born mean or whether she studied long and hard to earn her PhD in Hatefulness."

"Life with you is gonna be a blast," he said.

He leaned down to kiss her lips. Then he kissed her ear and her neck, his hands clutching her waist.

"I've got a hankering to make love to you."

"First, I have to…"

"Don't tell me. You have to get your ducks in a row."

"Not ducks. I have to get some birth control pills in a row."

She could see his mind chugging.

"You're right, of course. And smart. And beautiful. And…"

She kissed him to shut him up.

*

Her new job at Sandhills High School was all that she'd hoped for. No more dreading going to work in the morning. Mr. Swaney was a great boss. The other office staff were friendly, the teachers welcomed her and the students didn't give a hoot who sat at the secretary's desk. In addition, she was relieved to be working with women again. She realized how isolating it was working in an all-male environment.

Audrey moved in, bringing a sofa and chair for the living room. They were compatible roommates, which didn't come as a surprise. When Audrey told her she was planning to invite Allan for a family dinner, Cheryl realized things were getting serious. Paul came too and it turned out the two men got along like best buddies now that they were no longer grudging adversaries.

That was the evening her guilt washed away for rebuffing Allan. During dinner she noticed he hung on Audrey's every word. There was a fervor in his eyes she'd never seen before. Thinking back, she had a hunch Allan mistook *liking* Cheryl and feeling comfortable around her for love. Then again, maybe it was a lesser type of love. One thing was certain: it didn't compare with what he felt for Audrey.

A week later Allan stopped by her desk one afternoon when no one else was in the school office.

"I've been meaning to thank you for some time now," he said.

"For?"

"For making it clear we were meant to be good friends."

She smiled.

"I was crushed at the time," he went on. "But now I get it." He did a quick check for eavesdroppers. "To be honest, I had never met someone who made my insides turn to peanut butter and jelly."

She laughed.

He saluted her on his way out the door.

She didn't mention she contemplated taking him up on his offer to test drive a romantic relationship. She hadn't told Paul either. Or Tina. Or Audrey. And she never would.

Paul paid for the two of them to fly to Oregon and rent a car for a visit the first week in December. It was easy to see that Tina and Peggy were euphorically happy together. The warmth in their eyes as they exchanged a glance and the way they touched as they went about their daily lives was proof of their deep affection. And there was plenty of joking around, the two of them exchanging one liners and teasing each other. They'd been forced to hide all this from Cheryl and everyone else when they were in Fayetteville. But here in their new home, they were free to be themselves. It warmed Cheryl's heart to see the love between them.

Peggy had succeeded in transferring her credits to an Oregon college with a dental hygiene program. She would graduate at the end of summer semester. Meantime, she found work at a restaurant to help pay the bills and Tina found a job as a keypunch operator.

As for Ricky, he liked his new teacher and had made friends. After school he stayed with a neighbor who had a son one year younger than him. Then Tina kept the boy in the evening so the neighbor could attend college courses.

Ricky conducted a tour of their apartment and yard. He was proud to open the shed door so she could see the hand-me-down bicycle Miss Darnell gave him that used to belong to her nephew.

"Mommy and Peggy are teaching me how to ride it!"

"As I always say – two heads are better than one."

"What I say is two biscuits are better than one!"

She laughed and hugged him.

"Guess what!" he said. "Peggy helped me teach Max to fetch!"

"Wow!" She was thrilled Peggy had thrown herself into being a second mama but couldn't deny she missed playing that role herself.

Ricky begged her to speak in her piggy voice when they played with the tape recorder in his room. She went all out reciting nursery rhymes in her nasal style.

Paul bedded down on the couch. Cheryl slept on a pallet on the floor of Ricky's bedroom, as promised. A small price to pay to be with her favorite little boy.

After a three-day visit, they packed their suitcases to go home. When they said their goodbyes, she hugged Ricky and Tina. This time around, she gave Peggy a big hug too, filled with affection and appreciation. It was the same as saying 'so long, see you next time' to family. They *were* family.

In the Christmas card from her parents, her mother included a clipping of a feature article she wrote for the NCO Wives Club newsletter. She hoped to submit stories to other publications as well. Her debut piece was about her good friend, Mrs. Lopez, who organized and hosted family dinners and barbecues for the single guys in her husband's unit. Mrs. Donovan was inspired to sign up for a big Thanksgiving dinner for a squad in Sergeant Donovan's unit. She was nervous about having unattached young men for dinner, that they were bound to flirt with Vicky who'd broken off dating the soldier she wanted to marry back in October.

Early in the new year the money laundering case went to trial. As expected, Cheryl testified. Her picture was published in the newspaper. She was surprised when Diane Coleman took the stand as well. Diane told her afterwards that the D.A. said her testimony would make his case stronger.

Eddie was found guilty of drug distribution and money laundering and given a stiff prison sentence. Mr. Carlisle was sentenced to community service plus a fine after cooperating with the district attorney's office.

As it turned out, Mrs. Carlisle stood by her husband and became the first woman sales agent at Carlisle Realty. In a newspaper feature about her, Cheryl was relieved to read that their son survived his drug overdose with only mild mental impairment. No longer playing football or other sports, he had time to focus on his passion for music.

The planned merger of Carlisle Realty and Odom Realty didn't happen. In fact, Perry Odom used Mr. Carlisle's misfortune in an advertising campaign, claiming Odom Realty was the most trustworthy realty company in town.

Cheryl was pleasantly surprised when she found a note from Mrs. Carlisle in the mailbox one day. In it, she apologized for the accusations she made at the Belk store, saying her husband explained that he only offered Cheryl the sales job to try to save her from Eddie's wrath.

As the trial wrapped up, an envelope was delivered to Cheryl's mailbox with a Los Angeles return address. She was bowled over when she opened it to find a letter from Nick Rossi, Tina's long-lost brother. He was trying to get in touch with Tina. He explained that he'd asked a friend to call his parents' number to ask about Tina's whereabouts. Mrs. Rossi said she didn't know where Tina had moved, but that she'd been living with Cheryl before she left town. He asked Cheryl to forward his letter to his sister. She sent it on right away, hoping the two of them could reconnect.

That was about the time that Audrey and Allan announced they would marry at the end of the school year. They had both applied for teaching positions at an American military base in Italy, eager to travel Europe together. Allan spent time brushing up on his French and Audrey bought some "Learn Italian" records.

On Valentine's Day evening, Paul took Cheryl to the Sakura Restaurant where they had their first date – the night they fell in love. She wore the same burgundy corduroy pants and jacket she wore for that first dinner.

"I knew you were different when you wore pants that night," he said. "Then that beatnik outfit for dinner at your house. I was yours, heart and soul."

She kissed her hand and touched it to his lips.

Like before, they talked non-stop about everything and nothing. She still got that tingly feeling when they gazed at each other across the black lacquer table as they sat on a tatami mat. As before, he held her hand, sending a current through her arm and into her body.

When they arrived at her house afterwards, she admired the bouquet of pink roses he brought her, turning to thank him with a kiss.

"Tonight's the night," she said.

"Tonight is what night?"

"I finally have my ducks in a row."

He gazed into her eyes, hypnotized, then pressed his body against hers.

She did something she hadn't done before, sliding her hands inside his back pockets, a seductive gleam in her eyes. Which prompted him to swoop her up in his arms and carry her down the hallway to her bedroom. Sitting on the side of the bed with her on his lap, he nibbled her ear. "I'm glad it wasn't far. You weigh a ton."

She slapped his shoulder. "Well, you're no Charles Atlas. You're a ninety-seven pound weakling."

"Whatever you do, please don't use that nasal thing you do. I won't be able to, well, to… keep going."

She responded with a sultry smile, unbuttoning his shirt.

Once they slid under the covers, they lay facing each other, eyes glistening in the lamplight.

"I'm so happy I followed my heart," she whispered.

"I'm so happy I persuaded a fiery cuss with brains and a very fine body to marry me."

"I'm not quite ready to set the date yet."

"Before the end of the decade maybe?"

She gave him a teasing wink. "By the way, you get an 'A' on your report card."

He responded with a sexy kiss. One thing led to another until their bodies vibrated with the electricity flowing between them.

They cherished every touch, every sigh, every moan of pleasure, savoring each and every precious moment, immersing themselves in the present as they envisioned their future together. A future filled with love and more tomorrows than they could count.

The End

Review it

Thank you for reading *The October That Changed Everything*. If you enjoyed it, please help spread the word by posting a brief customer review. Or tell your friends, in person or on social media. Thanks very much!

About the author

Connie Lacy writes time travel fiction, speculative fiction and historical fiction, all with a dollop of romance. She worked for many years in radio news as a reporter and news anchor. She and her husband live in Atlanta.

Acknowledgements

Huge thanks to sensitivity reader Beth Williams for her insight into the lives of lesbian women and the challenges they have faced historically. Thanks also for her excellent feedback on plot, characters, scenes and language. She is a retired metro Atlanta high school history and psychology teacher.

The character of Ricky is based loosely on my three sons when they were little boys. However, I borrowed one of Ricky's mispronunciations from my sister-in-law Sandy Dudley's daughter who died as a young woman. When she was three years old, Jennifer Yost would beg to go to her favorite BBQ restaurant because she loved the "cold slop." Her version of "coleslaw." One of the cutest childhood mispronunciations I've ever heard.

Note from the author

Historians say the Cuban Missile Crisis may be the closest humanity has come to nuclear war. Over the course of thirteen days in October of 1962, many of the scenes included in my novel actually occurred, including school children practicing "duck and cover," protests, and empty store shelves. Soldiers from Fort Bragg, North Carolina (recently renamed Fort Liberty,) were deployed to Florida as preparations were made for defensive operations and a possible invasion of Cuba.

My father was stationed at Fort Bragg with the 82nd Airborne Division for a number of years and we lived in Fayetteville. But he was stationed in Okinawa during the Cuban Missile Crisis and my family accompanied him for his tour of duty.

Sign up for newsletter and get your FREE copy of

The Engagement Ring, A short story
When Ethan pops the question, Lydia pops some questions of her own. A 21st century take on a marriage proposal with a pinch of humor and a dash of the unexpected. **Sign up here**: www.connielacy.com

Also by Connie Lacy

Livvy and the Enchanted Woodland
Rural Georgia, 1930. Pursued by a wealthy neighbor while she dreams of a mysterious Englishman, Livvy escapes to her secret woodland where everything may

not be as it seems. Historical fantasy, magical realism, romance.

A Suffragette in Time
Thrown back in time to the 1850s, Sarah Burns becomes a suffragette who finds danger and romance where she least expects to.

The Time Capsule
An unlikely journey through time brings Hannah Myers face to face with a man like no other. But she doesn't belong in 1918 with a killer flu epidemic raging and the KKK targeting the newspaper reporter she's fallen for. Can she rewrite history to protect the man she loves?

The Going Back Portal
She avoided the Trail of Tears. But can a young Cherokee Indian woman of 1840 survive the white man intent on owning her? Can a time traveler from the 21st century help?

The Time Telephone
What if you could save your mother's life by calling her in the past on a time telephone? An intriguing coming of age story. Teen/Young Adult Fiction

A Daffodil for Angie
It's 1966. Angie's got a lot on her plate – the women's rights movement, school integration, the Viet Nam War, a cocky anti-war activist and a sexy quarterback. A

coming of age story that drops you right into the social upheaval of the 1960s. Teen/Young Adult Fiction

VisionSight: a Novel
Seeing the future is a curse for Jenna Stevens. A heartfelt novel of secrets and unexpected love.

The Shade Ring Trilogy
A compelling Climate Fiction trilogy in the year 2117, a time of runaway global warming. A love story in a hotter, more dangerous world.
The Shade Ring, Book 1
Albedo Effect, Book 2
Aerosol Sky, Book 3

Contact/follow

Newsletter sign-up: www.connielacy.com

www.connielacy.com
www.amazon.com/author/connie.lacy
www.Facebook.com/ConnieLacyBooks
www.Goodreads.com/ConnieLacy
www.instagram.com/connielacy_author/
www.pinterest.com/cdlacy0736/
www.tiktok.com/@connielacyauthor
www.youtube.com/@connielacybooks/featured
Email:

WildFallsPublishing@outlook.com
connielacy@connielacy.com

Made in United States
Orlando, FL
02 July 2024

48548115R00200